CIRQUE

A Literary Journal for the North Pacific Rim

Volume 14, No. 1

Anchorage, Alaska

Cover Photo: David A. Goodrum, "Set in Concrete"
Table of Contents Photo Credit: Nard Claar, "Lines"
Design and composition: Signe Nichols

ISBN:
979-8324885649

Independently Published

Published by

Anchorage, Alaska

www.cirquejournal.com

All future rights to material published in *Cirque*
are retained by the individual authors and artists.

cirquejournal@gmail.com

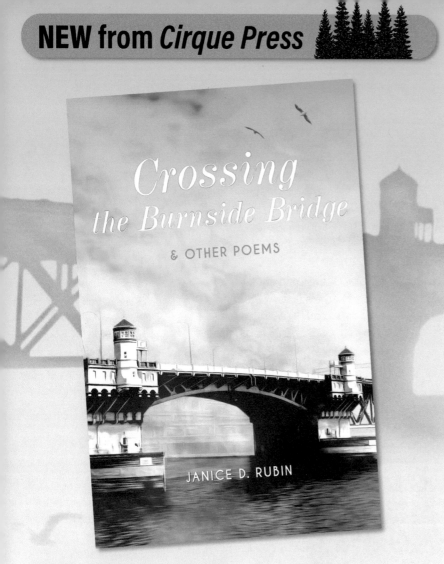

In the Winter *of the* Orange Snow

In the Winter of the Orange Snow captures a era of freewheeling adventure in southwest Alaska, beginning in 1955, when Diane and Bob Carpenter embraced the wild with curiosity and courage, and the phrase "only in Bethel" was coined in response to events both mysterious and magical.

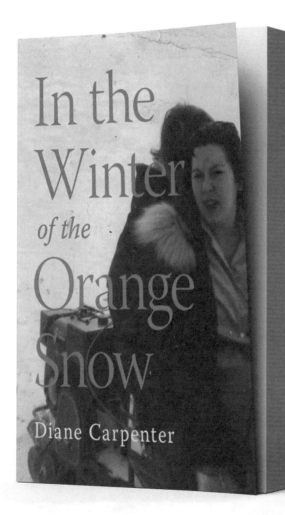

Diane Carpenter captures the spirit, the oddities, the bizarreness of characters and happenings, as well the unique and beautiful environment and indigenous people of the Kuskokwim. She does so with humor, sensitivity, and clear recollections. It's a tough land. One cannot help but greatly admire this woman. No tourists here in Bethel, Alaska, where primitive ways became modern times in the span of a lifetime.
– Clif Bates, author of *Sky Changes on the Kuskokwim*

Diane Carpenter's book is a delightful tramp through the Alaska bush country in the 1950s and sixties through the eyes of a great storyteller. The tales are sobering, hilarious and very informative, each a window into the details of the storyteller's life and times. For many Alaskans, the book will be nostalgic. For others, it will bridge the gap between those who live on the road system and the bush. For readers in the Lower 48 states, this book will be an astounding ride on boats, airplanes, and dog-sleds through the Alaska wilderness. – James H. Barker, author of *Always Getting Ready / Upterrlainarluta: Yup'ik Eskimo Subsistence in Southwest Alaska*

The tough landscape of the Yukon-Kuskokwim Delta required someone like Diane Carpenter. As the decades passed, Diane was a teacher, a social activist and statewide leader. She was elected mayor of Bethel. She chaired the Alaska Humanities Forum and the Counsel on Domestic Violence and Sexual Assault. She was a state delegate to the National Women's Conference in Houston and lead organizer of the Alaska Village Electric Cooperative (AVEC). She taught in public schools and the local college. As she approached retirement, she set up the Pacifica Institute, a non-profit educational organization that developed many innovative programs. In 2007, Diane retired and moved from Bethel to the historic town of Alamos, Sonora, where she renovated a 250-year-old villa. She recently celebrated her 90th birthday there.

CIRQUE PRESS

Available on

$20

IF SINGING WENT ON

GERALD CABLE

Gerald Cable's poems are so full of life—exploring, inquiring, imagining—that it's still hard to come to grips with his too early death. There is a wonderful spontaneity here, as the poems twist, weave, dart, and land in unexpected places. As they offer up verbal and sensory revelations, these poems express the full richness of one man's experience.

— John Morgan, author of nine books, including *The Hungers of the World: New and Collected Later Poems*

Jerry Cable's poems capture what it is to live and work for twenty years in Interior Alaska, all the while navigating between one's past and the future, the cold and warmth, the fun and not. Spare and   honest, Cable's poems explore what lies beneath the moment—vivid, poignant, ecstatic, unsayable.

— Carolyn Kremers, poet, and finalist for the 2014 Willa Award

Paperback Published February 2024 on Amazon

Cover Art by Tami Phelps, "Polychrome Pass"

Gerald Cable

Gerald Cable's widow, Martha Ferris, kept a promise to herself when this collection was published in 2024. Cable passed away in 1988, after a life spent in work, poetry and wild Alaska. Jerry grew up in Northern California, served in the Army, and after discharge, earned a BA from Chico State in 1965. A few years later, looking for adventure, he flew with a pilot friend in a small plane to Fairbanks, Alaska. Over the next 20 years, he worked in Alaska as a surveyor, built a cabin with his partner, and made a close community of friends. All this time he wrote, radio plays, journals, and poetry. In 1982 he earned an MFA in poetry from the University of Alaska, Fairbanks. In 1987 he was diagnosed with cancer. He passed away a few months later, breaking the hearts of many who were close to him.

RON MCFARLAND

A VARIABLE SENSE OF THINGS

NEW FROM CIRQUE PRESS

A Variable Sense of Things is sometimes wry, sometimes downright funny; sometimes elegiac, sad, or rueful, and always, always smart. They do not strain, these poems. They are wise. They mean exactly what they say, and more.

— **ROBERT WRIGLEY**,
author of *Earthly Meditations: New and Selected Poems* and *The True Account of Myself As A Bird*

Intensely personal poems, studded with unexpected ironies like grace notes, which illuminate the depth below the surface.

— **MARY CLEARMAN BLEW**,
author of *Think of Horses*

RON MCFARLAND was born in Bellaire, Ohio, grew up in Cocoa, Florida, took his bachelor's and master's degrees in English from Florida State University in Tallahassee, taught two years at Sam Houston State in Huntsville, Texas, garnered his doctorate at the University of Illinois with a dissertation in 17th-century British literature, and embarked on a nearly 50-year teaching career at the University of Idaho, where he acted as impresario of poetry readings, served for many years as faculty advisor of the literary magazine *Fugue*, and helped create the MFA program.

Learn more about Ron and his writing at: cirquejournal.com/cirque-press-books

CIRQUE PRESS

The Andy Hope Literary Award 2024

This award is the brainchild of writer Vivian Faith Prescott. Vivian co-directs Raven's Blanket, a non-profit based in Wrangell, Alaska, whose mission is to enhance and perpetuate the cultural wellness and traditions of indigenous peoples through education, media, and the arts, and to promote artistic works throughout Alaska of both Native and non-Native Alaskans.

Andy Hope, an influential Alaska Native political activist and writer of prose and poetry, died after a brief battle with cancer in 2008 at the age of 58. The $100 annual award will go to an author of prose or poetry published in *Cirque*.

The winner of the Andy Hope Award is DJ Lee: writer, artist, and English professor at Washington State University. This is from the winning essay, "The River Decides." "People are drawn to the river because it is difficult. It has forty-one named rapids, places where the gradient steepens, flow increases, and the water becomes dangerous. Many of the Selway rapids come from 1960s slang: Holy Smokes and Galloping Gertie. But some—Wa-Poots—-are Nimipuutímt words. Others are warnings."

Cirque Pushcart Nominees

Issue 13.2

Cynthia Lee Steele

Publication in The Pushcart Prize: Best of the Small Presses is awarded annually for works of poetry, fiction, and creative nonfiction published by literary magazines or small presses during the current year. Editors may nominate up to six poems, short stories, novel chapters, or essays published, or scheduled to be published, in 2023.

CIRQUE PRESS

Cirque Poetry Contest.
Poems About Puppies! (And Other Pets)
Winners to be published
in *Cirque*, #27.

Blind Judged by Cynthia Steele,
MA English Literature
Cirque Assoc. Editor,
Providence Therapy Dog
trainer/team, dog foster

Featuring Alice
AKCATANDDOG
MEDICAL RESCUE
Adoption Pending

Winners

Christianne Balk, "Wild Grass"
Joanna Streetly, "Playing God"
Randy Bynum, "Charli the Fierce"

Chosen for Publication

- "Dragged Back", Carol Kaynor • "A Stitch in the Heart", Dale Champlin
- "My Heart, My Mare", Penny Johnson • "Only in the Kitchen", Robin Woolman
- "Set in Concrete", David A. Goodrum • "Other People's Dogs", Jim Hanlen
- "Trinidad Stray Dogs", Joanna Streetly • "Infidelity", Joel Savishinsky
- "Breathless", Juanita Smart • "Because", Katherine Poyner-Del Vento
- "Fat Kitty Trilogy", Leah Stenson • "Seeking Buddha", Teresa Carns
- "Love of Season", Shauna Potocky • "Three of Nine", Shirley Martin
- "In Dreams", Shirley Martin • "My Chicken Heidi", Judith Duncan
- "You're the Reason I'm Wearing a Torn Tennis Shoe", Sue Fagalde Lick
- "Listening to Patience", Wanda Wilson • "Replenish", Warren Rhodes
- "Driving with the Windows Down", Patrick Dixon

From Unsolicited Press:
Cormorant
by Elisa Carlsen

Cormorant is a work of contrition. The poems are political and personal. A response to the federal government's plan to kill thousands of cormorants in the name of salmon recovery and a tribute to the person who died from heartbreak because of it.

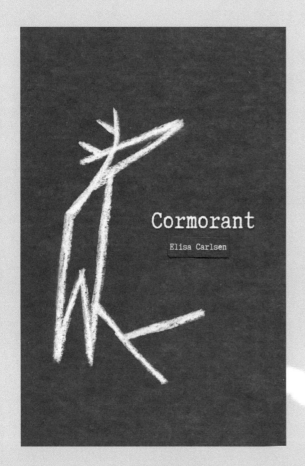

To support wildlife, we are donating the profits of this book to The Wildlife Center of the North Coast.

Cormorant is available at Unsolicited Press, Bookshop.org and Amazon.

Elisa Carlsen is an outsider artist and poet whose words have appeared in *SixFold*, *VoiceCatcher*, *Anti-Heroin Chic*, *Nevada Arts Council*, *Oranges Journal*, and *Brushfire*. Elisa won the Lower Columbia Regional Poetry Contest, was a finalist for the Editor's Prize at Harbor Review, and Best of the Net nominee. Elisa is the author of *Cormorant* (Unsolicited Press, 2023).

BOOKS FROM CIRQUE PRESS

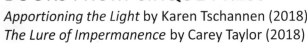

Apportioning the Light by Karen Tschannen (2018)
The Lure of Impermanence by Carey Taylor (2018)
Echolocation by Kristin Berger (2018)
Like Painted Kites & Collected Works by Clifton Bates (2019)
Athabaskan Fractal: Poems of the Far North by Karla Linn Merrifield (2019)
Holy Ghost Town by Tim Sherry (2019)
Drunk on Love: Twelve Stories to Savor Responsibly by Kerry Dean Feldman (2019)
Wide Open Eyes: Surfacing from Vietnam by Paul Kirk Haeder (2020)
Silty Water People by Vivian Faith Prescott (2020)
Life Revised by Leah Stenson (2020)
Oasis Earth: Planet in Peril by Rick Steiner (2020)
The Way to Gaamaak Cove by Doug Pope (2020)
Loggers Don't Make Love by Dave Rowan (2020)
The Dream That Is Childhood by Sandra Wassilie (2020)
Seward Soundboard by Sean Ulman (2020)
The Fox Boy by Gretchen Brinck (2021)
Lily Is Leaving: Poems by Leslie Ann Fried (2021)
One Headlight by Matt Caprioli (2021)
November Reconsidered by Marc Janssen (2021)
Callie Comes of Age by Dale Champlin (2021)
Someday I'll Miss This Place Too by Dan Branch (2021)
Out There In The Out There by Jerry McDonnell (2021)
Fish the Dead Water Hard by Eric Heyne (2021)
Salt & Roses by Buffy McKay (2022)
Growing Older In This Place: A Life in Alaska's Rainforest
       by Margo Wasserman Waring (2022)
Kettle Dance: A Big Sky Murder by Kerry Dean Feldman (2022)
Nothing Got Broke by Larry F. Slonaker (2022)
On the Beach: Poems 2016-2021 by Alan Weltzien (2022)
Sky Changes on the Kuskokwim by Clifton Bates (2022)
Transplanted: A Memoir by Birgit Lennertz Sarrimanolis (2022)
Between Promise and Sadness by Joanne Townsend (2022)
Yosemite Dawning by Shauna Potocky (2023)
The Woman Within by Tami Phelps and Kerry Dean Feldman (2023)
In the Winter of the Orange Snow by Diane S. Carpenter (2023)
Mail Order Nurse by Sue Lium (2023)
Infinite Meditations: For Inspiration and Daily Practice by Scott Hanson (2023)
All in Due Time by Kate Troll (2023)
Getting Home from Here by Anne Ward-Masterson (2023)
Crossing the Burnside Bridge by Janice D. Rubin (2023)
May the Owl Call Again: A Return to Poet John Meade Haines, 1924-2011 by Rachel Epstein (2023)
A Variable Sense of Things by Ron McFarland, 2024
Tiny's Stories: An Athabascan Family on the Yukon River by Theresa "Tiny" Nellie Demientieff Devlin

CIRCLES Illustrated books from Cirque Press

Baby Abe: A Lullaby for Lincoln by Ann Chandonnet (2021)
Miss Tami, Is Today Tomorrow? by Tami Phelps (2021)
Miss Bebe Comes to America by Lynda Humphrey (2022)

Order via Amazon or your local bookstore.
Venders may order from Ingram or via email to cirquejournal@gmail.com

NEW from *Cirque Press*

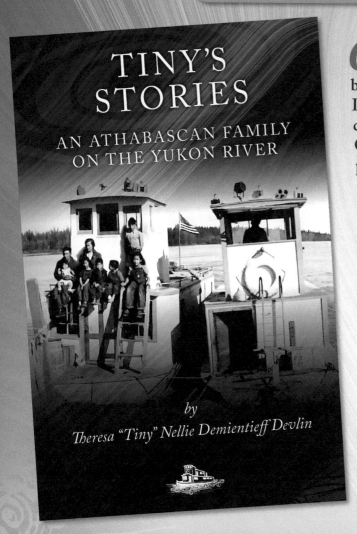

TINY'S STORIES

AN ATHABASCAN FAMILY ON THE YUKON RIVER

by

Theresa "Tiny" Nellie Demientieff Devlin

*C*limb to the pilot house roof with Tiny Demientieff on her parents' paddlewheel riverboat, the *Sea Wolf*, to bask in sights and sounds of the broad Yukon and winding Innoko. Number eight of Nick and Nellie Demientieff's ten children, young Tiny loves her family and her town of Holy Cross, Alaska, but is not afraid to steal her sister's birthday party or laugh with her mother at the neighbor who is certain she sees black bears on skis—black bears who turn out to be nuns from the Holy Cross Mission! Through child eyes and her family's stories, Tiny takes us up remote rivers to glimpse gold mining towns in their last days of fancy ladies and storekeepers. When her family barges freight along the Yukon after WW II, Tiny enters her school days in Fairbanks and learns to be a town kid. She schemes with her siblings to join the Empress Theater "Space Cadets" in the brief neon glow of that historic movie theater. Tiny's stories take us into her young adulthood at Copper Valley School. At CVS, Tiny is still the lively prankster, but she asks hard questions of herself and others as she encounters heartache in her family's first great loss. Readers will relish the first-person voice of an Athabascan youngster in these true tales, set against the dynamic backdrop of Alaska's history.

Praise for *Tiny's Stories: An Athabascan Family on the Yukon River*

These stories draw an intimate portrait of an amazing family, nurtured in the love of parents who gave them a firm grounding. Drawn immediately to the riverboat stories, I was soon also struck by the wide exposure Tiny and the other children gained in different aspects of post-WWII Alaska. Tiny's brother, Sam, has talked about how the freighting life fostered friendships all along the rivers, friendships that became important when he later served in many important positions in the state. Finally, Tiny's vignettes from the Copper Valley School, where she and several siblings attended, are a window into Native schooling that will take readers beyond simple good or bad characterizations of the religious boarding schools.

—WILLIAM SCHNEIDER, PROFESSOR EMERITUS, ALASKA AND POLAR REGIONS · UAF RASMUSON LIBRARY

What a joy to hear Tiny's voice! The book is beautifully written— warm, humorous, and lively—just like the Tiny I remember!

—IRENE ROWAN, TLINGIT ELDER, ALASKA NATIVE MEDIA GROUP

CIRQUE PRESS

MAY *the* OWL
CALL AGAIN

A Return to Poet John Meade Haines, 1924-2011

An intimate correspondence of words, writings, & letters with
reflections on life, death, and friendship

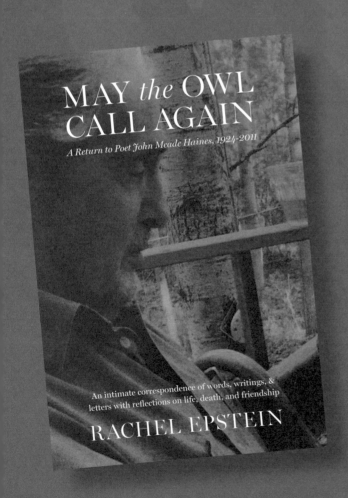

May the Owl Call Again is a moving and
memorable collection...

– MARC HUDSON, POET AND AUTHOR
OF *EAST OF SORROW*

May the Owl Call Again bears witness to
the last years of Haines' life...But above all
it is a meditation on friendship and the
solace of intimacy that can be found on the
handwritten page...

– FREYA ROHN, POET AND FOUNDER
OF ARIADNE ARCHIVE

John Haines will be remembered as one of
Alaska's greatest thinkers and writers.

– ANNE CORAY, POET AND AUTHOR
OF *BONE STRINGS*

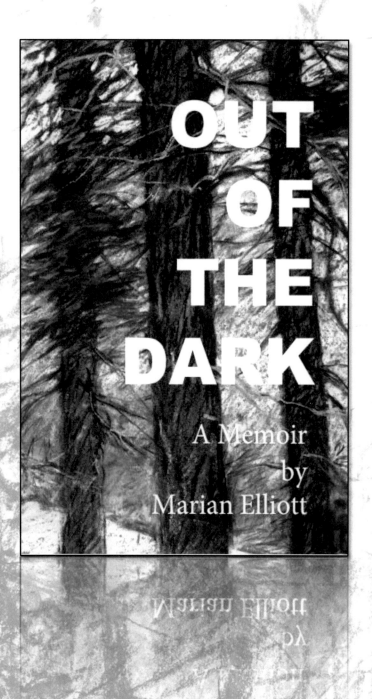

From the Editors

Leveling Up

The complex challenges of celebrity follow each of the talented writers and artists who appear in our twice-yearly *Cirque* issues. We are collectively at work elevating those we publish. For some contributors, the goal is to have the work alone achieve recognition, while the creator peeks from behind a curtain. "Are they gone yet?" Once the lovely thing is done, artists/writers really must face the ditch digger's sweaty job of promoting it through readings, book signings, interviews, book club visits, and giving little talks with slides.

Getting the Word Out

Book tours sound amazing but check in with any writer… they are quickly arduous. Are you ready for Ted Talks? Interviews where you describe your "process?" Exposure can be hard for one who prefers a room of their own and nothing beyond it.

A memoir writer can meet a stranger and mention growing up in Sequim. This random reader might say, "I know. I read your book." You can find yourself thinking, *What else did I tell them?* You know what you did to create your opus: you "opened a vein and bled." Soon you will be getting "cards and letters from people you don't even know." Mixed blessings.

Writers/artists quiver about the self-serving chore of posting events and achievements, but I believe a commitment to the work is required, a deep and motivating belief that calls for a level of what feels like shamelessness.

Rewards

This just in: Tami Phelps, featured artist in this issue, had two cold wax pieces accepted in the international fly-fishing exhibit (L'arte della pesca… La pesca nell'arte") and with it came four nights room and board to attend the event in Italy. See one of her entries (pg. 145) "Viva la Santa Nonna." Such rewards come from bravely releasing the work into the world.

Creative Partnering

Let's go public together, like this. Shauna Potocky has been at work with others creating the Seward Poetry Festival. Cirque Press poet Sandra Wasillie (*The Dream That Is Childhood*) is traveling from Oakland, CA, as the featured poet. Potocky is in pre-publication for her next book, *Sea Smoke, Spindrift and Other Spells*. Sean Ulman (*Seward Soundboard*) will interview Wasillie on his local radio/live stream show. There is a partnership in this and evidence of the dictum, we all rise on the same tide.

Fifteen Minutes! or, For Us, Even Twenty!

Feeling excited and half-embarrassed, associate editor, Cynthia Steele and I will soon be on the cover of *Southside Neighbors*. This is a slick ad-filled publication focusing on our, also slick, neck of the woods. With a circulation of thousands, this prominent placement will bring area attention to *Cirque* and Cirque Press putting Cynthia and I a bit more into the local public eye. With modesty and aplomb, we will manage the new experience of getting recognized at grocery stores and garage sales.

In This Issue

Readers will get some feels when reading the winners of the contest, Poems about Puppies (and Other Pets). Resident dog whisperer, Cynthia Steele served as judge. Our Pushcart nominees and the winner of the Andy Hope Award are applauded here. Tom Sexton, former Alaskan laureate and our elder statesman, graces us with two poems. The second one ends, "I have no idea how to end this poem." There is a review by Alaska writer laureate Heather Lende of *May the Owl Call Again: A Return to Poet John Meade Haines, 1924-2011* by Rachel Epstein, published this year by Cirque Press. Check out the story and photos from last summer's *Cirque* adventures in the air and on the ground, "For Poetry's Sake: Packed Cafés and Summer Soirées." Cynthia Steele has captured the wonders of the best kind of book tour.

Moon Kiss   Sandra Kleven

Cirque: A Literary Journal for the North Pacific Rims

Sandra L. Kleven, Publisher and Mike Burwell, Editor
Cynthia Steele, Associate Editor
Paul K. Haeder, Projects Editor
Signe Nichols, Designer
Published twice yearly near the Winter and Summer Solstice
Anchorage, Alaska

Our mission: to build a literary community and memorialize writers, poets and artists of the region.

CIRQUE A Literary Journal for the North Pacific Rim

Volume 14, No. 1

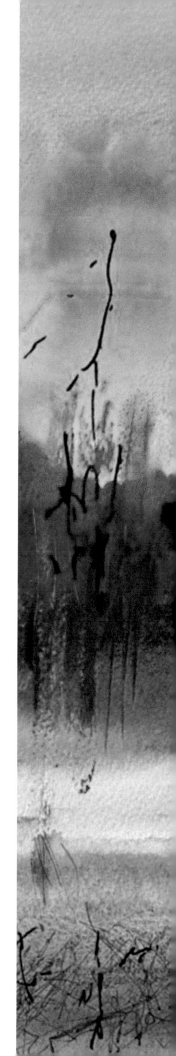

FEATURES

REVIEWS

TRIBUTE

FEATURE

CONTRIBUTORS...163

POETRY CONTEST: Poems About Puppies (and Other Pets)

Cynthia Lee Steele

How I Became a Dog Advocate

The story of puppies and other pets is dear to my heart. As a child, I grew up moving from apartment to apartment with my mother and sister and, we had litters of puppies for which I volunteered to care. Those puppies changed me. I could have been a less heart-full person. I could have been harder. But, the smell of puppy breath, and open, loving warmth, a yearning for closeness brought me around. Raising pups, with their near-constant need of cleaning and our own worry for them bonded me forever to the idea of them. Their clinging-to-us affection destroys any wall we put up, if we let it, and I did.

As with many people of the 1970's, puppies and other pets often went without medical intervention or shots. I wasn't 10 when 1973 began the nationwide rabies vaccination mandate for dogs, driven by fear of harm to people and *not* care for dogs. Medical care for people was far less than routine, and for household pets was often for the wealthier pet owner. Shake it off, walk it off, endure, and we will see how it goes—that was the idea. If a dog could not tough it out, it was unfortunate. We had several dogs contract distemper, and one of them, a black dog named Puppy died in my arms, twitching.

Getting dogs "fixed" wasn't something we had money or inclination for all the time, either. I often fed and brought home strays.

Our dogs were free range, like us free-ranging children, doing whatever and reporting or not reporting it to parents who were quite caught up in the hippy movement in a very radical sense. Dogs followed us around, kept us safe, barked at strangers, and waited for us at all hours at every place we went. They were our constant companions but often for less than their allotted life spans. Knobber ate a hashish ball and walked very slowly into the road where he was hit by a car, and we were unable to stop it from happening. This was the 70s.

Blondes   *Linda Lucky*

When we moved to the Mat-Su Valley, we owned a wolf mix, Gray, a cat-killer. We had a few who kept getting within his line of the chain. The law of survival ruled. Darwinism for felines and former sled dogs. Eventually, we had cats who could tow Gray's line. My mother had a short-term slew of 20-some sled dogs that I cooked fish-head stew, barley, and rice for in huge drums over an open fire. I knew the hunger of sled dogs as well as the love and the chain they lived on.

Cody was one: a medium sized reddish-blond dog the neighbors wanted to shoot because he had eaten their rabbits. I saved him. At our small, and also short-lived, farm one night, Cody got loose and killed all our rabbits, pheasants, ducks, and chickens—animals I fed and grew to love and need. I learned that for the sake of a farm, all animals cannot be kept or maybe even saved. I learned that we must accept that some characteristics of animals just exist. Cody was blood thirsty and instinct driven. He didn't mean to be that way; he just was. The silence of that morning was deafening. No rooster to crow, no clucking, no calls from birds from whose nests we would take eggs to put under warmers to hatch. We put the unhatched eggs in with the pigs to recycle life.

These unforgettable incidents made me a champion, a fighter for dogs and their care and training. I have quite nearly always had a dog, except for a brief period when I had rabbits. I have owned a dog who lived to age 19—throughout my children's lives. I determined this to be "the way to go." We are their necessary caretakers because they are domesticated.

Never do I ever want a dog to shiver and die from distemper or any other illness that is preventable or curable. Nothing is guaranteed, though. Over the past several years, we have taken six dogs into our home—two heartfelt and true rescues and four definitely intentionally planned breeds. Consistently thereafter, we fostered some 13 dogs—one or two at a time (as with bonded pairs). We "failed" one foster (Kona, a Husky-Great Dane-Mastiff mix), giving us a total of seven, by adopting her instead of letting her go because no one applied for her. A pet grieving the death of an owner brings on strange behaviors. The risks she took to love me grew into my first dog poem "I Am Kona's Landscape"—playing off the great "I am" of the Bible and describing all we are to our dogs—their higher power and protected property.

A year after her adoption, our pack, minus an older dog, caught Kennel Cough, likely via dog parks. This happened even though they were all vaccinated, something that unnerves me still. How can they not be protected? It happens, the vet says and just shrugs. Somehow, Kona and Hawk contracted pneumonia. Hawk healed, but Kona's turned into the dreaded lung plague that has swept a good part of the nation, morphing into necrotizing bacteria.

They asked if she had been out of the country. Was this a COVID spoof spinoff? Out of the country? She'd never been out of the state, to my knowledge. The bacteria ate a hole in her lung, and she was hospitalized for a week, expected to need a lobe removed.

She took on air between her ribs and lungs over and over and suddenly didn't. The vet called to ask if we could pick her up that Sunday as she had suddenly healed, and her health was not overly compromised. Again, we felt punked. The hole had closed on its own.

We still occasionally hold our breaths as we watch her ribs rise and fall and imagine her in the hospital and all that that includes. Their eyes, their breaths, their steps—the things we memorize without trying to.

Kona returned to chase moose off the trails, and there's nothing that will keep her from it. She's ardent, prideful even, letting the moose know in low spoken undertones from the Dane and Husky in her that the moose must abide, move on. The moose listen. They mosey like domesticated horses. The fact is that protecting me is her responsibility, and she takes it seriously. As do I.

Thus, this contest is near and dear to my heart. Still, I asked myself, can I handle or do I even want to read the poems that deal with losing a dog or cat, especially with my most recent dog health crises? I felt it might be too much. But the words of a poem are different than the explained reality of life. These poems have humor, contain wry silliness, and discuss the personalities that vary so widely in our canine, feline, equine, and even chicken friends. I am inspired by these poems to think of the story or poem of Little Miss Fluffabutt, a chicken we once had that was fluffy beyond imagination right down to her little ankles. Is there a silliness to it all? You betcha. But, there is also a seriousness.

Pets make whatever hovel we have into a home, those of us who invite in the animals. It's their warmth, already there, that brings us home. Our dominion and responsibility over them that makes their home complete for them. We are forever in their debt to protect us from predators or to rid us of mice or even bring us some. We just say "Thanks." And to you who submitted poems for me to read during my difficult time with Kona, I say "Thanks," you sustained me, as well. ◪

CONTEST WINNERS

Christianne Balk

Wild Grass

At eight-weeks old, we named him Kobuk,
Athabascan for big water, and held his
soaking wet, perfect blackness in our arms
to keep him from crashing through the Chena's
ice. How he loved to run! He tricked the yellow
flag iris, fox tail, and wild grass, leaving
long rifts in the field to close slowly over.

A farmhouse dissolving into the landscape.
The Palouse, eastern Washington, 2023   *James Pearson*

Randy Bynum

Charli the Fierce

In the forest surrounded by the city
surrounded by the greener forest,
tinted by the passing years, July's
alabaster marble moon goes full,
throws a bone down
to all those sleeping this night,
even that tiny chuckling chuffy
white-curled Bichon doggy next door
who today passed on, his race run,
poodle front porch finally guarded in full,
sprinting with all fifteen years
catching up to those elusive beams
that now stick to his paws like
magic water. He leaps around, amid
the sad stunned family, yelps he's
met the lunar pack, and sends
back his love, but they do not see.

They remember, and weep,
tears telling the lessons left
of our lives in the forest,
surrounded by the city,
surrounded by sentinel
trees who also mourn but quietly
hear a small kindred become wind,
move their branch limbs in applause,
welcoming him home, enveloped
by his well-kept life, loved, held, fed.
May he now ever more freely roam.

Friends   *Shauna Potocky*

Joanna Streetly

Playing God

After our moment at the beach, everything changes.
Smiles fade. Drift logs and sea foam shear away, too fast,
out of sight. In my rearview mirror a pale fleet of gulls
glare at me from their runway of shining sand.

Do they know where I'm taking him?

Does he know, too? Warm white muzzle rests
on my shoulder, pink tongue flaps in the open window,
licking last lungfuls of air. Rushing wind sweeps away
the stench of infection wafting from his tumour.

I watched this dog born, a slippery grey ball, falling onto straw.

I push songs into the stereo, reach back to ruffle
his ears, but he pulls away. Judas fingers hang in air.
I shut off the music. In the new silence I hear my name
as a distant cock crows.

Who am I to make this choice?

The road to the vet is rutted and bumpy. One big clearcut.
Stygian, fire-blackened stumps loom and creak.
I could turn back, race home euphoric in a fanfare
of trumpets, tomorrow watch him suffer.

I stop the car, start again, stop, start.

The plunger goes down on the final syringe. Pale
liquid pushes the light from his eyes, leaves only the heavy
grey sand of the beach. Seagulls rise and scatter. Their wings
beat turbulence in the heavy grey sky of my mind.

Sand Stories   *Mandy Ramsey*

FINALISTS

Carol Kaynor

Dragged Back

you come in tangled, flat, a soft black rug
dragged by unheeding teammates
toward the finish line
no rider on the tipped-over sled

your eyes bulge wide, staring, black and empty
your tongue a bloody, fat protrusion
snow stuck to lips, to legs, to face
a tinge of blue, faint halo speaking death

some ten of us block the incoming team
stop the other dogs, grab the sled
unclipped from lines, your body waits
to be reclaimed from those who dragged you here

cursing—I have seen this once
and wished to never see again
I bend to your limp form, lift and turn
from the crowd with their curious, pitying eyes

seeking someplace quiet to lay you down
my arms hold lifeless shape against my chest
I step away: one, two steps, maybe three
and out of stillness comes a quiet rasp

of remembered breath
…and then another
and my arms are cradling your life
instead of your ending

Tumbling   *Sheary Clough Suiter*

Dale Champlin

A Stitch in the Heart

Fleet of foot, sharp of claw
A bag of bones, a bag of tricks
Brought back from the dead
Frankenstein's dog

First the teeth come out
"Like a string of pearls,
One following close behind another"
The canines and front teeth left to nip and pierce

The tumors compile, one on top of another
Grape clusters under the skin
One the size of a peach, overripe
No pit, no substance

The uterus ready to rupture
Swollen and bloated
Scooped out, eviscerated
At the doctor's whim

One week, then a month
The tumors are worse
Take them out too,
An inch strip of flesh on either side

A septuple mastectomy
Whip stitch! We'll stitch her up!
Put in drains, shunts and staples
There's not enough skin!

It'll be a little tight
But never mind
(Please don't fall
apart at the seams)

Dress her in onesies
The sad seeping darling
Railroad tracks down
Each side of her chest

Sleep with her
Comfort and spoon her
Water and feed her
She's fragile, she's mine

The staples come out
Shunts drop down useless
Stitches removed
But for one attached to my heart

She uses her front teeth to
Eat artichokes like I do
She uses her canines to
Pull up her blanket

Diagonally running
Whimpering in her sleep
She has learned to talk
She is civilized now

She is stitched to my ribcage
But what is that black spot?
What is that cough?
My darling,
My beastie,
My monster

Quilted Portrait of Brooks   *Lucy Tyrrell*

Set in Concrete   *David A. Goodrum*

David A. Goodrum

Set in Concrete

Paw pads dark with age
emboss the cement sidewalk
Memory unleashed

Jim Hanlen

Other People's Dogs

I stop at Lisel's porch step
and we run down to Petra,
the chihuahua, who doesn't
keep up, but she tries. Then
It's over to Eddie, greyhound,
racetrack-retired, but ready.
He couldn't find his way back
without us. We stop by
the police dog's house.
He actually was a policeman
In New York City. Like his owner
they retired to the easy life.
We run to the end of town
and back. We ran Main Street
once, but the cops chased us.
There's not much talking.
I've sniffed the other end
and the French puddle
was disgusting from gobbling
prosciutto and braunschweiger
and I hadn't had breakfast yet.
No time to talk. We move,
We go. We stop at the corner
of the library and leave
a contribution for canine culture

Hiding from the Rain   *Annekathrin Hansen*

Joanna Streetly

Trinidad Stray Dogs

There were always stray dogs
fleeing stones, hit by cars
dogs whose unloved bones
saw invitation in my open hand
dogs who cringed and scarpered
dogs who *could be rabid*, my dad said

My favourite was Tramp
his dull fur called out
over muddled street chaos
tentative tail-wag
eyes that took in distant threats
even as they trusted me

I kept meal scraps safe from ants
tiptoed back & forth
house, street, house
dustclouds chasing blackened feet
hot weight of secrecy

After dark I listened through
the streetlight's loud buzz
for sudden sighs, the ridding of fleas
his bed a rooted hollow
amid barbs of pink bougainvillea

I trusted those thorns to keep him safe
too young to know the chronicles
of street dogs, volumes of them peopled
with feral Fagins, streetwise Dodgers,
men, sticks, cars
& other tragic endings

Juanita Smart

Breathless

I race after River
my galumphing, honey-colored dog
who chases the fawn
round
              & round
& round—
the earth clabbers into butter
beneath their feet.

The fawn curtsies to the dog
before she collapses,
chop stick legs folding
underneath her like a TV tray,
her face, a morning song.
She holds the shine
of dewdrops in her eyes,
pants, silent as a star.

Then River folds her body too,
splashes swales of grass
where she flops beside the fawn,
two engines huffing
                side by side.

Underneath the clouds' white blouses,
their bodies are a pair of commas
stalling time, pink tongues
dripping light.
I dive towards River,
click the snap-hook to her collar ring—
The fawn rockets

         away,
            away,
              away,

shimmer of gold vanishing--
already a wish, salting summer air.

Warm Light   *Nard Claar*

Joel Savishinsky

Infidelity

It is the season of promiscuity,
of open doors, shadowed streets,
evenings that invite conspiracy,
that dare disappointment
for the sake of danger.

We've been together years
I no longer count. She shares
my bed but pushes the boundaries,
takes too much of the blanket
for her own comfort.
At uncontrolled moments,
her face moves into my cheek,
she licks my ear.

I beg her not to leave me,
plead I will ignore her snores,
overlook the restless legs, forgive
the soft cries of her dark dreams.
It does not matter;
she won't listen.
I wake at midnight to find
the cat is gone again.

Katherine Poyner-Del Vento

Because

Because when my twenty-year-old cat
is confused by the shaking bed
and tenderly starts scraping at our skin,
you take one hand off my hip
to pet her.

Leah Stenson

Fat Kitty Trilogy

Fat Kitty Trilogy

I. How Fat Kitty Got Her Name

The stray cat appeared one day
in the field across the road.
Demanding affection,
she flopped down in front of us,
attempted to rub her
mangy body against our legs.
We spurned her advances, unkindly
called her Fat Kitty, refused
to stroke the tangled fur
matted with clumps of mud.

Despite our rejection,
Fat Kitty hung around.
One day, we watched as she sat
for hours by a mole hole,
not moving a muscle.
When the afternoon turned chill,
she curled up into a ball
to continue her vigil,
an impossibly long wait,
longer than most humans wait
for love.

With moles in our garden,
and mindful of the proverb
about pragmatic alliances--
*An enemy of my enemy
is a friend of mine--*
we welcomed Fat Kitty
as our friend
yet still I wouldn't pet her.

II. Cat Bodhisattva

One sweltering summer day
my hubby took pity on Fat Kitty
and brushed her.
The cat loved to be brushed,
loved it so much she lashed out
and scratched him when he stopped.

Brushing her was like shearing a sheep—
her hair soon filled a pail.
Rid of the winter coat that ended up
in her throat as supersized hair balls,
she began grooming herself with gusto.

When cleaned up, Fat Kitty
wasn't fat after all.
She was a long-haired Nebelung
with a rich silver-tipped blue-gray coat
covering a multitude of scars,
some still fresh with scabs and blood,
evidence of a hard life in the wilds.

The more we learned, the more
our affection for Fat Kitty deepened.
She seemed to have weathered
myriad trials in her search
for someone to love and feed her.
The cat bonded with my hubby,
curling up in his lap,
licking his fingers.

Like Bodhisattva Never-Disparaging,
Fat Kitty had weathered our rejections
and found acceptance in this lifetime,
and we in turn were blessed
with a new friend.

III. Fat Kitty Sensei, My Teacher

They say it's impossible to train a cat
but Fat Kitty was a quick study.
She learned to circle a post
three times to receive a cat treat,
never entered the house unless
invited in, waited patiently
on the doorstep.

I began to feel a soft spot
in my heart for Fat Kitty
whose intelligence
and loving nature won me over.
Her name, once a mark of disdain,
became a term of endearment.
Every morning I looked forward to
Fat Kitty bounding
across the lawn to greet me
and I was happy
to pet her.

One morning we missed her.
She didn't show up the next day.
Or the next.
Could the frightful yowling
we heard late one night
have been Fat Kitty fighting
for her life with the coyote
that had been killing
the neighbor's sheep?

For five long nights and days
I worried about our precious kitty,
meditated on the duality
of love and loss, and when
our Beloved finally returned
I greeted her with open arms
and rejoiced.

KitKat Looking Through the Blinds   *Patrick Dixon*

If I hadn't let Fat Kitty into my heart,
I would never have missed her
or realized how much I cared.

Fat Kitty taught me to reflect
on missed opportunities,
to look beyond surface appearances,
even when I don't like something, and
to be kind to all people and creatures.

Patrick Dixon

Driving with the Windows Down

for Spencer

Prologue

Tonight's stroll around the lake
was comfortable, cool and calm.
We took our time sniffing the start
of sweet-scented spring.

We walked in a weave with you,
pausing at the picnic table when you looked tired.
You laid at my feet in the shade.
I scratched your white face, and thought,
We can do this for a while.

But when we walked back to the car
I was watching as your leg gave out
and you fell hard onto the crushed gravel
of the path, filling the side of your mouth
with stones. Your legs trembled as you
rose, leaned against me, panted while
I cleaned pebbles from your mouth.

You took a few steps, sighed,
lowered your head and pushed on,
me matching your slow pace,
my eyes big and wet as your tongue.

First Visit

The next day
the sky was blue and the trees
were the lime-green
they only have in April,
spring's opening act.

I hurried to get Spencer in the car
for his appointment.
The wind's bluster bent
the treetops – made me look up
to see where the soft roar was coming from.

He's getting old,
said the short man in the white lab coat.
*He isn't as coordinated as he once was.
No wonder he's falling. My eighty-year-old
dad did the same.*

I wasn't comforted. Spencer panted
and looked away, haunches
on hard linoleum, expression tolerant:
*I'll put up with this guy, but don't expect
me to like it,* was the message
I got, but the doc didn't seem to.

He looks like a good dog, he placated us,
and I knew the session was about over.
We were relieved to pay
the bill and get out of there,
drive with the windows down,
ears flapping, tongues out, leaning
together, into the wind.

Last Visit

I'd rather have a different doctor, I said
into the phone as I made another appointment.
I thought perhaps someone else would see
Spencer's balance problems differently.
He was limping more, and my confidence was sliding
down the dark tunnel from concern to worry.
I needed help with the landing if despair was the outcome.

We'll X-ray the shoulder, the new doc smiled,
and see if we find anything. I was the one who said
the word: *My last golden had cancer.*
I got a sympathetic look. *It's common in them,*
she answered gently, *and often shows in the shoulders.
We'll see what's there.*

I waited a long time outside
on another cool and breezy day,
then went in to wait some more in the lobby.

The pleasant, welcoming atmosphere
behind the counter had changed tone.
Only one person was left attending the clients
who were sitting, standing, barking and meowing.
The assistants who showed their faces looked troubled
and disappeared quickly. I watched one gentleman
and his dog get turned away until the following day.
We were next.

Spencer Portrait   *Patrick Dixon*

Spencer was led back to me with apologies,
We've had an emergency. Can I schedule you for tomorrow?
Her expression was dark as she worked the computer,
and I leaned in. *Is someone in trouble?*
She nodded. *We've had an emergency.* Her hands shook,
her smock was covered with light yellow hair.

Epilogue

We returned for the X-ray, and you seemed
pleased to be back, despite my apprehensions.

The vet slid the film onto the light table mounted to the wall.
She pointed at a small white speck
and spoke to you.
Looks like a bone chip in your shoulder, Kiddo.
She rubbed your head as you licked the last of the peanut butter.
Probably some arthritis broken away.
The good news is, it's not cancer. You licked her hand.
We should be able to manage the pain until it eases.

At the counter, I asked again,
and was told someone else's Spencer
had reacted badly to routine anesthesia yesterday
and didn't make it. Someone had departed the clinic
with an empty collar cradled in their hands.

Home, we lingered side-by-side
leaning into one another under the cedar,
where in just a few short months
I'd lose you too.

The Last to Go   *Sheary Clough Suiter*

Penny Johnson

My Heart. My Mare

I am the vase left to collude with dust mites. A metal so tarnished, I pit. Now bitter with dried yarrow and mullein that is bared to its skeleton. But the animals

tamarack furred dogs
caramelized onion, the yellow cats
dijon ruffles of scythe horned goats

and on farther, past these, look to the ones sold off-property. Please return and hover clear as water after slaughter. Suzie-Q. Popeye. Vaporous. Please slick my skin. Smoke this lanky white hair as I make my way, this low barn, the frost crusted roof

each one of you, hold tight this vigil
and the ones who fell dead at my feet

the black and white collie. Not one more step in him with all his pack lost and haywired. Like springs sprung and launched. Hung from beneath their shoulders, each dog flies into the wild umpire green. Where the lights shimmy. Where the lights shiver in a fever of Aurora Borealis and the sequester of cold cold stars.

Every single night, down these three wooden-porch steps. Watch the ice. Step resolute. Tamp flat-footed to reach the allowance, the wide swing of the metal gate and

this sky is so jimmy-jammed with stars waylaid and backed up in magic-mirrors. With edges ragged in an endless current of ghosted mice and their tissue-nibbling shreds cast on a concrete floor.

Mare. You so young to my old. Your neck arches over the rail. Statue-still in night with one pink hoof cocked. How do you never question my complicity? Your sable nostrils against, this my pale, fleshy nose, smaller than a scarlet-nante-carrot now sandpapered with contact dermatitis. Please

breathe the fugue of my dinner. Cautious. Sipped in shallow, skin-flint draughts but this is

chickpeas and orange peel
honey and raisins
Mediterranean olives

nostrils quiver and then their caverns swing wide. This is the tidal salt of you as I am pulled forward until my knees buckle.

Robin Woolman

Only in the Kitchen

The litter of puppies scrabbles about the worn porch as she passes.
Like a magnet, they draw her up the steps to sit among the licking and wagging,
the needle teeth gnawing.
"Want one? Free to a good home."
She strokes the black silk of their coats, remembering all the puppies in her past.
"Yes! So adorable…well, no. Things are difficult right now.
"So we've heard. Your husband has cancer? How's he doing?
"Brain tumor. Not good." A puppy is licking her neck.
"Hey, would you mind if I just borrow this cutie for the afternoon?
Might be a nice distraction. He was raised with dogs. And my son Sam would love it."
"Of course! Keep her a week. Whatever works. Just let us know."
"You are so kind!" She summons a smile and cradles the puppy on home.

…………

"Last thing we need, Babe, you know that," he says sliding his tired hand
over the drowsy puppy curled in his lap.
"I know…it's just for the afternoon. For Sam. After school."
"Sure." He fingers the thin marvel of the puppy's ear. She shakes her head
then rests her muzzle back on the patch quilt.
"Dogs shouldn't be in the house," he mutters. "Our dogs were never in the house."
"I should take her back…"
He lifts his gaze to his wife. Sees his own stern sorrow mirrored back.
He summons a smile. "Not yet, I guess. For Sam…"
She nods not trusting her voice.
"Is Hospice coming today?"
She nods.

…………

"You're up!" Surprise replaces her daily fear as she returns from work.
She tosses the pharmacy bag of pills on the counter and kneels
by the puppy and her husband who sit on the kitchen floor together.
He shrugs. "It's a good day. Been in the kitchen with the puppy. She knows
her boundaries already. Only in the kitchen," His finger draws the line
between linoleum and hardwood. The puppy licks his hand.
"My mother let one dog in the house once, just for the week
before it died. Got into some poison. But only in the kitchen."
"Okay, then…so she's staying?" her breathing shallow with hope.
"I need to let the neighbor know…"
"She can stay…for Sam…only in the kitchen."
"Only in the kitchen. We'll let Sam name her?
He shakes his head, "It's Scout."
"Oh, okay. Scout. Like in *To Kill a Mockingbird?*"
He shrugs. "It's a good book."

....

She sits on the floor of the kitchen, throwing the tennis ball to ricochet
off table leg, fridge, cupboards, dog bowl. Scout scampers and slides after it.
From upstairs the rush of shower water and the hospice nurse's cheery voice
float down. She feels useless in these final stages.
She scoops up the puppy and stumbles down the basement steps.
Neglected laundry lurks in baskets, mesh bags and on the cement floor.
She dumps it all as if it were a pile of fall leaves and she and the puppy
burrow and roll in the smell of the family until her tears are spent
and the first load agitates in the machine.

....

They drive to the cemetery on this day every year,
Scout in the passenger seat, sunflowers in the back.
Sam is not with them; he has his own life now,
his own fussy breed of dog—all care, no boundaries.
After flowers are laid, she and Scout hike among
the gray stones and shade trees, flush a deer,
watch the birds feed on new seed the grounds keeper
keeps planting. Scout whines but doesn't chase.
There's arthritis in her shaggy legs. Scout
stays close to her master's side always, except at night
when she sleeps in the kitchen…
only in the kitchen.

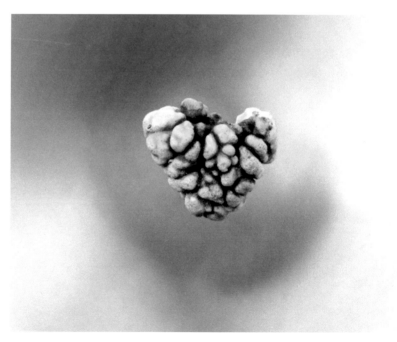

I Heart Coral   *Jim Thiele*

Shauna Potocky

Love of Season

Siku knows—

She knows the difference between cold rain
and the bliss of swirling snow

She stands in the yellow glow of street lights
kaleidoscope snowstorm, its twisting shadows

mouth agape, catching crystalline bits of magic

She knows the word "ski" and the turn off
to Exit Glacier and Bear Lake

Clipping into her line is an act of trust as much as folly
our adventure hinged to the strength of our bond

and the power of words

She is a woven line of genes; working dogs raised
on the edge of the Bering Sea, she was born to run and pull

so she does—

She knows the lag of slow snow and expects me to pole hard;
on fast ice, it takes everything not to be filled with fear

She'll chase down the snowmachine, grooming the track
if you ask and when she catches it, the groomer laughs

while she twirls around, proud

She'll stand on her long back legs to fetch a wider view
of moose or lurking bear, keeps watch, smells hard

If it has snowed all night, the trail brimming
she'll break it—bounding or with a steady pace

some things she knows without being taught

Into the Woods,
a Belgian Tervuren's Final Walk   *Cynthia Steele*

Shirley Martin
Two Poems

Three of Nine

Life # 1
Bit of grey fluff on the pebble beach
catches my eye –
not gull feathers, not flotsam or jetsam
but?!!
I barrel-ass down the yard
seize our itty-bitty-kitty Mungo as
enormous bald eagle
ceases circling downward –
foiled, lifts up,
fierce onyx talons gleaming in the sun.

Life # 2
Grey cool cat
rebellious teenager
constantly demanding to go out –
tonight he missed his curfew.
2 a.m. – godawful caterwauling –
night air shudders with hissing,
snarling, gnashing,
with crashing of branches –
I shine flashlight out bedroom window,
beady yellow eyes blaze back at me,
crimson drips from razor claws –
raccoons can be vicious.
Early morning trip to the vet,
(will we have to remortgage the house?)
then cautiously drive Mungo home.
He slinks from room to room,
skulks behind the couch,
mortified by
his punk rock haircut, his
fluorescent orange-red mercurochromed scalp.

Best of Luck   *Richard Stokes*

Life # 3
Aging grey cat sunning on grey pavement –
not a good idea.
Neighbour phones to say, "I ran over your cat. He
ran for the bushes by the beach."
Three days, three nights, of searching, calling
and then a faint "Mew…. mew."
Husband steps into bushes,
straight into a wasp nest, emerges running
and catless.
Husband (aka Fire Chief) dons full turnout gear
enters wasp inferno –
emerges cradling broken cat.

Reconnoitering:
Husband – nine plus wasp stings, and a revelation – a wasp sting allergy! Luckily, next-door-
neighbour is a nurse, administers adrenaline shots and antihistamines, reverses his swelling
features, his closing windpipe.
Mungo – no wasp stings! recovers from a broken pelvis, damaged left eye, but forever after pads
through the house with pirate-like visage (his outer eyelid will not close – family reassures him
that the closed left inner eyelid is creepy yet debonair.)

(Lives #4 to #9 – fingers crossed.)

In Dreams

You are dreaming again,
muscles flexing
beneath your sleek grey fur,
whiskers twitching,
faintest 'mew'
exhaled with each breath,
through tiny needle-sharp teeth.

Where do you go in dreams?
Do you relive the pursuit, the kill,
the depositing in the kitchen sink
of your first unwanted gift to me,
the hapless fieldmouse
with sweaty ash-grey coat,
chubby body still warm?

I recall the day you caught a duck
larger than you, on the beach,
dragged it by its neck up the hill
to the front door.
I can see the glare of your topaz eyes, hear
your incredulous yowl as we set your offering
free to fly away.

Now you extend stiff legs, arch your back.
Do you dream of the morning you fell
from our bedroom window, landed
on soft padded paws, sashayed off
triumphant tail waving,
to play tiger in
the tall cool grass?

Sue Fagalde Lick

You're the Reason
I'm Wearing a Torn Tennis Shoe

Or sneaker or athletic footwear, whatever the heck we're supposed to call them these days. Me, I could call them work shoes because I wear them to work. In fact, I wear them everywhere but church. But you, you dog you, you incredibly tall and agile canine, one day I got poo on the bottom of the left shoe, yours I presume. I scraped it off on the lawn, but there were remnants stuck in the grids and I thought, mistakenly, that if I left it on the table to dry, it would just fall out and I wouldn't have to, well, touch it. Ha.

It's a tall table, white plastic, mold-mottled, tall, and you were only three months old, so I figured, again mistakenly, that you couldn't possibly reach it. Then I looked out and saw you standing on top of this impossibly tall table eating my favorite shoe. I ran out, screaming obscenities, threw you down, grabbed my sneaker and slammed the door in your innocent-looking face. The shredded shoestring lay in pieces in the yard and that little loop thing on the back of shoe was gone, stuffing sticking out.

One good shoe, one trashed, still with poo. Perhaps I could wear them for gardening or cleaning the house. I washed off the poo and saliva in the sink, dried it for about a week, bought new strings, too short but they tied, and put my shoes back on. I'm wearing them right now. And you, you canine chowhound vet-visiting checkbook-draining alligator, you're the reason my left shoe slips as I walk you, shouting, "Heel!"

Teri White Carns

seeking buddha

distracting
from enlightenment
dog's wagging tail

Arctic National Wildlife Refuge, June 2023 247   *Nancy Deschu*

Wanda Wilson

Listening to Patience

He has seizures
grand mal
they're messy & bewildering
for both of us

The age of them
wrestles the skin
of our dependencies
into exhausted cracked stones

Yet I remember rainbow days
racing in the tundra
crushing cotton & star flowers
twisting legs until entwined falling laughing

This big yellow hugger
smiling against my hip
after swimming in icy Aleknagik
giggling sighs over our wetness

He often told me our favorite
zoomie stories of hidden moose bones
& treats & running so fast so far
until he found me & I wept in love

for Bisq - my love I miss you

June 2023

Warren J. Rhodes

Replenish

The North reeks of smoke and fear.
Two ghost towns haunt Yukon's Silver Trail,
Elsa since 1989 and now Mayo,
evacuated
to Whitehorse and cots on the ice rink
as hungry flames lick a few klicks from doorsteps back home.
The people send *gunalcheesh* to the YPS wildland crews
and hope their town is spared.

To the north,
past the iron creek that runs red like blood,
other heroes risk all to save
the only lodge on the Dempster
(and its world's largest cribbage board).
When their long day is done,
and they can fight the dogged foe no more,
men and women stumble back to the hotel,
exhausted, eyes bloodshot,
spitting ash from desert mouths,
summer thunder mocking,
promising new fires tomorrow.
Anticipating a shower, not enough shut-eye
and another day
or week
or month on the front lines,
the crews give thanks too:
for cool water, the rest,
buffet chicken that fuels their inner fire,
strength to ignite
a mundane conversation with friends
despite blistered throats.

In their line of work,
the unexpected rarely bodes well,
but tonight the red twilight of Eagle Plains
is different:
An hour snuggling with squirming puppies
recently born to a mutt
clawed back from the inferno,
their fevered kisses on delighted faces
returning a small portion
of the moisture lost that day.

Canon Light   *Nard Claar*

Judith Duncan

My Chicken Heidi

is named after my lover's ex-girlfriend
whom I live in fear will return for him.
I am not inclined to be too fond of
her–this Heidi Chicken.
She has gaudy golden, silver feathers
far too bright to hide from eagles.

She's sort of like his ex with her blond tresses
glimmering smile, big eyes attract all men.
She steps with a prideful swagger.
Does he still love her–the ex?

Heidi Chicken clucks, scratches for worms,
ruffles feathers. She is not an ideal pet
she offers no cuddles, or kisses.
Kisses! Does he long to kiss his ex?

Yet I yell when I spy a diving hawk.
I holler *incoming-Heidi-incoming*
she scurries for shelter of shrubby bushes.
Hides until I holler *come out Heidi, come out.*

We have reached a truce, his ex and I
I warn her of predators
she does not poop on my deck.

Crowded House

Sheary Clough Suiter

Flowing Path   Mandy Ramsey

NONFICTION

Judith Lethin

Dappled Light

I returned to Anvik in the spring of 2000, and Angela Young invited me to stay with her and her mother, Grandma Mary, in her new log cabin near the school. When I came into the cabin, I found Grandma Mary sitting in an overstuffed royal blue chair near the window, humming and gently rocking. With dappled light falling across her face and her pale green hooded parky and the hand crocheted blanket at her back, she looked for all the world like a painting by Claude Monet. Her hands were pressed together, as though she'd been praying. She looked up when I sat down beside her. I smiled and nodded hello, and began to move my own generous body in time with hers.

"I want the children to know that Jesus was Mary's son," she whispered. Her words seemed to float on a numinous wind that moved in chorus through the trees and through the tiny cabin and through my heart just then. "She wants us to love him." I smiled and nodded yes, as she looked deeper into my eyes and appeared to see me for the first time.

"She wants us to love him, and follow him," she said more urgently.

Again, I nodded, and Grandma Mary smiled and her face broke into a million wrinkles, and the soft skin around her eyes crinkled, and her brows floated up, and she leaned toward me and gently took my hand. Willingly, I followed her into that unfathomable place where she knew the love of Jesus and his mother.

Grandma Mary was born during the 1918 influenza epidemic to a young woman known as Diva Xidoy, a name that means *"who's that at my door"* in Deg Xinag. She was later called Julia by the white people who lived in Anvik. Diva Xidoy could not take care of Mary, so she gave her baby to Clara and George Reed. The Reeds raised Mary up the Yukon River in a place known as Bonzilla until it was time for her to go to school, then they moved to Anvik so Mary could attend the Mission at Christ Church.

I felt humbled by Mary's devotion to Mary and Jesus. I was aware that before first contact with Christianity, the Deg Hit'an people had their own cultural and spiritual beliefs about Dinaxito' that were taught to the children by the elders and the shaman. After contact the diseases brought by the explorers, missionaries, and gold miners killed over half of the Native population in Alaska, leaving many children orphaned. It was a time of great suffering.

I wondered if she'd been spared the terrible effects of boarding school because she had been adopted.

When Katherine, my ministry partner from Shageluk, and I came back to Anvik a few months later, Grandma Mary was lying in a hand-made spruce box at home. She had fallen and broken her hip, and died a few days later. Her extended family and friends had come to the village to help cook the traditional meals that would feed the village for the four days before the potlatch. Men and young men set to work building the spirit house and digging the grave. Women and young girls sewed the skin boots, and hat and gloves that she would wear on her final journey into the light. A steady stream of workers and visitors came to the cabin to eat and visit and speak well of Mary.

On the morning of the potlatch the men brought Mary's body to the community hall. Marsha, Susan, Julie, and Melody gathered to help Angela dress her in her new clothes. Katherine and I were invited to help. I had participated in a number of funerals on the Yukon, and had been allowed to watch the dressing of Grandma Alma in Grayling, but this was the first time I'd been invited to participate in this sacred burial ritual of the Deg Hit'an.

We all gathered in a circle around Grandma Mary. The two oldest elders, Marsha and Katherine, stood with Angela near her head, ready to give instructions and to see that everything was done according to the old traditions. Julie and Susan, Marsha's daughters, were on one side of the box and Melody, the health aide, and I were on the other. Julie was the head teacher at the school. She often invited me to sing or play games with the children when I was in the village. Susan had a store in the front room of her cabin on main street and sold chips, sodas, candy, and canned goods. It was my go-to stop when I needed chocolate. Melody had invited me to help her dissect a fetal pig once for her medical certification and we'd laughed late into the night. Everyone here had children who came to Sunday school and took turns being acolytes during the worship services at Christ Church. I felt a warm kinship with these women who had invited me into this sacred circle.

Julie looked at me and nodded, "Judith, take her pants off."

I looked up in disbelief. Sweat broke out on my forehead. My mouth went dry. The only time I'd actually touched a body was after it was dressed in its traveling clothes, and then only to shake the gloved hand so the person's strength could come into me. I wanted to cuss. I wanted to run. I scanned the circle. Everyone calmly waited for me to begin.

"Okay."

As I leaned into the handmade spruce box, I became aware of two remarkable things: the unforgettable scent of death, and how still the room had become. The first caused me to hesitate, but the second caused me to look up. Grandma Mary's face held such a quality of serenity that I was immediately transported back to the morning the sunlight dappled her face and she'd told me we were to love Jesus and follow him. Follow him? Yes. Wherever he leads us? Yes.

"Thank you," I whispered.

I took a deep breath, grabbed onto her navy-blue pant legs and began to pull. The polyester didn't budge. I pulled again. This time the waistband moved about two inches. I leaned deeper into the box, held my breath, and slipped my hands around the sides of her waist and began to pull back and forth, back and forth until the cold, wet pants slowly began to slip free. I dropped them into the black garbage bag that Melody was holding, stepped back, and gasped.

I wanted to run outside and gulp in fresh air. I wanted to wash the wetness from my hands. I wanted to shake off my shame for hesitating. I also wanted to shout, "I did it! I did it!" But I couldn't move. I was mesmerized by the tenderness with which the women began to prepare Mary's body for her new clothes. She was their mother, their auntie, their elder. They loved her.

The gentle, yet confident, actions of the women dressing Grandma Mary and the soft murmur of voices as they discussed the right way to fold the handkerchief and tie on the belt began to flow over me like a gentle wind or a beam of sunlight. My breathing deepened, my shoulders began to relax, and in that moment, I realized we belong to the things we love the same way the trees belong to the wind and the fox kits playing in the forest belong to the sunlight. The things we love inform us and dwell in us and make us who we are.

Where do love and belonging come from? Where does gentleness come from? Where does the wind—as it curls over the hills—come from? We do not know, but we do know the sound the wind makes as it stirs the trees, and the feel of it as it brushes past our cheeks, and its undulating dance with the spruce boughs dappling the light that lifts the veil from an old woman's face when she smiles and talks about Jesus.

When Grandma Mary looked into my eyes and

said she wanted the children to know Mary and Jesus, I somehow knew Jesus in a new way, too, and I was filled with joy and wonder. In that revelation, I could see that her desire to teach the children was not born of the fear, which so many Christians harbor, that the children would somehow be "lost" if they didn't know Jesus. No, there was a serenity of spirit that seemed to say, *even if we don't know Jesus, Jesus knows us, and Jesus loves us, and invites us to follow him into the way of love.* And we know, in that very moment, that we belong to love just as the trees belong to the wind, and we welcome it and we gulp it in, hoping to hold onto that mystery when times get tough.

Arctic National Wildlife Refuge, June 2023 42   *Nancy Deschur*

Grandma Mary didn't choose me or choose any of the women who served her in that sacred way, but her faith and her cultural traditions assured her that she would be dressed with love and respect for the potlatch and her final journey into the light. Marsha and Susan and Julie and Angela and Katherine and Melody had welcomed me into their circle of love, and we belonged to each other from that moment on.

At last, I found soap and water and washed my hands, but by then a kind of peace had begun to replace the shame. I knew I was called to be at Christ Church as the Deacon who would officiate at the Christian burial rite the following morning. But it was also my privilege to be invited to participate in one of the oldest Deg Hit'an Athabascan rituals—preparing the dead for their potlatch—and, in that, I was changed. I felt humble and more alive. My work felt more hallowed. I was rooted to that place, a spruce tree undulating in the wind.

The following morning at the Anvik cemetery I noticed the patchwork of paper birch and black spruce standing watch on the hill facing the Yukon River, and the wildflowers that graced the family plots clustered here and there, and the spirit houses marking the individual grave sites; some standing straight and tall with a new coat of paint even as others melted into the landscape from age and neglect. Tall grasses and wild roses and purple Siberian iris pushed this way and that, greeting Grandma Mary and the Deg Hit'an people with an elegant sagacity. *Thank you for still being here, on this river, on this land, with your language and your culture and your traditions, old and new, showing us the way to love.* ☐

Valkyrie Liles

Hungry Bear

I walk the forest every day. I look at the trees. I see the dead and dying but also the thriving, sometimes side by side. What makes a survivor? One wild turkey poop? One rodent engulfed in owl wings under a pine bough and the blood soaks into the mossy ground? The rain comes and this one tree gets some precious thing that the one next to it didn't? And that pine tree has perfect branches, up high, for owls. The needles fall year over year and the forest floor becomes a deep cozy layer of litter for mice. It all works and maybe it seems random but it's not, it's complex. The puzzle pieces unseen yet fitting together perfectly. Some say God and I say yes. God lives in the forest and my cells, and in my magical, broken body. God lives in the blood of rodents and turkey poop and the wheel turns. The wheel turns. Endlessly it goes round and round. Do not always ask why. Just breathe in the mystery. Just wash your hands in the river of not knowing, forget the 2 am tossing in sheets, wide awake, trying to catch yourself, trying to know the things… which are still beyond your knowing.

No curse words for the things you cannot control. No hatred for the big world of mysteries. No place for hopelessness. No rage unbalanced; there is always love on the other side. Feel the association of cells and miracles that you are. Strip off your doubt and run naked through your life like a leaf falling from the sky. Open your heart to this impossible maze of choices and consequences. It's not easy. Big world, small person. Big feelings and one small life to contain them all.

I struggle with the practical world every day. Junk piles, too many projects, not enough money, not enough time, an aging body and flagging motivation. The oven breaks, the washing machine won't agitate. My husband orders the parts and he fixes the oven, the washing machine. He gets up and goes to work every day, he carves timber and builds houses, he's tired, he's inspired. His hands are rough, large and full of little splinters. His thumbnails are cut so short. He works for us and I work for us. The dirty shirts agitate now, I run the machine that sucks dog hair and mud from rugs, I make meals upon meals. I prepare seemingly endless calories to keep us going and it makes sense to me, these predictable moments fit together perfectly but they are not the whole puzzle.

So many pieces unseen. I feel them floating around the edges of my life. Things sliding out of control but also into place. I stopped trying to see them, to move them. I think of the trees, one thrives while the other dies. A little blood and a bird's feather. The wild rabbit digs, the coffee tastes good. The blood soaks in. The sweat and tears soak in. I move the earth in spoonfuls and tuck seedlings into little open pockets that I made with a trowel. No different than a mouse beneath the pine. I have made a home, a place in the world, and it is both secure and dangerous. It's all moving together, though I don't know how; I can't see the whole picture. I don't know how to change or when to change and I don't have to. Change just happens and I adapt and transform. I've already lived many lives in this one small life. All magical, all ragged.

Sometimes I wish I could disappear, but we never disappear do we? And sometimes I wish everyone could see me, but most people never see us do they? They only see us in fragments and so in a way we are always disappearing and reappearing. Even with ourselves we do this: disappear, reappear. From the things we forgot we loved to do to the hobbies that we no longer wish to pursue to the choices we can't fathom we once made. That was a different person. Where did she go, I wonder? I don't wonder long. I look back and the road behind is so much more clear than the one ahead. This is always the way. Always. The road ahead may be planned, but you still can't see it.

Pieces unseen but still moving. Life never stops, it feels like a line but it's no line, it's a pine tree sprawling toward the sky. I am tangled, mangled, I am irritated but it is also beautiful. Our lives intersect with other lives, branches that cross or grow together. Giant limbs fall and some holes never heal; we just eventually abandon them. As the tree grows upward and in all directions; it feels more chaotic. Let's see…choices, choices, plans, progress, decisions, guilt, fear, more choices, wrong choices, right choices, moving in all directions but it looks like a line. We are not finite, we are endless. We are puzzles of ten thousand pieces, we are just one broken piece of something bigger than us, one mouse in a pile of pine needles. We are small.

But also the whole universe in one decrepit body. Light explodes from our owl wings and eye sockets and darkness pours from our chests and pulls at the fabric of reality. Move cautiously. Do not forget that it's all happening right inside of you. One step forward and you break the world. One step back and you disappear forever. It feels like this sometimes. We might be paralyzed in some ways, trapped in a construct, a chaotic creation. Surely I am not responsible for this mayhem. Surely I didn't make something so ridiculous. Surely I am just happening to the world as it is happening to me.

I have crafted and toiled endlessly to arrive where? I ask of no one again and again, but what does it mean? Oh just stop! Yes, just stop. I think it's best to just stop asking. The wheel turns. Some say God and I say yes! My Grandma said God but her God and mine are different. No wrath too small said my Grandma because they all mattered to her angry God, because her God only seemed to love certain people and there was no mercy, only religion as a weapon. Her God of wrath and judgement made it hard for me to love her which I felt was wrong because my God said love and only love.

The whole world is inside of us and we pretend we can't remember. We forget we are the land even as we tread all over it, We say "don't tread on me," but we are already letting our boots crush our own lungs with every step. We have so many promises inside of us: everything holy, but also the dirty, the grotesque…all of it kept hidden under some ridiculous bouffant that's framing a forced smile. Don't pretend you have it all figured out. Just let go. Soil in your veins, seeds in your mouth. So many seeds that you should not be able to get a word out. Some thrive while others die, and everything in between…there are levels of thriving and many kinds of dying. Owl wings beating against the night sky, talons pierce a mouse, blood spills on the land. If something exists, it has a place and purpose.

Like my cousins, the bears. As a child I knew them, and I knew what they ate. I knew that when I foraged berries or caught salmon that there were still plenty for the bears. We didn't fight over food and the bears were not hungry and I was never hungry. Not like I am now with things disappearing and land going barren. Now I don't trust a bear, the bears are different, the world is leaner for all of us. When the bears go hungry it's only a matter of time before we all go hungry. Everyone eats or very soon, no one eats. The puzzle is not a mystery at all. The hungry bears are not a mystery, they are a lesson. A lesson in balance. The people crying for justice and equity are not a mystery to imprison or kill, they are a lesson in balance.

Give up your ghosts, your founding fathers, your hastily written partial history. Inside of you there lives a whole planet, a puzzle of 10 million pieces. Trust the puzzle, trust your anger but don't let someone else give it words. Can't you hear the sound of your own blood? It's a river, it's an ocean, it's a lake. It's the owl, now dead, sinking slowly into pine needles and moss, filling the forest floor with layer after layer of life and death and this is the cycle we are meant to be a part of. No conquerors! Only pine needles to fill the empty space of generations. Only stones to roll over the dead.

And an axe to bust up Grandma's bones and the memory of her bones. I ground them all into dust, yes, the soil that feeds the land can be made of rotten stuff. I am proof.

Hungry bears to remind me of my own unfulfilled hunger. God lives in the blood of rodents and turkey poop and the wheel turns. The wheel turns. Endlessly it goes round and round, do not ask why! Just breathe in the mystery. Just wash your hands in the river of not knowing. You are that river. Everything that exists has a purpose, a reason and is connected. I tell myself this and oh I know it's true, but how does it all fit together? I feel the weight of my questions and I embrace the weight, the burden, but I have no grip on it, it slips through my hands. I spend my life trying to hold the truth but I am lost. Earn more, have more, be more. It doesn't make sense to me. I feel mediocre, trying to shove puzzle pieces into places they don't fit. I am me but I am also the man who lives in a tent on the side of the freeway. His garbage is my garbage, his pain is my pain. He starves and we all starve, and I cannot turn away because there is nowhere left to look. Every sideways glance takes me back to my own reflection.

I walk the forest every day. In between chores and work days. I always make time, even when I am tired, sick or the rain is pelting down. I say it's for my dog. She needs the exercise and that is true. But I need it too. My fingers on fir needles, green moss on gray rock, prickly hoar frost on the manzanita. Empty seed husks on the rabbit brush, Mullein spires, grasses folded sideways where the deer have slept, oak leaves scattered, paw prints in snow, the small vole carcass of a coyote kill. The position of the sun in the sky and how the shadows run. I need these things that make sense to me, the grand puzzle. I need this ordered chaos, everything in it's place, everything connected. I need silence.

So many other lives and I've tried to be good in all of them. Even when I was wounded or confused. I didn't always do it well. It's not that I don't trust the bears exactly, it's just that they are hungry. I have been hungry too, and trying to learn how to manage the hunger. We have all always been hungry and often feeding that screaming place with violence. Humans boxing other humans, humans capturing the land and caging it, humans ready to hunt the bear that tips over their trash can instead of working on the puzzle of their own heart. Humans hungry to fill the void inside but looking in the same fruitless places they've always looked. Divorced from the source and carrying on the illness of manifest destiny. Reveling in the unabashed, empty hubris of the conqueror, unwilling to flex away from their spiritual desert until the dry burnt land of their soul comes straight out of their dreams and becomes our nightmare.

An axe to bust up Grandmas bones. I took it to her long ago, years before she died. I learned what I could, but I trusted her less than the bears. She was shot through with hate and fear and we can't abide it, not anymore. And if it continues, we won't survive it.

I live in such a beautiful place. I mean every day I am awe struck by the brilliant wide sky and pine forest. The smells, the sounds, the feelings I get when I immerse myself in the wild of this place are indescribable. Yet my small community is toxic and out of balance. There has been rampant and vile hatred stirring for years and now it boils over. Targets go on backs quite easily in these parts and we are all marked. There is hatred seething, hatred burning holes in the land, fear is growing in the congregation of the country church and there is hatred on the tiny school board. It is a blind, vengeful hatred for "the other," and we have found endless "others." It seems this hatred knows no bounds or limits and across the country and in every tiny community we are building black holes. Black holes where no life can thrive and soon every single last one of us will be sucked in.

River Heart   *Jim Thiele*

I sometimes feel like hating too, but I know it's a disease, so I drive it out. I drive it from my heart and mind whenever I am strong enough and I will myself to strength. I will not abide hate in my heart. I will never let it pull my being apart from the seams even as I watch so many around me ripping themselves up from the inside out. I have watched over the last several years as the smiles and bright eyes of my neighbors moved to grim, tight lipped, hard lined frowns and furtive scowls and oh I ache for what was. And I ache for what has been lost.

We must seek love and the company of those who love all of humanity and life on this planet. And we must fight: against ourselves succumbing to apathy and the outside forces tearing us into bits and we must fight the wedges between us. This is what I've learned from my life here among the ponderosas. My life as it hangs just now, presently, in this time and space. And this is my practice of acceptance but also rebellion. This is my practice for revolution. I have called out for help and none came. I have been out walking and hidden myself in the trees away from the trucks of those who I knew would happily hurt me and when that failed I put a pistol on my hip so that we could find a common language. I don't always do the right thing, but I won't stop trying. And I will say it again, for all of my frustration, longing and grief; hate is not my weapon nor the weapon of my God. My God is love. Pure, blinding, all encompassing, planet and people healing love and it's defensible. It can be protected and nurtured. Anything outside of that love and liberation is a door to darkness. Oh yes, it's in you, that door, but you can turn the other way anytime. You can walk back out of it even if you've already passed though.

No hatred for the big world of mysteries. No place for hopelessness. No rage unbalanced, there is always love on the other side. Feel the association of cells and miracles that you are. Strip off your doubt and run naked through your life like a leaf falling from the sky. Open your heart to this impossible maze of choices and consequences. It's not easy. Big world, small person. Big feelings and one small life to contain them all…

Do not give up for it's a gift. A wild and terrible gift that will open itself without you, so why not pull at the string? Why not wrap your arms around the knotty trunk and climb the tree. You can do it.

And keep doing it.

The puzzle of your own heart first, this small thing perhaps not so small. What have you given shelter there, are you harboring hate? Fear the weight of a black hole? Can you let it go, let it burn up and fade away? Find instead a daily practice of love. Love only, love always, love for the sake of love. Love for the mouse and the owl, love for the bear and his hunger. Love for the trash and the man in the tent. Radical acts of love for yourself and your own culpable, disastrous life.

Love for the beginning, the middle and the end. Born in chaos and then turning to dust, with at least a million choices in between. ◧

Mike Hull

Hunter/Gatherer — Another Perspective

There was a bear. I was climbing over the last stretch of sod leading to the ridge when he came up behind me and woofed. I turned and saw a large black bear stretching to lift his nose to catch my scent. I waved and called out, "Hello, companion."

I do not carry a rifle on these trips, I do not need the extra weight. My only concern was the heavy pack on my back and the uneven ground at my feet. I turned and went on. He resumed his journey, catching up to me, and we walked parallel for a few minutes, then he veered over the side of the hill. Had he wished to remain unseen, he could have. I appreciated his gesture. We are simply two creatures who share the same burden of crossing the tundra.

I had built a small cabin in the most remote area of Alaska's tundra I could access by a float plane. A friend had accompanied me on this venture, and when we completed the cabin that I planned to spend the year in, we hiked out five days to the Yukon river and caught a ride on a barge to make our way to Fairbanks. My friend went home, and I flew back in with some materials for the cabin and enough food to carry me into winter. The nearest the pilot could get me to the cabin was a small lake 13 miles and a modest range of hills away. I would make six two-day journeys to carry my stash from the lake to my cabin.

I took no books; I did not have a camera. My purpose was to silence the arrogance of reason. A handy tool, but just an afterthought for most of our realities. Not the attribute that defines our humanness. I was here by invitation to watch and listen, to learn from the natural environment, and find my place within it. All the science that our species has acquired, and is justifiably proud of, started in this manner, and in places like this. Before we had much of a vocabulary, perhaps before we even had words, we learned to adapt to the patterns and rhythms of our living environment. We acquired knowledge and understanding. And we made decisions that kept us alive.

These are excerpts from the journal I kept during that time alone.

Misty morning chill, and a bright sun melts its way through the fog that swells from the river and climbs the forest hillside. The wolves howl again, full-throated, echoing, and sometimes there are distant answers. There are many wolves and quite close. Within two hundred yards of the cabin. And they have come to be comfort like the owl who fills the evening. I suppose it is the reassurance of more kindred companions. We who stay. For there was a frost and that morning the first large flock of geese gathered and flew east. Now they are all gone and only a few ducks too young yet for the journey remain.

There grows that quiet trust in the land as provider and teacher. It gives as I need in time, and for that I am learning more about its animals and plants, its skies and forests. More for my need than if I had supplies enough to keep me cooking all day in a warm cabin. I am about the land food gatherer. Sometimes, like last night, a lady pike, swollen with eggs, grabs my line. She'll carry me three days.

And within that, the moose teaches me, coming to my front yard each morning. I stalk, he moves as though unaware of me. Each time, I learn more, and he moves away. But this morning he crossed the river, turned to look straight at me. Then he went into the brush. The moose knows, but still he will teach me. And when I've learned well, I will be ready to take him. He knows that, accepts it, and goes on teaching me.

I had grown comfortably to feel that I would take the moose with the first snowfall. This morning light snow, barely more than a heavy frost, covered the ground. I grabbed my rifle, checked the chamber and stepped outside. Immediately I heard the moose splashing into the river. I ran a short way up the hill and saw him walking the path to my cabin. I went down and braced myself against a tree. Thirty yards from my cabin, and thirty feet from me, he rounded a tree, stopped, looked at me, lowered his head, and fell quietly with one shot.

I brought my rifle home, emptied it. Happy that I won't carry it again for a long time.

I was sitting on the morning hillside, as I frequently do, to listen to the community discussion of my neighbors. It is a very interesting family dynamic among the wolves. All have a voice in the discussion. I hear even the yelping of the pups. And when all have had their say, the alpha male makes his last pronouncement, and then all fall silent.

I had brought a small tree saw with me this morning, and when the discussion was over, I started sawing on a small dry log to take home. The whole pack erupted in protest. "Papa has spoken, how dare you break this silence."

I quickly stopped, feeling very apologetic. The family protocol applies to me as well. I am honored, and humbled.

During the coldest part of winter the wolves were absent. Nothing moved. For nearly a month there was an inch of ice on the inside of my window that did not thaw even with my wood stove burning for several hours. I had just one visitor.

This evening I watched a spider make his way across the vertical ice field that has formed inside the cabin beneath the window. Slow - cautious - struggling. He'd pause to rest often, then continue so slowly I could watch the muscles flex in his front legs. Lifting himself up, dragging himself forward, straining, slipping. He fell once and went on again and again. Finally he came to clean, dry wood, but in the short trip of a foot and a half to the top of the window he had to stop and rest three times. Now he hangs head down, fast asleep.

Such heroic determination to cling to the few moments and little space that life has granted him.

In the evening, I walked on the river and stopped to watch Winter where he worked in the forest making new layers of frost for the spruce, and I was amazed at what he had accomplished in a day. He knew my thoughts and addressed me without turning from his labor.

"I am not here to impress you nor to teach you. You are not a concern to me. Mine are the trees, the land, the river, and the sky. My work is perfect, and in it you will find both beauty and wisdom. You will find these because you need to experience such things to reassure yourself that you are neither blind nor dull. I am not concerned with perfection nor beauty, nor wisdom, nor you. I am winter, and upon those who are given to me."

I remained silent because it is not yet for me to speak in the presence of any master. But I understood better my attraction to him. It is his cold, deliberate indifference that I find so captivating. In such a strength, I find the easy comfort of a companion. Strength understood, accepted, and brought to its mature fullness in act. Perfect execution, and pure, with never a moment's hesitation to take pride, or receive praise. A being of obvious greatness, yet unmoved by that because greatness lies beneath the realm of his concern.

Arctic National Wildlife Refuge, June 2023 21　　　　Nancy Deschu

About the time the sun inched its way above the horizon, the wolves returned, and stayed a good while. We still had an understanding, the wolves and I. I was not to enter their camp, and they would not enter mine. We abided by this understanding all through that year. They moved to another area a few times, but always returned. So I got to listen in as pups grew and matured. And by springtime, the morning discussions seemed more of a planning session for the day's hunt. They would go out in separate groups, and in the late afternoon I would hear them call to each other as they made their way home.

I like wolves. Snowfall gives to silence a softness, and the wolf brings a sense of companionship that enriches rather than violates solitude.

A lone wolf howled late at night, and then again in the early light, but still there was no answer. There seems both hunger and sadness in his cry.

The other wolves returned. There are many voices, the tone is conversational.

I had seen tracks leading to where the wolves gather upriver within sight of the hill behind the cabin. This morning they were howling from there, and I ran up the hill to catch sight of them. They must be awfully sensitive to my movement. A little way up the hill, their chatter cut short. I turned and saw them all on the run, looking white in the early morning light, flashing through the stunted trees of the muskeg. Perfect disciplined stride, knowing and unafraid.

There were many lessons learned from the land, the seasons, and the animals that year. It seemed all of Nature abides by one simple command: Grow. And what is it that drives the response to that command? The Will of Matter.

Winter's valiant spider, the woodpecker on frozen spruce, trees that bloom even though the added weight quickens their destruction. The creatures I have met here— plants, insects, animals, gods—share one outstanding virtue: dynamic indifference: be who you are where you are. Do not be bound by concern for purpose or significance, do not seek understanding, appreciation, or praise, and above all, do not save yourself. Spend your whole strength in every moment.

Among the Hunter/Gatherers

I did return to civilization after sixteen months on the tundra. A few years later, my wife and I began a 27-year career teaching in remote Native villages in Alaska. The people filled in that gap in my education. This was the time to come to know the human beings that this land had generated. And they provided a greater understanding of the context of my experiences.

For nineteen years we lived among the Yup'iks, the last people on the planet who still hunt with an atlatl, a spear thrower, that they use to hunt seals. To strike a seal is like trying to hit a target the size of a bowling ball at 150 feet. And this is done while standing in a boat bouncing through the waves of the Bering Sea. Statistically, highly improbable.

The Yup'iks explain that the seal knows the heart of the hunter, and if this is a good person, the seal will give himself to feed this hunter's family. Riding in the boat with these hunters, one comes to believe this is the only possible explanation for their success.

The bear had welcomed me. The wolves accepted me. And when the snow covered the ground, the moose walked the trail to my cabin, looked at me, and fell quietly. That pattern continued on so many levels throughout that year. The Yup'iks (whose name means: The Real People) further explained that all of their world is conscious. Plants, animals, the land itself. Nature is the great provider,

protector, and teacher.

When living with the Inupiat up on the Chukchi Sea, I learned that the relationship with their environment was much the same. These are whale hunters. In the spring, when the ice begins to open, Bowhead whales swim north to feed in the Arctic Ocean. These are hunted by the people in the coastal villages. Hunters go out in large sealskin boats and hunt with harpoons. All boys 12 and up leave school in mid-April when the head whaling captain says it is time to set up camps on the edge of the leads. When I visited one camp, I joined the men who were settled in an ice shelter, resting on caribou skins, and playing backgammon while waiting for the whale. I had read books about whales and whaling when I was young. I asked if any whale had tried to crash a boat when it is struck. The men looked confused and discussed this in their own language. Then the captain turned to me with a puzzled look and asked, "Why would a whale do that? He is coming here to feed the village."

For the indigenous peoples I have had the opportunity to be among, all creatures are family, and the land is the source of life, and it is their provider. All that makes up their environment is spiritual and conscious and connected. When people share their concerns for animals, it is generally a statement of the connectedness they feel with these wild creatures. The indigenous peoples offer us a view of how the animals feel about us.

Let me return to the occasion of my leaving the tundra.

My closest and most endearing contact with a wolf occurred that summer when I was on my way to rejoin the society of people. There was a dream that showed my way forward, so I packed the canoe and spent 20 days meandering along a twisting tundra river. I beached the canoe one afternoon and hiked over the mountains to visit a hot springs where I had been told a couple had built a lodge. Thinking to spend a few days, I stayed four months. Wonderful folks, but the man was dying of cancer. When they had to fly out, they asked if I would take care of the place until they could return.

They had built a very nice log lodge heated by a hot springs. There was a twelve-hundred foot airstrip used by bush pilots to bring in supplies and guests. And there was a sawmill, a tractor and all the tools needed in such a setting. I kept myself busy with projects. But having been on the tundra for a year, a person becomes sensitive to other things. I knew I was being watched. So I was careful to make my actions outside slow and deliberate, so that whoever was watching me could get a good sense of my behavior and patterns.

As I was washing dishes one evening in the kitchen, I

saw a large black wolf walk into the woodyard just beside the lodge. He was cautious but confident. As he drew close, he looked at me through the window. He was familiar with me, and not threatened.

I went outside and stood on the porch. The wolf then walked over and stood at the bottom of the stairs, just a few feet from me. I can sense when I am in the presence of a being more knowing than myself. We just stared into each other's eyes for what seemed a long time. From my seasons with the wolves, I knew that they are highly social creatures. It is not good when one is alone. He seemed to look deeply into me and let me know—neither is it good for you.

There was a large dog at the lodge. Part Malemute, and easily twice as heavy as the wolf. He started to stir, and the wolf, hearing this, turned to walk away. The dog burst through the screen door and went after him. The wolf merely stopped and looked back over his shoulder at the dog. That dog dropped and went down on his belly like he was trying to disappear. He knew who was in charge.

For a period of two weeks, the wolf would come by, or I would see him in the forest and call to him, and we would walk together. He even showed up at the screen door a couple of times, looking for me. The dog never made a move.

It was beyond special to share time together. I was very appreciative that the wolves I had lived near accepted and respected my presence on the edge of their community space. Their values and behavior were in many ways a model family. We could learn something from them. And now with the black wolf, it was clear that we solitary creatures have something to share. A simple, unspoken companionship.

In time, a plane arrived with some visitors to stay at the lodge. And the wolf came no more. But he had offered a fitting closure. Yes, I am welcomed as his companion. We have walked together. But now it is time to move on. ◪

DJ Lee

The River Decides

Since the first day I bathed in the Selway, the water washes over my consciousness whenever it pleases. I'll be teaching an English composition class in Pullman, Washington, or checking out sale items at a department store in Vancouver, BC, or strolling around the Museum of Contemporary Art in Chicago, and the Selway will appear, snaking through the Bitterroot Mountains, steep as skyscrapers. It's as if the river chooses when to materialize and when to disappear in my mind. Sometimes I'm visited by the white-and-gray granite razoring through the alder and serviceberry that frame the river, other times by the grassy meadows dotted by hawthorn and clover, glowing neon green. Often I recall the sound of the river's animals, the trill of cedar waxwings on an spring day or the shy cough of a whitetail in autumn, or I find myself wondering if that goshawk who built her nest on the river near Shearer airstrip, or some relative of hers, still dive-bombs hikers who get too close to her territory.

It's not surprising the Selway rides roughshod on my imagination. I spent twelve years hiking its corridors and trails, tagging along with fisheries biologists, foresters, hunters, backpackers, fire scientists, friends, family members, and strangers down Rhoda Creek or up Wylie's Peak, on horse and mule trips with outfitters to Bitch Lake and back, along Bear Creek and those two-thousand-year-old cedar forests, over to the Crags and across that glacier-carved border between Idaho and Montana. The Selway, one hydrologist told me, is the least contaminated river in the lower forty-eight states, as measured by parts-per-million, meaning its ecosystem is the least impacted by humans. Part of the river's power is that it runs entirely through designated wilderness, on the homelands of the Salish and Nimíipuu.

Maybe I think of the river because it takes lives. Tradition says Selway means "slow water." Yet the river is anything but sluggish. All forty-seven miles of it is fed by a massive watershed, larger arteries like Meadow Creek, Surprise Creek, Boulder Creek, and thousands of other trickles, seeps, and streams. Echoes and roars drum the ears where the Selway meets Moose Creek and it doubles in size. People have lost their lives there. In 1988, a man in his late thirties fell from his raft and hit his head on a rock in Ladle Rapid. His friends, who had gone to the top of the rapid to help him launch, watched him float out of sight. He was next seen fifteen miles away—face down. In 1989, a middle-aged woman was thrown from her raft in Double Drop and never seen again. In 1996, two young men were tossed from their raft immediately after put-in at Paradise Creek. Water levels were too high—six to ten feet—to allow anyone to save them. In 2004, an elderly woman's boat capsized in Ladle and she went under. People in the other boats couldn't find her. She just disappeared into the great, turbulent hole of the water. Even as early as 1850, history records the Nimíipuu tribesman Black Bear rafting the Selway with his daughter and niece. As they traversed the rapids at Selway Falls, their boat splintered to pieces. Black Bear was found, days later, downstream.

Selway Falls

He was a large and fleshy man. They dragged him from the river and buried him close by. Later, when the railroad was being built, workmen unearthed Black Bear's skeleton, causing people to wonder why the river took such a giant spirit.

People are drawn to the river because it is difficult. It has forty-one named rapids, places where the gradient steepens, flow increases, and the water becomes dangerous. Many of the Selway rapids come from 1960s slang: Holy Smokes and Galloping Gertie. But some—Wa-Poots—are Nimipuutímt words. Others are warnings. Ham Rapid is named for one group of rafters whose canoe broke into three pieces and they lost their food—their prized meal was a canned ham. Still, among whitewater enthusiasts, the Selway is the crown jewel. For wilderness protection and safety, the forest service strictly limits the number of people who can run the river. It is the hardest river in America for which to score a rafting permit.

But perhaps the Selway occupies my thoughts so often because it gives life. For one thing, the river supports spring and fall Chinook salmon. I've watched those taut silver bodies jumping up the huge cataract at Selway Falls, flinging themselves again and again into the spray with complete passion so they can migrate high upriver

to the exact spot where they were born. Nutrients from those spawning salmon sustain the ecosystem along the banks and beyond, from the tiniest honeybees suckling yarrow to black bears gorging on huckleberries. The salmon who return each year to spawn transport nitrogen, phosphorus, and energy as protein in their tissue. As their flesh breaks down after spawning, these nutrients feed riverbank vegetation. Scientists say river ecosystems can get anywhere from twenty-five to seventy percent of their nitrogen from decaying salmon. One study found that trees growing on the banks of spawning rivers grew three times faster than those rivers without salmon.

Or maybe I'm drawn to the water because thinking about it has a nurturing effect on my mind and my body. That first time I waded knee deep into the confluence of Moose Creek and the Selway, the cold cut through my skin, bone ache ran up my calves and thighs to a freeze in my head, and I knew this was some different kind of place. My sightline contracted as the two channels merged and shot down the canyon, a dense phalanx of Douglas fir and white, lodgepole, and Ponderosa pines. By now I've entered that river hundreds of times. Still, every plunge jolts me, goosebumps plumping even on the hottest day of summer when purple butterflies land on purple asters, a pop of color like the snap of wet cold and the sudden quickness of mind. Once I catch my breath, microscopic nutrients from salmon and other organic material—mica flecks, oxygen bubbles, and the vanilla scent of Ponderosas riding on the wind—intoxicate me.

In the Selway, my senses grow keener, seem to stretch to the beyond, especially the gasp of breath as I pull my head under and emerge to rub stars from my eyes. The enormity of Selway makes me aware of how my everyday life limits my senses, how narrow my field of vision, how incomplete the range of colors I see, how few sounds clatter into my ears, how bland my touch. In the water, my body seems to dissolve, transform. I sprout scales, gills, become a transitional creature, water and airborne at once, a quantum wave of being, taunt and slack as the current rises and lifts me, pulling me in its tow, and the surprise of rocks on my buttocks as the water shallows and eddies me to shore. Then, I let myself become solid again. My scalp tingles as I dry next to the campfire, having freed myself from harsh city water and chemicals of grocery store shampoo, soap, and sunscreen before I even touch the river.

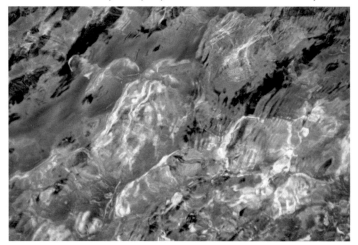

The Selway at the confluence with Moose Creek

The first time I bathed in the Selway, I didn't want to wade more than ankle deep. The turbidity scared me. I hadn't yet acclimated to the river's extremes. But since that initial dip, I've splashed right in with a scream, bright sparkle of the sun on the ripples, the green and green and deeper green of water, trees, shrubs, mountain tea and that momentary trance of clarity: how delicate and fleeting it all is.

Or could the Selway slip into my thoughts so habitually because it feels like protection? I spent those twelve years along the river trying to figure out why my grandparents had migrated there in the 1920s and helped build a wilderness preservation infrastructure, in some cases with assistance from Nimíipuu elders. My grandparents' marriage began along the river and partly broke apart there. I published a book about some of my family's dark past in an effort to free myself from the place, trying to understand what my grandfather was up to and why my grandmother rejected him. Even though I never solved that mystery completely, it turns out the place is wedged in me like the giant rock that it is. The entire region is undergirded by the largest area of exposed granite in the world, the Idaho Batholith. The stone makes poor soil for human development—farming and mining are almost impossible in the Selway drainage—but it creates gorgeous beaches of comminuted granite for the life it sustains. It as if the Selway has chosen to protect itself. But more than that, it feels as if it has protected me. I've swum in the Selway every year since my first bath, even the summer I had cancer. Within days of my oncologist giving me permission to hike again, I was back at the hole below Selway Falls because the river has a curative effect that I can't explain.

But, no, the real reason I think about the river so often is its mystery. That's what I can't get out of my bones, especially its complex of whirlpools and vortexes, which, strangely, sit right beside its unhurried, quiet, and wholly intentional flow. Once I interviewed a wilderness ranger who was on duty in 1979 when a DC-3 full of people and supplies crashed in the river near the confluence of the Selway and Moose Creek. The ranger said he'd never been on such a strange search-and-rescue mission. In the helicopter, hours after the crash, he was hovering over a whirlpool. The water was high but clear. He could see some of the plane's cargo—a saddle and some lawn chairs—churning around, but no bodies. As the copter pilot was getting ready to leave, the ranger noticed the sand moving in the bottom of the eddy like a puff from an Aladdin's lamp, and a human body emerged. Pretty soon, he saw two more, and then the sand covered them again. "The water looked to be about ten feet deep, but it was actually about twenty feet," he told me, "and the currents were so strong. We'd never seen anything like it. The sand was moving in such a way. These people would rise out of the sand in the bottom of the river and then disappear." In and on the Selway, human history thrives and decays in the river like salmon that feed it. The Selway decides when to conceal and when to reveal, what to protect and what to destroy. It chooses which stories to tell and which to secret away in its wild heart. ◪

Diphylleia Cymosa   Jack Broom

FICTION

Sarah Birdsall

Some Kind of Lucky

I was there the night Max and Marleen blew into town for the first time, standing right there in the fresh cool air of the ramshackle patio of the pub, drinking a fast glass of red wine on my break when their old dusty car pulled up in front and they waltzed toward me off the equally dusty street. I noticed the remains of the dust covered and smeared "Just Married" paint on their back windshield.

I felt that twang inside, like the pluck of an out of tune guitar string. Tom and I were like that once, long before we fell into that fucking-or-fighting life our marriage had become, which turned into the fighting-loudly-or-fighting-silently life after the fucking stopped. And being the good Christian man he was, he took me to court and got the house, the kids, and 100% of his North Slope paychecks. I got the old car and a sleeping bag. I spent that first summer in the parking lot by the railroad tracks, pissing in the bushes and feeling the car shake when those midnight freights came through, blasting their horns in my ears. I would visit our two kids when he was on the Slope and my mom, *my* mom, was living there with the kids. (She who named me Zelda—who the fuck would name their daughter Zelda? It's hardly a name of positive associations filled with the promise of good things to come, and don't give me any of that what's-in-a-name-crap.) Of course they'd take sides, my mom and Tom. *Zelda drinks too much. Zelda's got a problem.* No one stopped to think that maybe Zelda's problem was Tom.

So after all that you'd think I'd feel bitter, begrudge people like Max and Marleen, new in town which made you a super star in and of itself, with their fresh-off-the-Alcan car carrying the dust of other roads and the way their eyes sparkled as they told their story: Met one month, married the next, then hit the road on the third. Bam. One two three. And now they were here.

That night I served them frothy pints of beer and big plates of burgers and fries. Thirsty from the traveling, hungry from all the hunger between them. You could see it, the way they looked at each other as they took bite after bite of those big juicy burgers—lust. They oozed with it, just like those burgers dripped mayo and ketchup and mustard back onto their plates. I thought they'd make a beeline for that car the second they finished eating, find a quiet place to park and get out the sleeping bag. But in the duskiness of the Alaska summer night-not-night the music started and they stayed on, like members of the gang now, joining in with the laughter at other tables and shaking the hands of fellow drinkers who wanted to meet them and welcome them to town. I finally acquiesced and did the same, bringing along another round and saying, "I'm Zelda. Welcome to our friendly little village."

"Max," the man said, and shook my hand. He was manly in a sweet-and-surly sort of way, like a friendly grizzly bear. He licked some ketchup off his lips, and I noticed the thick tufts of chestnut hair in the V of his road-weary t-shirt.

"And I'm Marleen," the woman said jovially, bosomy and blond with soft round cheeks and big hoop earrings in her ears. She shook my hand, too, long pretty fingers decorated with sparkling rings and I wanted to say, *Aren't you lucky,* thinking of that grinning bear beside her and that cozy-looking chest hair, but I bit my tongue on that.

I was blond once, not natural like Marleen, but I used to get my not-really-any-color hair done on a regular basis, back when I was a small-town diva. Wicked—a wicked shade of blond. I loved it. Now I go red, out of a box, do it myself when I can get my hands on an empty bathroom with a good sink.

"We're so glad to be here!" Marleen beamed, her long hair swaying across her shoulders. I'd had long hair once, too, but I've learned that shorter hair is easier to wash when you get the chance, and I keep it right around shoulder length so I can ponytail it when I have to and still feel like I've got something of it left.

Looking at Marleen that day, and her so-happy-to-be-here gush, I thought about adding something like, "Glad to have you," but fortunately I didn't imbibe in that over-the-top, too-many-glasses-of-wine friendliness that so often happened out there on that deck, in all that fresh air and the saturated smells of mid-summer at midnight Alaska—

Love this place. I hated it when I was a teenager but I love it now, even after what happened to my marriage and then, of course, that far worse thing that was yet to happen to Max and Marleen. That wasn't the fault of this place, now... was it? They brought what happened to them with them, and there was nothing any of us could have done.

Right?

Anyway, I'm getting ahead of myself. Max and Marleen proceeded to settle right in and cozy up to everything small town Alaska: Max got a job right here at the pub, cooking up the same burgers and fries like he and Marleen consumed on their very first night, and Marleen began volunteering at the local radio station right away and soon got her own show. She also got a job at the local one-stop-gas-and-other-assorted-crap, located at what we call the "Y" where our little road intersects with the Parks Highway, a river of asphalt that cuts north and south through the center of everything, and they rented a cute little place off a dirt road that was plowed in winter and was by the big lake out there.

"Watch out for bears," I told them. "They come around to the lake sometimes."

"Bears?" Marlene looked startled at first, her eyes searching for Max. But then she remembered something. "We've got a gun," she said. "I mean Max does. A handgun."

At that Max turned toward us, grinned, and made like he was drawing a pistol from a holster. "Bang," he said. "One dead bear."

I wasn't thinking they'd have to shoot one, not that a handgun would do much good. "Don't leave your garbage out." That's all I was gonna say about it, but I felt like I had to add, "And don't try shooting one with a handgun."

"Oh! Okay. Good advice," Marlene said, but Max looked disappointed, and I felt for a moment like one of the know-it-all instant local dickheads who've got to tell all the new people what's up, ignoring the fact that they themselves hadn't been here very long either.

Then Max laughed and slapped Marlene on the ass and made some joke about which one of them was the fastest runner and made some moves that cracked us all up and I felt forgiven.

I liked working with Max. He had the endless energy of a hyper two-year-old and lots of smiles. Grins, really. He won us all over: Gary the main bartender, Shirley the other server, Stubbs the owner—who would have guessed that—and yours truly here. He sang a lot when he worked and had a great whistle. Without fail Marleen would come in after her own workday ended, pull up a stool at the bar and wait for Max to be done with his shift. Then they would share his shift meal before taking off in their little dusty car. It was like clockwork—until it wasn't.

Sometime after the cold weather started Marleen quit coming in to wait for Max. Max said it was because sharing one car between their two jobs was just getting to be a bit too much, and Marleen had taken to walking home to the place by the lake even though night came swift and early in the growing dark. Max stayed his cheerful self though, and at first he packed up that shift meal and took it home with him to share with his bride. But it wasn't too long before that came to an end, too, and he started eating the whole thing at the bar and following it up with a few tall beers. Sometimes a few more. "Jesus it's cold," he'd say, and I'd say, "Damned right it is." Then we'd laugh and I'd slosh back my third or fourth glass of wine and get back to work. I never flirted with him—no, at least I didn't think so. I felt like we were comrades-in-arms of sorts, fighting the growing crankiness of winter-weary customers, fighting the cold that crept along the floor, fighting the damned snow every time you went to drive somewhere. We were the pub crew, and we stuck together through the dark days of winter.

Needless to say, I was no longer living out of my car. In winters Stubbs let me stay in a small room above the general store—or "trading post" as it was quaintly called—in the front of the building. My favorite time of night was also my loneliest, saddest time: I'd get off, have a few final drinks, and come up to that little room and stare out the window that looked over Main Street. This was my town. I grew up here—mostly. The people here had known me since I was a bitchy-as-hell teenager. They knew me in my glory days of early marriage, when Tom and I were like some small-town superstar super couple, our kids on the basketball team, me in every musical or theatrical production the town could cough up, and young handsome Tom the super provider with all that slope money filling our house and filling our bank accounts. My town. Yet now I felt outside of something, everything, there in that little room while Tom and my kids were in that little castle of a log house on the other side of the railroad tracks, my own mother there maybe—probably—a nice fire in the woodstove and lots of laughter around the table where I was no longer allowed to be. Sometimes the pull of the Clearwater Inn, right across the street, was too much for me and I would leave the little room and cross over to the other side. It was always better when I didn't do that. Once you enter a place like that in the dark of a cold winter night, it's not likely you'll be leaving anytime soon. I'd wake up the next morning, head hurting like Hell had gone crazy, and wish. Wish for everything. Wish for my town to still be my town and for me to get my life back.

One such day after one such night, when I showed up in the pub feeling like dog shit on the bottom of a boot, Max said, "Hey there Zelda. Hey, come here. I can fix you."

I managed a laugh at that. "I'm afraid there's no fixing me, Max," I said. "It's been tried many times."

"Come on," he said, and grabbed my hand. That got my blood pumping; that hand was big and warm. But I put the brakes on those thoughts as I remembered Marleen. He pulled me into the tiny cold cube of a bathroom and I said quicky, "So where's Marleen these days?"

"Marleen? She's home mostly. Or at work. She don't like the cold much."

"She should come out. It's a bit better if you socialize."

"Ah yeah. I'm working on that." He pulled a bunch of stuff out of his front pocket. A tiny mirror, a little vial, and a rolled-up dollar bill. So that was how he stayed so chirpy.

"Nah, Max, that's not for me," I said. I wanted obliviousness, not awareness. No way I wanted to be up at all hours, listening to nothing but the frantic beating of my heart.

"It'll do you up good, Zeld. The night will fly right by!"

I thought about that, the night flying, like it was some big giant raven swooping past. I felt I could just be honest with Max—we spent five nights a week together, after all—so I said, "Max I'm not looking for that. Nights I need my mind to stop. Or else I'll go crazy. I'll suffer through my shift, and it'll be okay once I get a little hair of the dog."

His big green eyes met mine, and I could almost hear the wheels turning around in his head, like he was coming to an understanding of something, like maybe of who I was. "Okay Zelda," he said softly, and put that big warm hand on my shoulder for a few fleeting seconds. "But just give a whistle if you change your mind." Then he poured himself out a big fat line and sucked it fiercely up one nostril and then the next. "Go 'til dawn, just on this." He smiled and raised his eyebrows, his face telling me how good that whole thing felt and wasn't I stupid to turn it down.

"Yeah well, you go cowboy," I said, thinking for a hot minute how things might have been if he'd come into town a single man. "We'd better get our asses out of this bathroom before people start talking." We laughed, and that little bit of comradery made me feel better. I had to wonder, though, where Max was getting the blow.

It's not that we were a drug free town, no, God no. There were rumors of a meth lab, right there down on my old home street. Tom must have been shitting his pants over that. And of course there was always pot—smokers, growers, sellers. It wasn't legal again yet, but people didn't worry too much about it and summer nights on Main Street you could always smell it, wafting through the air.

But not a lot of people in this town had the money it took to keep themselves in blow. I wondered if Marleen did it, too, and I found myself wishing she'd just start coming in again, like the old days. Seeing Max's blow made me wonder about Marleen working out at the one-stop, and about the owner, who was always rumored to have made all his shithole buying money from drug deals down in the states, and who had a thing for busty blonds.

I got my wish, about Marleen coming back in, soon as February surfaced and the days got a little brighter, like a crack had formed on Old Man Winter's frozen gripping hand. "Hey girl!" I said when I saw her slide onto her old stool. "Where the hell you been keeping yourself?"

"Oh!" she said, smiling. "Didn't Max say? I picked up the night shift at the gas station. So I go from one shift to the next."

No, Max hadn't said but I hadn't exactly asked. Oh wait. I had. Well, maybe she hadn't had that second shift yet. I said, "Ahh. So you've been pretty busy then? Good plan to get through the dark months."

"Tell me about it," she said.

"Still doing your show?" I asked, but I already knew she'd quit that. Why the hell did I ask? I guess I wanted to hear what she said.

"Nah—it was getting too complicated, with the work schedule and just the one car." As she lifted her wine glass to her lips the sleeve of her thick loose sweater fell back up her arm only a little bit but enough for me to see a ring of bruises around that delicate wrist. Damn you to hell, Max, was my first thought but I cautioned that with an image of the one-stop owner that flitted through my thoughts. Scrawny scarecrow of a guy, but I always had him pegged as someone who could be a mean fucker behind closed doors.

"Job good?" I casually asked, pretending like I noticed a greasy smear on the bar top.

The Great Fall   *@tjinalaska Toya Brown*

"Oh yeah," she said. "Just—I don't think I was prepared for winter, you know?"

I nodded. "No one ever is," I said, thinking I saw a sadness now somewhere in her round blue eyes and uncertain smile. "Just hang in there. It'll be over soon enough, and all this white will turn into a big sloppy mess then we'll be shit deep in mud and then before you know it, the roads will be nice and dusty again."

"Thanks, Zelda," she said.

"Look forward to the light," I said, something I later regretted.

There was a Max and Marleen renaissance, right there before the end. Brought on by summer probably, and the sweet memories of their first months here when it was light all night and the birds were everywhere and every breath held the smell of the ferns and the river water and the wild roses when they came out. The return of midsummer, and the magical spell of the simmer-dim, even though by then we were already losing it as each day took some away and brought a little less of it back. Marleen must have quit that second shift because she was coming in again at the end of the day and she and Max were back to sharing that shift meal and I forgot all about the bruises on her wrist. There was music again out on the deck, and that last night I watched them swaying together in a slow simmering dance in a quiet corner while everyone else stomped around in the center of the deck. It was a local band, real simple, bass, drums, guitar, and before the end of the night they'd pulled me over and had me sing a song with them. "Summertime," that's what I chose, and as I sang, I felt myself rising up above that deck, above the town, and catching a puff of a gentle breeze that took me all the way down to the end of Main Street where the river ran and everything was that great gray swath of glacier water and wild roses and seagulls and salmon. Then the song ended and I was back on the deck, back to being Zelda again, and when I opened my eyes Max and Marleen were gone.

The next day Max didn't show for work, and it didn't take long before we were getting in a big panic about it. "Hell I'll do it," I said. "How hard can it be to throw some frozen patties on the grill?"

"We serve more than just burgers here, Zelda," Sheila said sharply.

"Hell I can throw some halibut on a grill, too. Salmon—no problem. I'm an Alaska girl, remember?'

"Maybe he'll show," Gary said glumly. Tourist time and we were looking at a packed night, though nothing like we see these days, a short ten years later. But even then it was a going concern, how to keep up with everything.

Then Stubbs came back from the front where the store was. "There's something going on at the Y," he said. We all stopped mid-sentence and looked at him. "What do you mean, something?" I asked. Car crash, likely, I thought. Some hot shot trucker speeding through. God—I hoped no locals were involved.

"Someone was shot. Troopers are all over the place."

"Shot?" we all said. Then I added, "Like what kind of shot are we talking about? Dead shot, wounded shot, accident shot—come on! What is it?"

"Someone was killed. Down near the lake."

I think we all went white, like those lifeless hunks of frozen halibut waiting in the freezer to be fried up for the tourists. "Max didn't come in," Gary said real fast.

"I heard it was a woman. A woman was shot," said Stubbs.

"What woman?" Sheila asked. "Who was it?"

"I don't know," Stubbs said. I could tell he was afraid of what we were all thinking. There weren't that many people living around that lake, and Max hadn't shown up yet. For God's sake he was nearly an hour late at that point.

And of course I was thinking about that handgun Max and Marleen said they'd had, and those bruises on her wrist, and I felt those thoughts land in the joints of my boney knees, my mind mixing up a deadly cocktail of drugs, guns, and lust.

"It sounded like Marleen. I mean, it sounded like it was their place," Stubbs said reluctantly, looking at the floor like he was somehow responsible for saying what we didn't want to hear. "Morty Wallace was out in his canoe, fishing. Heard some yelling. Then, well, maybe some screaming and yelling. Heard the shot but didn't think it was a shot. Then things quieted down. He didn't realize anything had happened until a while later when the troopers showed up."

And that was the beginning of something, the unfolding of a story with missing pages that was Max and Marleen, who blew into town on a summer's day, lasted a year, then both left in different ways: she in a coffin, and he on his own two legs, to go on and live his life God only knows how, knowing what he knew, what all of us eventually decided we knew, too, which was what the troopers knew but couldn't seem to prove.

Say what you will about my ex-husband, the non-Christian Christian creep, but he never put a bullet in my head. I guess that means I'm some kind of lucky. Damn. ◪

Russell James

Gooey Ducks

Waves, slight and soft, pat rhythmically on the shoreline. They emanate from nowhere in the gray-green-brown sea, no swells birthing them. Only wake from passing bowpickers in the shipping lane could have caused them, but they're at least half a mile out. The boy is talking to his sister, but she isn't listening. It has been a long time since she's listened.

"Look at Mount Baker. It's so clear today," Sister says, and shades her eyes with both hands, looking across the great distance of water and land to the rivulets of snow high off the horizon, draining from that great and mighty hill into the northern Cascade foothills, the Skagit, and eventually emptying right here into the Sound. This is what she is thinking about when her brother interrupts her.

"You're not looking!" He is imploring. He wants to share something with her. She turns abruptly.

"Ok, what? Where am I looking? Can you tell me what to look for?"

"You'll know it when you see it," he says, his big front teeth shining. "Those rocks, right there. Like, this whole area," and he passes his hand in front of him.

They sit silently for a minute. The seconds feel longer to her than him. Then, a silver spray springing from the rocks shoots five or six feet into the air. She exclaims; he laughs.

"See? I told you!" He is laughing his laugh, the one she's known since they were both toddlers in the crib and would make faces at each other. There, they slept close like sardines, and when they woke they did everything together.

Now she is wearing the same toothy grin as her brother. "What is it?" she asks with more excitement than she realizes.

"It's a geoduck," he says, articulating the pronunciation– gooey duck.

"No way. Look, there's another!"

"Yeah, it's a geoduck." He rests on his haunches.

"I thought you couldn't get them in the wild anymore, that they were like, farmed now."

"They are," he says, "but there's still pockets up and down the Salish Sea if you know where to look. Seems like I found one."

Brown Pelicans, Oregon Coast   *Jack Broom*

A group of teenagers arrives on the rocky shore with tandem kayaks in tow. They are loud and shouting instructions to one another. Sister is distracted by their exuberance and remembers when she and her brother would take the old green canoe on the water and set crab pots by the western beach. They haven't been out on the water together since they've gotten older, since high school when boys and girls and the separation of interests wedged between them. He was always sitting in place while she was eyeing the door.

"*We* found one," Sister corrects and directs her attention to Blue Heron: it glides slowly with its tired wings and lands near the flats towards the eastern shore. It does its yoga pose on one slender leg, stretches its wings in a loud flap: once, twice, and then offers the hoary croak it is known for, and its ancient echo finds its way across the still water to where two slender teens are sitting.

"*I* found it," Brother says sternly. Sister laughs. Brother always takes everything so seriously. Sister thinks about pursuing the bit, then is distracted by movement on the Canadian side of the water. There is always something pulling her attention away from her brother now.

"Lotsa action over there," she muses.

"Gotta be a geoduck," he says quietly.

She wonders what life is like in Vancouver, the glass city to the north. Her mind wanders the streets and hills, tastes the foodsmells in the neighborhoods, imagines ordering a pink cocktail at a bar on the Burrard Inlet.

"Did you know geoduck is spelled G-E-O-D-U-C-K?" Brother asks.

Sister watches a ferry turn into the Canadian terminal. She wishes she were on the boat.

"Don't you think that's crazy? GEO-duck. Why not G-O-O-E-Y-duck? Stuff is like that all over the place up here. Sequim is pronounced 'squim' but spelled S-E-Q-U-I-M. Makes no sense."

Sister turns back towards the mountains and thinks about how far away they are, as Crow flies, and how impossibly close they look right now. "Makes no sense," she says softly. Heron sits and watches the flats intently, moving its head from side to side in almost imperceptible movement.

"Why don't we take the boat out anymore?" Sister asks gently. She moves closer. Their thin shoulders almost touch.

"They gotta be huge." Brother stands and moves away from her, still gazing at the rocks on the shoreline, watching each spray. "And no wonder they're still here, look at these rocks. No one is digging down to get them, it'd be way too hard. How many do you think are down there?"

Sister watches one of the tandem kayaks launch awkwardly. The long, slender blonde girl in the back falls into the water before she can get into her cockpit. Everyone laughs and the fallen girl laughs with them. Sister wishes she was the fallen girl.

"We should go out tomorrow and set the pots. We could surprise mom and dad," she says.

"You know that's shit and piss, right?" Brother turns to see her reaction to this vulgar detail.

"What?" Sister says, surprised.

"The spray. That's the geoduck's shit and piss, that's how they do it," Brother says.

"What are you talking about?"

"The geoduck, dummy."

"Oh. Well, what about the crabs?" Sister asks, slow sun setting behind her.

"What?"

"The crabs. We should go out and set the pots tomorrow, like old times."

"What are you talking about?" Brother says, shaking his head. "You're so random sometimes."

A cool breeze blows in from the Pacific, scalloping the surface of the water. Beyond, in the orange frame of the sunset, a line of brown pelicans glide and dip, then settle one by one onto the mottled sea. ◧

Colten Dom

Immovable Tangible Property

We couldn't do it alone: there is no further frontier, no more free real estate, and even the homes that dot the shittier streets of your far-flung hometown are reserved for millionaires. Ten years after graduating, I work a good job—she doesn't, but I do—and now there's mold in the basement suite. We wake up with stuffy noses, listening to the dripping windows and the leisurely gurgle of a sink that doesn't drain. It's a strange taunt, hanging Christmas lights on someone else's house. And she wants a garden; we'd have to ask permission to plant a single tulip.

Housing market? D'you mean the thing down the street with apples, oranges, and tampons? Or an entity that hides in newspapers, jumps from burning bed to burning bed—Toronto, Victoria, Vancouver—and sloshes around inside of you like a dark, breathing sea, numbers and currencies flowing through your ventricles? Soothsayers ride the waves: sirenic realtors with blonde hair, suntans, and razor-sharp teeth, surfing through your life like a cannonball. Can you spit it out? Vomit it up? Just once, I'd like to see someone grab a home off the grocery store shelf and cram it into their shopping cart...

One day, we baby-talked throughout high school, *I'll live in a great big mansion*. But now the kids in the break room—even the gals with business degrees and the guys with accounting jobs—all agree: there will be no castles, no penthouses. Their eyes grow moist as they spell out a little standalone with a petite backyard, a second floor for their parents, and a suite for an international student. Bunkbeds downstairs and Lego bricks in the dining room. A frenzy of stray cats and rescue dogs.

I had a nightmare about death, a dream about my inheritance, and woke up, retching, to the sound of the gurgling sink and the slow blink of the Christmas lights. She doesn't have a good job, she has a great job, but no teacher gets paid much in their twenties. We want kids but not specifics, realities like *when* and *where*. We don't talk about it; we can't say that the next rung on the ladder is a headstone. It's unspeakable.

Then the glacier shifts, a recession rippling across the country, then the province, then the city. For some families, the revelation arrived alongside a diagnosis—diabetes, or one of the less lethal cancers—and the promise of at-home care. For others, it appeared alongside a surfeit of historical inquiries, front pages dedicated to headlines like "Defining Multi-Generational Housing," or "Refusing to Sell After a Century." Awkward, even embarrassing, at first, to re-acknowledge that great, antithetical need—kin, clan, house, home—and the contradiction in the center of a sociopolitical creed. After all, wasn't it as simple as reaching down for your bootstraps?

My family wandered through a darkened neighborhood. Like great ships in the night, homes buoyed atop the curling driveways as if the cul-de-sac were one giant concrete marina. Passing the *For Sale!* signs bobbing atop the frosty lawns, we suddenly stood outside the two-story craftsman we had come to see. *Been inside yet?* my mother asked. *It's open house.* My parents looked pale and old. Feeling sorry, weak, you waited alone at the bay window until you overheard the women glowing about the low-slung living room and the dense kitchen, already sailing ahead and offering each other the master bedroom, giggling, and you lock eyes with your father. A gentle transmission, his clouded irises like smoke signals, blinking a wordless acknowledgement, an approval to grow old and die there in that ancient house (we'll fix it up), on this cold street (we'll meet the neighbors), in this gentle, infant town.

Together, we make a single millionaire. Who would've guessed that, in the end, the near-entirety of human history had been correct? That the grandiose economics of spreading peanut butter across some four-thousand kilometers of toast—two centuries of stolen space carved into states and provinces; a continent of long whooshing hallways, empty living rooms, and throaty elevator shafts—could be wrong?

But when the glut of things subsides, whistle, and let us find each other. Let us meet back on the sidewalk in front of the old abode; we'll remember how to do it, how to be it, that family, again. Pheromones and genetic memory will aid and abet, taking us back to Dad gargling in the bathroom and Mom kicking us out of the kitchen. The generational helplessness was not learned but shared—and most of the retirement communities have sunk, are sinking, or will sink beneath the white-hot sea regardless.

The banks hurt as the mortgage market fell apart but fuck them anyways. They couldn't match the petty cash tucked on the mantelpiece, hidden under the four-legged jar of Clive's ashes, nor the late nights across the dinner table, your parents in their chewed-up slippers, secret pains all over their aging bodies, diving into their retirement fund and saying *Okay, we'll help you out.* The op-eds tracked the fall, miles of print and talking heads wailing, trying to write away the flood, to legislate against the new weakness. But how could a news channel understand the infinite strength of helping your mother weed the backyard? Of your father handing you the sledgehammer to knock down a dividing wall, inhaling the gypsum together? Of bobbing amid the currents of a Sunday morning kitchen—around the pot of coffee, over the sink, across the cutting board—and cooking omelets for the sleepy-eyed relations grumbling in the hallway?

The market grew still, financial waterways now an anchorage: a flotilla of concrete, rebar, and wallpaper embarking on one long stationary voyage, sailing through the days and decades. After the boxes emptied out and the moving trucks rumbled away, the real work of patching and painting began. The attic needed re-insulating; we blocked over the squirrels' doorways and portholes. We steadied ourselves in the galley, sealing the countertops and pulling up the rotting boards. In no time at all, sailors are signing on: international students, cousins, or the odd tenant at reduced rent. Stowaways practically spring out of the woodwork when her job goes steady and she gets pregnant. Once, twice, the years turn. A dog shows up, then a cat. Soon enough, the kids have become mariners, manning the curtains, cleaning the ribald mess, and protesting the chief officer's bunk inspections.

Inside, outside, the generations resonate; a thousand times, a million times cleaning and refilling the hummingbird feeder. The compost bin has been there longer than any of us, an entire civilization of worms with border-town anthills and raiding groups of spiders. We survive in the cross-section of a song, a symphony of voices: the wind snickering in the chimney, the croak of the stairwell, icicles snapping inside the gutters—plus the human instrument of steps sneaking through the house for late-night leftovers, or to scroll porn on the family computer. Who needs photo books when your chipped tooth records the patio step? When, for three months of the summer, the barbeque clocks overtime, etching the siding in chicken burger soot? Arteries fail; Grandma passes; her dented mattress is dragged downstairs; the teenager inhales the dust of her dead skin every night. He sleeps with his first girlfriend atop it.

Heading Out   *Cheryl Stadig*

The walls do not listen (but they do), and the floors cannot breathe (yet they must), existing in the preternatural *now*, in the tide of an entropy that neither a dozen renovations, new countertops, nor fresh bathroom tile can stop. For the house, there are only these people and this time. Carve your initials in the attic beam; in a century they will only be lines. Hairballs grow in the shower drain. Saltwater moves to fill the space, be it a cup, bowl, or jerrycan; love, likewise, can flood a drafty mansion, a stuffed apartment, or the tent atop a concrete sidewalk. Beneath the bedroom nightstand, we still have our cookie tin of vibrators and lube, just a little quieter with the kids down the hall. She giggles as I lock the door. I stare at her forty-year-old breasts. *Do you think Dad will knock?*

The news gets worse, uglier, as you grow older and warmer. So come on home—the diaspora is over. Dreams, nightmares? Come back and kiss the rolling deck, sniff the familiar carpet. You can finish your university courses from the bedroom desk. You can check in on telework from across the ocean. There was once a time when you could say, *I planted my father in this paddy; I raised my son in this field.* Not a movie or a novel but a bleeding script; your grandparents didn't know how to narrate. *Australopithecus,* in their herds, could neither read nor write. They didn't text across the anthill.

How else can I tell you? Don't hate this house with its leaks, copper pipes, and creeping mold. Try and see it for what it is, existing somewhere in the process of material between a thatch hut and a starship. Sure, there are the too-hot summers unsuited for the architecture, the flooding basement, brownouts humming in the walls. But it goes on, be it a tent or a mansion, a hovel or a flying saucer.

And so what of apocalypse? So what if they go and drop it, that final bang? Then the house only becomes dust, or glass. This home may end, sinking to the bottom of a still-darker sea; many will not. You hand the international student a glass of wine at Thanksgiving dinner. They look well-fed and frightened. *If you get out of school early,* you tell the sailors, *come straight home.* And, *If you're hurt shooting hoops in the road, come right on back.* And if the world should end while I'm sitting downtown, let me struggle past those burning highways, sparking powerlines, and drowning people. Just let me make it home in time to tack up the Christmas lights.

The outhouse feeds the tulips. The moths eat Grandma's furs, then her daughter's fakes. Please, let me rot here, fading out beneath the lawn—at worst, spread my ashes in the garden where the racoons walk so when they lick their paws, they taste me. We never told you about when you were in diapers, did we? And those same bandits got into the trashcan and boom, exploded it into a million pieces, all across the carport? Don't feel embarrassed; there is no glory here, only a house. There is no fantasy, no dream, and we are not sick dogs—come in from the outside, come and die in the burrow. But don't forget, after you bury me, to exhume my lower jaw. Wash it clean with the garden hose, then submerge it in the bird bath so that, when spring comes again, I can kiss the robins, tooth to beak.   ◪

—Originally published in *Broken Pencil Magazine*, 2023

Making it Right   *Sandra Kleven*

Jennifer Carraher

Primal Landscape

The old blue house is the first place Jane remembers seeing an elk tethered from its hind shanks, tied with a half-hitch knot, like the calves her cousin Jason wrangled at the county fair, the piggin string taught above the forehooves in a ropey coil. Every winter, the smell of fresh blood and cold flesh splayed open would cuff her awake as she trudged in her stocking feet out the back door and down the three steps to where her folks parked the '71 Bronco that she'd later learn to drive from her uncle Roy, and the rusty brown Chevy that Jim had been working on for as long as she'd known him. In front, nearly against the bumpers, hung the elk, fur matted with blood where the first shot went through, just above the right shoulder, ruining all that good eating, her grandpa said, and the second shot, between the eyes, tongue lolling out between black lips, teeth bared, dripping blood onto the concrete floor.

Jane and the twins and the littlest, who she always called the baby even though she wasn't a baby for very long, had a meal of choice cooked by their mom for their birthdays. The twins requested stuffed hotdogs which Jane couldn't understand because there was cumin in the mashed potatoes cushioning a carefully severed beef frank topped with a glistening slice of orange cheese, baked in the oven, a confusing and almost appalling way to mark a whole year of life. The baby chose venison, fibrous and gamey, covered in flour and spices like Alpine Touch and cracked black pepper, fried in butter.

Trudging up the walk from the bus stop after school, through deep snow and over ice patches that knocked you off your feet if you didn't mind your steps, Jane would catch the heavy pong wafting out the door of the old blue house, jogging her memory of a birthday she'd forgotten to commemorate with a handmade doll or a cross stitched handkerchief like her grandma had taught her to make; so she dropped her backpack, parka and kicked off her winter-worn sorels, careful not to let the screen door slam, and made her way down the stairs. With a fine pencil sketch on the front of a five point elk frolicking by the riverside through a meadow of wolf's bane and snowberry, Jane concentrated hard on the details, like the rough gray triangle depicting the Mission Mountains which loomed, snow covered all year long, behind the old blue house. Opening the card she stenciled freehand in chunky block letters, each a different shape and color, H A P P Y B I R T H D A Y beneath a grimacing stick figure holding a rifle aloft, both arms raised high, the cartoon elk cleaved open, anus to neck, and hanging from the ceiling over a floor of blood-stained cement, burnished under summer-bare feet.

Happy Birthday, baby.

—

Jane's father was born in a small northern town into a circle of sisters, to a gentle and pious mother who grew up along the lake where she picked and sorted cherries until her father moved the family up to homestead, south of the park where glaciers still stood and grizzlies trudged through Junegrass to look for sedges or clover growing around the one-room schoolhouse and log cabin where they made their life back then. So too was he born of a severe and exacting father who, Jane was told, more than 70 years ago, taught at least half of the valley's young men to fly a single-prop airplane over the length of the lake, up past the Cabinet Mountains and the Kootenai forest where Canadian lynx and wolverines still trudge along the nine months of rutted winter trails. He made those boys cross low through the Purcell Range, teaching them that the tremors of current were just friction from air moving against the summit, calling them mountain waves, which, to the boys felt like tsunamis, making sweat cloud their vision, imagining plunging into the depths of Lake Koocanusa below.

—

Jane's father's town stands on the edge of that feral backcountry, the little of it that still remains up north, run through by the great Kootenai river, coursing above the tree-line. It's here that the drift boats take prune pickers out to fish for cutthroat and rainbow trout when the current pulls at the bank and flows deep, after the snowmelt makes the Silver Bow run rich for the trawl.

The mines of this town, once heavy with glossy soft vermiculite sloughing flakes of layered rock so dense that you could run your fingers through, nearly killed the whole town when her father was growing up. Ore was shipped across the country, back then, and scattered round to fertilize soil or fill attics, fortifying the houses against ice storms, hot topping the wood burning stoves which stood in the corner of every living room, reeking of burnt creosote. They called it Zonolite to hide the misdeeds that lurked in offices above dark mineshafts where men spent days and nights digging into the earth, extracting its poisonous core. These mines, now and forever, hold within them specters who walk the pit, recounting the killing of half the town before anyone knew why their children were coughing up blood and their brothers couldn't race them down the block anymore without stopping, bent at the waist, holding hard to their knees until their knuckles turned white and over years their nail beds curved and rose while they tried to just breathe. People in the town watched without eyes as fibers escaped the mines, on currents or miners' shirtsleeves, boot bottoms or coveralls and sliced into pleura, drowning almost the whole town with each breath of its fresh mountain air.

—

When Jane was pulled into the world with cold forceps scraping and scarring her temples, her young mother with a slight build, so much smaller than Jane at that age, reached to wipe her own blood from Jane's head and saw the dark trickle came from the place where the steel had clamped down hard and rotated Jane's little body with a force so great that her skin gave. She'd have scars there her whole life and as a child, when her grandmother would talk to her about afterworlds and other lives, she'd imagine invisible threads extending from the scars, pulling her back to a life she'd known, or one she had yet to live. These strands, filaments through her brain, intertwined like a helix, trailing all the way back to this mythic place. She couldn't know it, she was told, because it wasn't in this mountain valley or up north by Indian Springs along the Canuck border that she first felt breath or found footing on land, trod by her father before her. It wasn't in Dupuyear on her great grandma's pig farm where the population would have been 56 if she had been allowed to come into the world there, like her cousins who rode their horses to school, slaughtered chickens, and shot rabbits in the meadow for supper.

She was born *back east*, said the locals, a place called Ohia by the folks who lived there. This made her an orphan, uprooted even in the comfort of her mother's womb, because you can't be made in one place and come from another, no matter how many times they try to convince you that your entire life won't feel like fiction when you return home. So Jane was pulled screaming into Hancock county, where the summers are stifling and the air heavy with fireflies, with weeks marked by Methodist Sunday dinners and the burning Cuyahoga. She had a dad there, a man her mom had married after two months of knowing him and not because she was pregnant with Jane, she said, even though Jane was born seven months later. Jane could never understand when this far-away Dad gathered up his family and traced the 2,000 white miles from there to here in a Bonaventure van, a new one every summer. She couldn't understand why he swept Jane up and took her with his children and wife who really didn't like her much but would allow her to play poker after the other kids were asleep at night, and let her keep the money, too. This Dad called this northern place his home. But Jane couldn't understand this, couldn't understand why she didn't look like him, didn't have his nose, his short legs or red hair; she didn't understand why he didn't stay if she was his and *here* was his too.

—

Off the high-dive over Flathead Lake, Jane stood on rickety two-by-fours bound together with rusty screws that the twins held twelve feet up and turned tight with a stubby, phillips head, until they created an upside down U for launching their bodies away from the swimmer's itch on the shore into the deep where sturgeon might be. From there, she could see through to the colored stones on the bottom, minnows swimming round the dock's mossy edge. She held her breath, arms outstretched against the blackening August sky, and let her weight fall, breaking the bite of this watery glacier, filled up by ghosts of the Salish people pushed out past the west shore all the way to Arlee where there is no lake at all, just the Jacko River and the sprawling, empty reservation. This lake carries these ghosts across its 30 miles, almost 400 feet down into its icy depths. Submerged, Jane felt the chill of souls within the *se'ulig*, the Salish word that her friend Henry, who lived on the reservation but didn't go to school there, taught her, where his people used to fish for rainbow trout and hunt across the shores, tracking elk and moose in winter. She felt it every time she broke the surface, every time she thought about being from a place where you are told you don't belong, even if you belong to it.

From below the wake, Jane remembered the story Grandma Lou told her, from her own mother before that, a story woven as the world was young, when a burning star jumped into the waters of Flathead Lake. The Salish people who lived along the shore heard the star crying out in pain, so they ran outside and saw the whole lake burning, the sky above it lit up amber and coral, shining like daylight, like the heavens on fire. But the star, burning and crying, hopped frantically into the lake, a huge gray cloud rising out of the water hanging in the air. The people believed then, as Jane believed today, that there was a water spirit in that lake who pulled the star from the sky, beneath the water, and if you got too close it would pull you in too. That's what Grandma Lou said and Henry said, and Jane knew this was true because once all the Salish, even Henry, still lived along the east shore but new people built cabins there, and these shoreline cabin-dwellers watched as his people were pulled away. Those new upon the shore listened to the crying and looked into the fiery sky and called it Nordlys, the northern lights, because legends of the midnight sun can't hold a fallen star and his people. But every time Jane broke through the water it scorched her skin cold and she imagined herself, like these souls, never being free. Jane knew the place she came from and knew the home she belonged to, knew she would spend her entire life and many lives after that even, trying to find her way, like the Salish and their *se'ulig*, souls tethered by the double helix thread, through the temples, binding each together, drawing them back again.

Nupeeka means spirit, said Henry. *Look at the nupeeka here, Jane. Look at them all, trying to get home.* ◨

Eve Müller

Strangers Paid to Pick Up the Pieces (August 2023)

<u>Delivering a Bed</u>

Steve arrives with the bed in the back of his pickup truck. He's black-eyed and handsome, not at all dressed for furniture moving. He's someone I would have courted had I been closer to life's beginnings. He slings the shrink-wrapped mattress over his shoulder and carries it into my bedroom. We peel back layers of plastic, and the mattress unfurls before us like a soft white petal. I don't tell him I left my husband this morning. That tonight I sleep alone for the first time in thirty years. Soon Steve is perched on a wooden box, strumming my battered guitar, and I am down on hands and knees in my dress, attaching the legs to the bedframe. I can tell he doesn't want to go, and that's fine. I enjoy the sounds of the guitar as sweat beads on my brow. Even more, I like that he keeps his hands and shirt clean while I squat here in the back of the house. Hem hiked high. Screws sticking out from between my teeth. As he leaves, he slips an engraved card into my hand: Steve Leopoldi – landscaper, guitar teacher, renaissance man. *Call me*, he says. *I'll teach your daughters how to serenade their sweethearts.*

<u>Stocking the Liquor Cabinet</u>

Ruth owns the liquor store down the street with her husband Feng. She is tough as hickory wood. Doesn't take shit from anyone. Sports a tattoo of a rat on her wrist, which according to the Chinese zodiac means she must have been born in 1960 – a few years ahead of me. Ruth says I look younger than she's ever seen me look before. *What's changed?* she asks.
Left my husband, I say.
I thought you two were happy, she says.
Your liquor store made us happy.
I place my bottles on the checkout counter. A ragged man in front of me runs his fingers over my whiskey bottle. *You gonna drink all that at once?* he asks.
Nope, I say. *It'll take me a couple of weeks at least.*
Ruth says, *Don't mind him. He's jealous. Wishes he had what you've got.*
A crummy divorce? I ask. *Two unruly teenage girls?*
The booze, she says. *I'm talking about the booze.*
Ruth laughs as she hands me my bag, her mouth open wide as a barn. It's January. COVID is already making its way across China. I have no idea how rare the sight of a stranger's mouth will soon become.

<u>Delivering Groceries</u>

It's the end of March, and COVID arrives in Maryland. Our lives are pitched into disarray. Nurses, childcare workers, and drugstore clerks are dying. Hooked up to respirators, unable to kiss their children goodbye, mowed down like meadow grass. I try to get my daughters to observe quarantine. They sneak out in spite of my warnings and come back after midnight stinking of weed and sex. I am afraid to venture out of the house to buy beer and eggs. I order groceries delivered straight to our door. LaWanda is late. I only know her name because it pops up on the screen of my phone. She is part of a new cottage industry, the first in a series of interchangeable delivery people. LaWanda carries three bags of groceries to my front porch, knocks hesitantly on the door. She whispers through the screen, *Mrs. Eva, I'm going to leave your bags right here.* I bring my groceries inside and wonder what LaWanda thinks about going into supermarkets all day long, delivering food to strangers. Does she have daughters at home who smoke and neck behind the garage? Whose wild laughter sends cascades of microbes into the living room air? Does LaWanda lie in bed at night, body clenched tight as a fist?

Unclogging the Sink

I let the plumber in. His given name is Barry, but he goes by Blink. His eyes shine bright as dimes, and his crooked smile reminds me of my dead brother's. I shake his hand and immediately regret this act of physical intimacy during a time of plague. Blink crouches beneath my kitchen sink. I flutter about behind him, asking questions, making small talk. In between replacing washers and using his wrench to tighten pipes, Blink tells me about his second wife. *She's just like the first,* he laughs. We talk about patterns repeating themselves. The illusion of freedom. Blink reaches into the drain and pulls out a clump of black, vile-smelling stuff. *Here's your problem,* he says, handing me what must have once been strands of my elder daughter's golden hair.

Tending to the Cat

The tomcat has dementia. He forgets to clean himself. His once-shiny coat is reduced to a tangle of matted orange fur. He shits on the rug and pisses on the furniture. The house is starting to stink. *We have to do something,* my daughters plead. I take the cat to the vet. Dr. McFadden used to front a punk band, and I admire the tattoo peeking from beneath the sleeve of his lab coat, a two-tailed mermaid whose hips twitch when he flexes his bicep. He checks the cat's temperature. As he palpates the cat's belly and examines his tongue, we talk about the indignities of aging. *There's not much we can do for your cat,* says Dr. McFadden. *He's old and he's set in his ways.* He suggests I move him outside. I propose building a tiny cat house beneath the dogwood tree, under the sun, the stars, the fat, white blossoms. We both reach out to stroke the cat's fur at the same time, and our fingers collide. I feel a small electric shock like the buzzing of bees. I yank my hand back as if I'd touched fire, and beneath my mask, my cheeks burn.

Dying My Hair

Working from home – avoiding movie theaters, coffee shops and crowded bars – I no longer need to make myself beautiful. But vanity persists. I look in the mirror and see a mass of grey, disheveled hair. Perhaps I'm not much different from the cat. I call Chanlina. She's cut my hair for almost twenty years. She is no longer cutting hair indoors but agrees to come and dye my hair on the back porch. It's cold outside. Chanlina wears a down jacket and sequined Uggs. We're the same age, but she looks much younger. Her hair black and shiny, her waist still shapely. She brings all her equipment including a hair drying chair and a garden hose. She spends most of an hour wrapping my hair in foil, transmuting my silver into gold. A true alchemist. We talk about our children, mothers, fear of death. She also tells me I need to wash my hair more often. She doesn't like to touch the greasy strands. *No man in his right mind would,* she says. *We're middle-aged women. We need to stay on top of things.*

Checking for Bruises

My daughters get into a fight with the police. It's 2 am. My elder daughter's boyfriend is arrested for driving down the wrong side of the road, high as the clouds. My younger daughter videotapes the cops because the boyfriend is Black, and the cops are rough. Another cop wrestles her to the ground, grabs the phone from her hand, grinds her face into the pavement. My elder jumps on his back and tries to pry him off her sister. By the time I arrive on the scene, both are in handcuffs. The younger screaming obscenities at the cop, her mask red with blood. I try to intervene. *Keep back, ma'am,* says one of the cops. *Your daughters have assaulted a police officer. There's nothing for you to do here.* A few hours later, I pick up both girls from the police station. Before we leave, Officer Jackson checks for bruises on my younger daughter's arms and abdomen, photographs the cuts on her face. She says, *That cop was an asshole.* Officer Jackson sighs and puts down his camera. *Yeah,* he says. *COVID's making us all a little crazy.* The girls and I drive home in silence. I'm hardly ever up before sunrise, and through my tears, I notice the sky is the color of plums, the moon an oily smear.

Administering Oxygen

My younger daughter crashes the car. She is in the intensive care unit for almost a week, unconscious for forty-eight hours. Because of COVID, we can only visit her one at a time. I sleep in a chair beside her bed. I hold her hand in mine. It's still the hand of a child, all ink stains and bitten down nails. Rebecca the nurse is young, ponytailed, and optimistic. She reassures me everything will be alright. But my daughter's oxygen levels drop into the danger zone. She trembles uncontrollably with cold. Rebecca slips an oxygen mask over my daughter's blue lips. Together we wrap her up in an inflatable plastic cocoon to keep her warm. The nurse touches my shoulder. *Just you wait,* she says. *She'll wake up fierce as ever.* But something inside me feels irrevocably broken, like a branch torn from a tree.

Assessing the Damage

The tow truck driver hauls what's left of our car to an auto body shop. I call an Uber to drive me to the shop so we can assess the damage. It's a wasteland out here. Nothing but weeds and automotive carcasses as far as the eye can see. I find my car and it's shattered almost beyond recognition. The door so bent out of shape, I cannot open it with the key. I feel a sudden urge to lie down in the grass and give up. Instead, I ask at the front desk for help, and Aisha bounds across the parking lot, big and strong as a house, long braids flying. She wears her mask around her neck, flashes me a smile as bright and audacious as the dandelions bursting through the pavement. Aisha uses an iron bar to wrench the door open. *You won't be driving this baby again!* she booms. The news is bad, and yet I want to throw myself at her feet. Kiss the tops of her boots.

Mask Option   *Jim Thiele*

Checking on My Safety

I'm losing my shit. My younger daughter finds me crying on the kitchen floor. A bottle of whisky beside me, and it is not yet noon. *I need you to be stronger than this, Mom,* she says. I call the behavioral health line. It takes half an hour to reach someone, and they tell me I can't talk to a therapist for another two months. I ask to speak to the manager, and I wait another thirty minutes for her to tell me the same thing. A tsunami swells inside my chest, and I scream into the phone. I accuse them of malpractice. I slam down the phone so hard the screen cracks and the floor is littered with a galaxy of tiny shining stars. Fifteen minutes later, there's a knock at the front door. It's Officer Chibudem. He's a slight man with a soft voice, kind eyes, hands like birds. He asks if everything is okay. *Kaiser called 911,* he says. I tell him I need a therapist not a police officer. I tell him my world is spinning out of control. *It's a tough time for everyone, ma'am,* he says.

Tattooing My Leg

It's Mother's Day and the Brood X cicadas have returned. Their shiny black bodies and angry red eyes are everywhere. We find them on trees and windshields. In gutters and floating in bird baths. My elder daughter suggests the three of us get tattoos of cicadas to celebrate surviving this endless year. It's a Sunday, and most of the tattoo artists are taking the day off. But Zach Schmidt is open for business in a warehouse parlor. *Gotta feed the wife and kids,* he says. He's practically a kid himself, all loose limbs and spiky hair. He tells us he's got more than seventy tattoos and rolls up his pants leg to show them off. The girls and I spot skulls and devils, hot rods and bloodshot eyeballs. But Zach doesn't seem to know what he's doing. As the needle pierces my thigh, he confesses he's just an amateur. *Whatever,* I think, *We're all just amateurs.* And I grit my teeth and brace myself for whatever pain is to come. ◧

Marble Pattern in Cliff Matt Witt

PLAY

Diane Ray

The Man With His Finger In The Door

CHARACTERS:

SPIRIT OF MORRIS: The dying patriarch, 88, until the last two years, ever fit and larger-than-life, now lying semi-comatose in his bedroom while his spirit, barefoot in pajamas, shows up kibitzing.

DENA: His soberly dressed daughter, a college professor.

ANYA: Dena's arty daughter, 18, flying off to Oberlin.

MR.: The Angel of Death, wearing a face-obscuring black hooded robe, carrying shepherd's hook and sporting wings, and underneath all that, a pale man in need of a shave, perennially forty-five.

FLIGHT ATTENDANT: Voice on intercom

TIME: The year 2000

Dena and Anya are seated on an airplane with a vacant aisle seat next to Dena. Mr. appears and disappears, lurking in back of plane. Spirit of Morris, barefoot and in pajamas, bursts in nearly falling out of airplane bathroom.

SPIRIT OF MORRIS: (CATCHES HIS BALANCE) Now you just hold on a minute here, Mr.! You dump me off in a john? On an airplane? I only wanted to see — And there she is! Thanks for the lift, on a wing and a prayer! By the way, it's drafty in here. Can't afford to catch cold! (LIFTS A BARE FOOT) Could use some shoes! (MORRIS WALKS OVER TO DENA AND ANYA) Dena, Anya!... Dena, it's your father! *(waves hand in her face; no response)* Oh, I forgot. Not part of the deal, eh Mr.? Just like before, when you beamed me to Daniel's place. (SEES EMPTY SEAT NEXT TO DENA) Oh well, don't mind if I do. (SITS)

DENA: I remember leaving for Vassar.

ANYA: Yeah, and I bet your parents helped you move in!

SPIRIT OF MORRIS: Can this be little Anya leaving for college? *(TO DENA)* I recall driving you upstate like it was just yesterday. Carcasses of bloody deer on top of car after car heading back to the city!

DENA: I'm so sorry about all this, Anya.

ANYA: I don't care! (SADLY) You're still not going with me.

SPIRIT OF MORRIS: Now why would city and suburban folk shoot beautiful, graceful deer when anything you need, you can get in the supermarket? It's like they're playing (SINGS OLD TV SHOW THEME SONG)) *Davy, Davy Crockett, King of the Wild Frontier!*

DENA: I'm really disappointed. I was so looking forward to it!

ANYA: Uh huh!

SPIRIT OF MORRIS: (TO DENA) I'll say one thing for your brother. Daniel never goes around trying to prove something like those phonies, and some of them may also be (MAKES SWISHY MOVEMENT WITH HAND) I mean, who would have thought Rock Hudson? It's true. Read it in *The New York Times!*

ANYA: *You* weren't dumped off with all your stuff in the fucking Midwest.

DENA: Actually (PATTING ANYA ON THE LEG), it's the fucking Mid-Atlantic!

SPIRIT OF MORRIS: Hold on, young lady! We never raised you to talk like that!

DENA: Look, Sweetheart, Grandpa is in and out of comatose, and the hospice people said—

ANYA: (INTERRUPTS) *I get it,* Mom! I just wish for once you guys would put me first!

DENA: (SPOKEN FAST, WITH CONTROLLED HYSTERIA) Considering we only found out about Grandpa at five this morning, and your Dad's stuck presenting in LA, we're doing the best we can! I think it's pretty great that despite you interrupting every five seconds and giving me the look, that by the time we got to the airport, *One:* I had reached your roommate's mother in West Virginia, and she's happy to take you both shopping for curtains or whatever; *Two:* I made it so we still get to fly this leg to Ohio together; and *Three:* My connecting flight to LaGuardia just might get me there before he—

ANYA: (INTERRUPTS SCREAMING) **Mom! Click on your listening ears!**

DENA: (RESPONDS SCREAMING) **What?**

SPIRIT OF MORRIS: Pipe down the both of you! Don't embarrass me!

ANYA: Click on your listening ears! like you used to say to me! You have all the words, but you're not hearing! I'm not a baby! I already flew by myself to all those admitted student thingies, because **I wanted to make the decision!** But now I am **really leaving!** Just this once, I *need* you to be there! Please, Mom!

DENA: I'm so, so sorry, Sweetheart, I'm not in charge of when my father—

ANYA: (INTERRUPTS) You're the one who felt so fucking empathic when you saw the robin mom return to her nest under our deck with a big fat worm to share, but meanwhile her last baby bird flew the coop, and you saw robin grief and confusion. I heard you tell all this to Katie, and you were, like, so sad, because—

DENA: (INTERRUPTS) But my Dad is still…

ANYA: Mo-om! It would help me so-o much for you to go with me. Please, Mom, please!

SPIRIT OF MORRIS: She's got a point, Dena. Your baby bird has got to fledge, and anyway, you're not missing much! Back there in the bed? I can hardly tell the real from the dream. But apparently, I flew the coop! I'm on vacation!

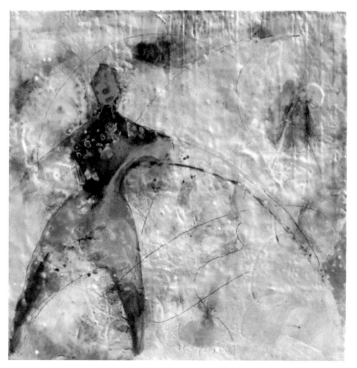

Spirit Dance   *Sheary Clough Suiter*

DENA: *Oy!* (SIGHS) You're right! I'm afraid I got on one of my tracks! Everything happened so fast, and I'm a little freaked out to leave my brother in charge of Grandpa now, but… you can't be in two places at once.

SPIRIT OF MORRIS: You'd be surprised!

DENA: OK: (TAKES A BIG BREATH) Good thing this flight's so insanely early! On to Plan C: What if I go with you for today and fly to Grandpa's on a red eye tonight? If I get there in time, I get there.

ANYA: Really? That's so great, Mom! Thank you, thank you, thank you! (HUG)

DENA: So when we reach Cleveland, you get the luggage, and I'll run to change tickets. Just don't drink the coffee, and you'll be fine.

SPIRIT OF MORRIS: Seattle people, always with the coffee! Remember when I came for your Bat Mitzvah, Anya, and you made me one of those mocha polka frappu cuckoo choochoos? Just a little slip of a girl! Never let on that to me, it's just a coffee.

ANYA: Oh my God, I am going to miss Grandpa!

SPIRIT OF MORRIS: I'll be there in your heart, but too bad I'll miss the rest of your story. On the other hand, Mr., maybe you'd get me a ticket in the celestial peanut gallery?

DENA: Remember when you were, like, six on a really hot summer day, and Grandpa challenged you to a race and took off leaping down the beach in long pants in his polished work shoes, and he won? Can't believe he would have wanted my brother to keep him alive for years on a feeding tube….

SPIRIT OF MORRIS: (INDIGNANT) How could I leave your mother! It's my job looking out for her!

ANYA: When you get to Syosset, for once, Mom, don't fight with your brother!

DENA: He is such a control freak! He hardly ever let Grandpa—

ANYA: (INTERRUPTS) Don't fight with your brother! Daniel is Daniel and you are…

DENA: I just think it's so much better to die with your boots on!

SPIRIT OF MORRIS: You getting this, Mr.? I ask, shoes. She upgrades me, boots! But you win: (LIFTING AND WIGGLING TOES) Bare toes!

ANYA: Uncle Daniel has a lot of good qualities and a lot of shticks.

SPIRIT OF MORRIS: My son, my son, always with the shticks and stones!

ANYA: Just don't fight with him, ok, Mom? Like Dad says, we're far away, and—

DENA: (INTERRUPTS) OK, you're right! He's had all the heavy lifting with our folks, (SIGHS) not that he ever let me weigh in my two cents about anything or help—

(ANYA TUNES OUT, PLUGS IN EAR BUD)

SPIRIT OF MORRIS: (INTERRUPTS) Just now when I dropped in on Daniel? What do you suppose he and his, uum, *partner* were doing? Oohing and aahing over chopped liver! Imported, and from a goose. Made a big production number, calling it pâté, but it was chopped liver, just like Mama used to make. I saw something, Dena. I saw their *comfort* with one another. Too bad they never told me. Did they think I was born yesterday, or were they gun shy? You would know, but Danny missed the boat. I knew they weren't business associates. So many missed opportunities…Maybe I should have broken the ice…We all could have gone on walks… (RECOVERING HIS EQUANIMITY) Anyway, it is what it is, and for them it is good, …and that's that.

DENA: (FIDGETS, PREOCCUPIED, UNABLE TO SETTLE DOWN) Anya? Ever hear the stories about Grandpa's Papa?

SPIRIT OF MORRIS: You mean, that **Bum,** my Papa! Gambling away Mama's happiness.

ANYA: I don't know, Mom. (REATTACHES EAR BUDS)

SPIRIT OF MORRIS: Ever tell her the story of my very first trip out of Brooklyn?

DENA: (TRIES TO SETTLE IN, CAN'T HELP HERSELF, POKES ANYA.) Sweety Toots?

ANYA: (ROLLS HER EYES) What **now**, Mom?

DENA: Did you ever hear the quintessential Grandpa Morris story about—

ANYA: (INTERRUPTS)This has totally got to be IT, Mom!

DENA: When Morris was young Morrie in East New York, where just off the boat Jews like his parents could hardly afford more than one set of school clothes for their kids, which meant no athletic shoes or shorts—

SPIRIT OF MORRIS: (INTERRUPTS) Just my second-hand school oxfords and knickers.

DENA: Another boy—

SPIRIT OF MORRIS: (INTERRUPTS) Murray Rivkin.

DENA: Challenges him to some big race around the reservoir.

SPIRIT OF MORRIS: Big shot, wants to bet me a whole dollar. A fortune of money for us kids back then. Ground's all slick and muddy, and he even has cleats, but I take him on.

DENA: And Morrie runs like the wind in a hurricane.

SPIRIT OF MORRIS: Lick 'em fair and square! I really cream that stuck up son of a gun!

DENA: And with the winnings, he buys himself an old bike.

SPIRIT OF MORRIS: That's right! Fixed it up and put a Macintosh apple and some nuts in my pocket and tied an old oilcloth around the seat for my first sleep out.

DENA: He bikes clear across Brooklyn and the Brooklyn Bridge and up Manhattan to the Jersey ferry–no George Washington Bridge back then, no highways, just a little road past the Palisades, the first country hill he has ever seen. Nobody around, he screams out: "Wheeeeeee!" — the summer breeze smells so sweet!

SPIRIT OF MORRIS: You listened!

DENA: And sees his first slopes and fields of storybook trees, and the wide, blue Hudson.

SPIRIT OF MORRIS: Now you've got the hang of it!

DENA: Pedals all the way on the old one speed bike and makes it to Bear Mountain. That's got to be at least sixty miles.

SPIRIT OF MORRIS: Bear Mountain takes the cake!

DENA: Sleeping under the stars.

SPIRIT OF MORRIS: *So* many sparkles in the sky!

DENA: And right then he decides to just forget about his Papa.

SPIRIT OF MORRIS: That Bum doesn't show for my bar mitzvah, his only son, and he was Orthodox, for crying out loud, and besides the rabbi, the only one in synagogue who knew what all the Hebrew meant, for all the good it did him.

DENA: And Morris decides that he will do whatever it takes to grow up and be someone.

SPIRIT OF MORRIS: And come home to a lovely wife and raise children where they'll have sweet, fresh air like this and wide-open futures.

DENA: He decides he will be whatever he wants to, do whatever it takes.

SPIRIT OF MORRIS: Which was eight years of night law school, and by the way, got a perfect score on the bar, but what New York law firm would even take a peek at someone named Morris Ratkowsky? So I went into business, worked six days a week til I turned 80. Did I ever complain? That ride to Bear Mountain was the start of everything.

DENA: Next morning, he starts back home, and his chain breaks shooting down a hill.

SPIRIT OF MORRIS: In the middle of nowhere!

DENA: He rolls in the grass, gets away with a scrape.

SPIRIT OF MORRIS: But that hunk of junk is toast!

DENA: By and by a man drives up, offers him a ride.

SPIRIT OF MORRIS: A gentleman in a Tin Lizzy. That's a Ford model T.

DENA: So Morris hops on the running board, but the door slams shut on his finger.

SPIRIT OF MORRIS: If I yell for him to stop, he could get mad, change his mind, kick me off.

DENA: So he rides silently like that for twenty miles before they stop.

ANYA: No way!

SPIRIT OF MORRIS: It hurt like shooting fire!

DENA: And to top it all off, Morris would always hold up his finger with the little bend in it and say with pride:

DENA AND MORRIS: (BOTH HOLDING UP THEIR INDEX FINGERS) *You know anyone else who could do that?*

ANYA: *Grandpa was paranoid!*

SPIRIT OF MORRIS: What's she talking about? You have to be on the safe side!

DENA: Oh Sweetheart!... Remember when your drama class did *Streetcar?*

ANYA: Uh, yeah.

SPIRIT OF MORRIS: Do I have to spell it out? I accepted a ride in the middle of nowhere from a stranger! From a **gentile** in 1927!

DENA: Grandpa never relied on the kindness of strangers.

ANYA: Good one, Mom!

DENA: Oh God, hope I get there in time!

SPIRIT OF MORRIS: She'll make it, Mr., right? You can arrange that?

DENA: (YAWNS) Let's get some rest. (ANYA AND DENA CURL UP IN THEIR SEATS)

SPIRIT OF MORRIS: So, on this flight, Anya, you get the double feature. No, the triple: First you get your mother to do right by you while she tries to do right by me, then you get your Grandpa's story, which after you learn a thing or two in college, you'll understand, and now, your Grandpa's blessing: (*MAKES A* CROWN OF HIS HANDS OVER HER HEAD) Anya-la, may you be blessed with a good life, a happy, fulfilling life, filled with love and compassion and doing right, and grow up to be a mensch like your mother, marry a nice, Jewish boy, and remember me to your children, name one of them Ethel after your Great Grandma, such an angel, and what she had to put up with (!), which should have been *your* name, not some Ruskie name out of Tolstoy, but that's Dena's mistake, not yours, and let us say amen. (BLOWS EACH A KISS, LIGHTLY STROKES DENA'S HAIR) You've always had my blessing, Dinkela, apple of my eye who truly blessed my life. (CHOKING UP) So long!

(MORRIS WILL TAKE TWO RUNNING STEPS AND A LEAP DOWNSTAGE TO FRONT OF PLANE, ARMS LIFTED IN EXULTATION, WHILE SINGING THE INITIAL WORDS TO THE *SO LONG, FAREWELL* SONG FROM "THE SOUND OF MUSIC")

SPIRIT OF MORRIS: (SINGS LOUDLY AS HE TAKES TWO RUNNING STEP AND A LEAP): **So long!**

VOICE ON INTERCOM: Please remain seated. We are experiencing some turbulence.

SPIRIT OF MORRIS: (TURNS AROUND, SOUND OF PLANE SHAKING WITH TURBULENCE/ MORRIS TAKES TWO RUNNING STEPS AND A LEAP TO REAR OF PLANE, SINGS OUT ON THE LEAP) Farewell! (CRASHES TO FLOOR)

(MR. APPEARS, HELPS SPIRIT OF MORRIS UP. MR"S HOOD FALLS OFF. SPIRIT OF MORRIS SEES HIS FACE).

SPIRIT OF MORRIS: *Papa? You're the—*

MR.: (INTERRUPTS) Hi ya, Morrie! They got a very good Anonymous up there. Been working the Amends some sixty-four years, and since I know all the prayers in the original Hebrew, I got this gig! (SINCERELY) Incidentally, good for you, going out with a bang!

SPIRIT OF MORRIS: You were terrible to us!

MR.: I know, I know. I was a shmuck, a putz, a goniff, a washout to your beautiful mother, to you and your sister….

SPIRIT OF MORRIS: (YELLING) **DO YOU KNOW WHAT IT IS LIKE** for an eleven-year-old boy to have to figure out all the fares and busses and ride from Brooklyn to the far edge of Queens to fetch his father out of the loony bin because Mama didn't speak good English then and was too scared and ashamed? You gambled yourself stiff as a board, forgetting to eat, to sleep, forgetting Mama, forgetting little Jenny and me.

MR.: I was a lousy dreamer, always trying to win big to take my beautiful Ethel out of the tenements (PULLS A TICKET OUT OF HIS SLEEVE). Here, you wanted a ticket, see how it all turns out? How 'bout third row center in the celestial peanut gallery?

SPIRIT OF MORRIS: (SPOKEN WITH AGONY) What did you ever give me when you were alive?

MR.: I admit it, I was never there when I was here. But since I'm gone, I never ever left you, always keeping an eye out. Like when you and little Dena were at that bus stop? And I told your mind to move back moments before the bus rode up on the curb?

SPIRIT OF MORRIS: Oh, Papa! (TAKES TICKET)

BLACKOUT

Raakmoor Surface with Flower   Annekathrin Hansen

POETRY

Claire-Elise Baalke

Waxwings

It is a clear, crisp morning
and the light clings to the hills
when a shrill war cry hits my ears—
the bohemian waxwings descend
upon few and sparse chokecherry
trees—the dance for survival of
nomadic kin—they pick them clean
like soot from teeth with bone.
I watch them here, enclosed,
as they flank and fold—
folding this figment of peace
within the seal of their wings
and flying away with it.

Droplets   *Jim Thiele*

John Baalke

Surface Tension

I lean back and draw the oars toward me.
The old fiberglass boat slips along the shore,
keel cutting a mirror sky

where painted-turtles clamber heavenward
and a mink scurries down a log, disappears in
clouds and brightness. It lingers

on the muddy bottom, holding its breath until
it re-emerges, moves effortlessly
between the elements. I maneuver

the skiff, and small eddies swirl beneath the stern.
The morning breeze sifts down-lake from the north,
rattles the bulrushes, casts

a deep blue pall over the surface. I drift under birches
that stagger from the cut bank, and set
the oars to rest. Here

the lunker walleye skulk in the cobbled shadows.
I let my bait bump along the reef, and wait
for a solid tug from below.

Overhead, an osprey angling in the wind
catches my eye. I begin to reel, and my line
plays out. I am taken up.

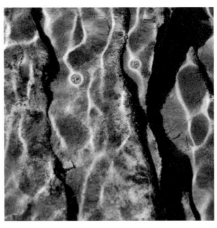

Bubble Eyes in the Creek   *Matt Witt*

Christianne Balk

The Beekeeper's Song

> *… palace beekeeper John Chapple confirmed to The Daily Mail that on Friday, he quietly told the tens of thousands of bees that are kept on the grounds of Buckingham Palace and Clarence House that the Queen had died …*
>   —CBC News, September 15, 2022

The Queen is dead, little sisters.
Dear dark London honey mongrels
who have tended her verbena
and fennel all these years without
falter—I've wrapped your hives in black
silk torn from her own worn dress hems
and tied lopsided bows to hang
from your walls. I've shifted your homes
just a few inches to the south
so your doors face ours and you'll know
everything has changed and you're not
alone. All these comings, goings—
no time to rest on the shaded

undersides of sunflower leaves,
not even at night. So many
of us, gathering as if grief
at her leaving cannot be born
alone. No wonder you're tempted
to flee to the cool rock crannies
and lodge in the fissured escarpments
far from here. Remember how she
sat with you, admiring your work
with the artichokes and lupine?
I have tapped gently on your domed
roofs to not startle you, whispering
she is gone. What song can I sing

to keep you from flying away?

Honeycomb   *Mandy Ramsey*

Joe Barnes

Old Dog

Deaf, he still tilts his head to a master's voice,
Though it is no longer mine.
There is a distance in his clouded eyes,
A longing for an otherwise, an elsewhere
That are not this cloistered life
Of sleep and stumbling through thin-lit rooms.
Ritual is what keeps him breathing:
The rising, the feeding, the walking,
The turn of days slowed to a creak.
I wake him gently now.

*Kona at the End of a Long Day
at Connor's Bog*   *Cynthia Steele*

A Squash Tendril   *Jack Broom*

Ari Blatt

In the Chest

A horse barreling through her chest. A horse galloping the racetrack along her ribs. A thunder horse; a fire horse; a horse in search. A horse lying in the grass, sun warming her side, breeze gracing her breath, a creek nearby. A content horse.

A fish sliding through his chest. A fish darting from trouble to hide in the overhanging curve of his ribs, cradled. A hungry fish; a knowing fish; a fish that's found. A fish deep in the pool, cool rich water, shadows and streaks of light. A fish at rest.

A river otter sliding swimming slippery in her chest. Swirling around each rib bone. A playful otter; a fierce otter; an otter that can turn on a dime. An otter sprawled out over a rock, crayfish in hand, lip smacking soul feeding nourishment. An otter momentarily satisfied.

A spider sitting in his chest, waiting. A spider spun her web from rib to rib, ready. A methodical spider; a savvy spider; a spider that is more than willing. A spider tiptoeing in the meantime, light tickly steps. A ballerina dancing. A spider in the throe of her life's purpose.

A jellyfish pulsing in her chest. A jellyfish slow and steady swimming rhythmically feeding. A calm jellyfish, a faith-full jellyfish; a jellyfish dedicated to their process. A jellyfish lit up, a jellyfish that stings, a jellyfish unperturbed until not.

A bed of moss softening their chest. A bed of moss growing along their ribs, catching every breath, every heartbeat. A bed of moss liked to be kept moist. A bed of moss that may jump ship if dried out too long. A bed of moss that will spring back when the drought ends. A giving bed of moss, if given just enough, not much.

A cedar sapling planted in her chest. A cedar sapling rooting around one rib, reaching up and reaching down, reaching out in all directions. A cedar sapling searching for light, searching for soil, searching for more to cling onto, to cling back, to connect. A cedar sapling expanding, deep breaths, breaking through. Her body the starting point, the open world, the end.

Eric Braman

The Scent of Sweet

our bathroom counter is a sugar ant highway
little legs traverse false marble
in search of something sweet
t h e y   w a n d e r
drawn by the false promises
of hand soaps and toothpaste
a pale peach olfactory mirage
where dust and scum texture
the path beneath their feet
but somewhere something sweet
                            pulls them forward

a layer of skin from my dry hand
swirls in the basin
as I lose track of my washing
trying to place wherever it is they
are coming from
nowhere, really, it seems
they are wanderers
s e e k e r s
lost in the flow of following what feels right
in a place that I'm certain
                            is wrong

one crawls into the bowl of the sink
and without thought I turn my hand
into a waterslide
creating a river to wash the little speck
                    down the drain

a twinge of sadness creeps in
from the corners and cracks of the room
l i t t l e   s o l d i e r s
in search of
something lost
                        someone lost

traveling what must be
s o   f a r
for things
s o   s m a l l
and I wonder
will they get distracted
by something sweet

                                        or travel
                                        down the
                                        drain
                                        seeking
                                        the source
                                        of sewer-bound
                                        cries

I re-lather my hands
to rid the smell of
crushed ant

                                        and lost thought

may this lavender
cleanse me of
m y   s i n s

House Bound   *Sheary Clough Suiter*

Randol Bruns

Anthony Completes His GED

In this day a solitary shot
from a high-velocity muzzle
makes small noise shattering but one chest,
one man, conscious but bleeding waiting
vigorous resuscitation.
Must have been a shock to his parents
downstairs watching TV when they heard
the report, ran to call EMTs
to patch this hole that grows toward the heart.

And then the autopsy, courtesy
of the State, to have out what went wrong
with Anthony, barely nineteen years
had just completed his GED
told his future was in computers...

His grandfather used to hunt the white
Arctic fox on the Bethel tundra;
it could take days following the tracks
waiting for the right moment to strike
when the fox lay asleep in the snow
Black knowing eyes buried in the white
on white, and then the silent arrow.

Man Bow-hunting

Suzanne R. Bernardi,
Penn Museum Archives

Shauna Potocky

Another Sort of Sun

Mark Burke

Parade For The Sun

The sun comes earlier now;
they rise for their god,
a parade in the cello of light.
First the strawberries, bright bells
peeking from the caravan tents
then blueberries, clusters of tiny balloons.
Raspberries arrive on the night train from Fiji
to an aria of sun and water
as currants appear from the air,
beads of black, crimson and champagne.
Bird song fills the golden plums,
egg-yolk tear drops,
honeyed ornaments in their mother's hair.
Blackberries begin their punctuations
along tales of vines,
jeweled pouches waiting for tongues.
Almost late, the rush of Asian plums
swell on the dark branches,
plump derrieres under wine petticoats,
each a kiss to purse the lips
as Damsons glow purple and lime
through the chills of mid-September.
And last, battalions of apples
marching four abreast; modest Jonagolds,
Pink Ladys, Fujis and Galas humming
through the longer shadows,
huddled in the branches as the days shorten
waiting the nights for hands
to save them from the cold ground.
So come the accidents of touch,
hands warming other hands, a thigh grazed
steadying the apple ladder,
the babe that comes in late spring.

Leap   *Sheary Clough Suiter*

Elisa Carlsen

Fade Into You

on the kitchen floor
our bodies soft and round like rolling hills.

we sleep in strange stratigraphy
old over new, me under you.

while the world outside
is waiting to unmake us.

I don't remember the dirt on the floor,
I only remember,

how I loved you then,
like light loves an open door.

Dale Champlin

Angels in the Wild

At first I hear singing—my heart clamps
  fiddlehead tight—a fistful of joy, a wild
  burr of hummingbird wings, the peppery
   scent of a skunk on the move, slinking

through a meadow diamon'd with dew.
  Do you dream the grass blowing as you pass?
  Listen. Stay still. Stealth forward. Break into
   the woodland with your panting breath.

Search the dapple for bird flit. Hear
  the first raindrops, a possum hiss in the
  underbrush, the devotion of fairyslippers,
   a chorus of blue-eyed grass. Why not touch

the gumdrop jewelweed sheltered by a granite
  outcropping, rooted feet first in rocky soil?
  Now cup your mouth into the curve of wolf howl.
   Crouch and run low to the ground. Skirt

the spring, laden with carnivorous cobra lily,
  a marshy reek of mold and decay, its foot-
  sucking slime. Duck beneath fir and willow,
   vine maple, and pine. In the magic hour

as the sun goes down, remember your
  children, your mother, your mate,
  one last time before light lets loose its hold.
   Tonight, ancient stars burst into brightness,

slide across the underbelly of speckled
  trout heaven. Return to the meadow.
  Kneel. To pray. To sleep. Tether yourself
   to our ever-rolling Earth.

Sunflowers   *Lucy Tyrrell*

Nard Claar

Pedal Tea

I live to ride my bicycle
down to the sea
to feel the air
to see it
and walk along the border
between worlds
to see and feel
to breathe
and maybe look beyond
the horizon
to possible
walk to change perspective
set to dwell and look
and maybe
to brew a cup of tea
and while boiling the water
setting out the leaves
watching each step
being within that space
and no other
to be on that border
and once it turns
the golden color
it is ready
the sip of something
so fine.

Receding Tide   *Mandy Ramsey*

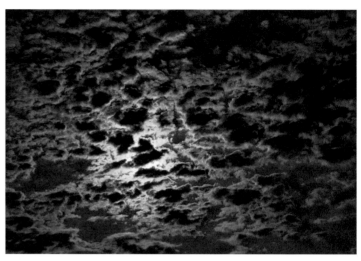

Afternoon Sun   *Matt Witt*

Joanne Clarkson

Beyond Darkness

Last horizon glow and a first planet
illumine the road past the old
fire station. Solitude and I companion
the quiet. Reach the high point
of the village from where I glimpse
lacquer black seas. Suddenly,
passing next to me, five does
with a yearling. They do not notice
me the way the falling dark, the distant
tides, don't notice me. They pause
in new grasses. They sample
leaf buds of the neighbor's apple.
They step up and into.
I want so much to follow, to leave
the way light has left, defined
by the invisible. Believing
in the chalice of tulips
the way last season's fawn noses
the first scent of gardens, starlight
buried under her coat. A muscle
moves under my right hand
with the nonchalance of fur.
I have forgotten my house number.
The wail of hope and sirens
is ten years empty. My vision
is less than breath. I am not even
sure they are deer.

Nancy Deschu

Unforeseen

Katmai National Park and Preserve, Alaska

The bear strikes down
one plate-sized paw,
then the next, over and over,
ten black hatchets
slice the frozen lake.

Why on this warm April day,
when he was hungry and lean
from winter hibernation,
why did he choose to walk
his 800-pound body
on to this capricious ice?

Now the long sunlight slips away,
snow glints orange, then blue.
In the middle of the lake
a brown image, head just above the ice,
a rhythmic cracking sound.

Nicole Emanuel

Tandeming

When you're up I'm up, when I'm down you're down—
down to go anywhere with you. A good stoker strokes
in sync, and I love to be in conjoined
cooperation with my captain.

Our routine rhythm has become synchronized
symphony, concerted concurrence.

Far from honking horns, far from cracking asphalt, where the sidewalk
ceases, the only paths that exist are desire
lines. We form some of our own, whenever,
wherever, we camp, making way through tall
or short grass, or across piney forest floor, or (once, by the banks
of the Missouri River) over sticky mud that the dogs brought
into our tent, when pitched at last. All grounds are good beds when
my mattress mate is you.

Team work makes the dream work and this is my dream team.
We know we'll get there at the same time, coming
and going simultaneously. Every landscape has your head in the center.
It looks much better than the view through a windshield.
Each ego-shielding car is a hard shell, all illusory speedings
sending some one some where, fast.

Our time takes us. Wherever I go, there you are.
An Eye requires an Other

to see your Self.

Monkshood   *@tjinalaska Toya Brown*

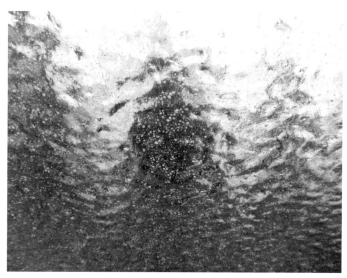

Ice Forest   *Cheryl Stadig*

Heron Leaving

Jack Broom

Mary Eliza Crane

View From the Apuan Alps

It would take stout boots
to scale this mountain pass on foot,
a thin road through a chestnut wood,
its dark trunks still bereft of leaves in early spring.
Far below, amid snails and wild primrose
eleventh century Castello di Montecuccolo
sits high on the horizon, taking in the view.
This was the front in World War Two.

In the east, rising steeply from the Ligurian Sea,
tiny villages persist, nestled into marble cliffs
which have been sculpted into Roman columns
and carved by Michelangelo to a smooth white genius.

Francesco tells us his grandfather
walked four hours every day to work the mines.
When he was a young man
his uncle perished in an accident
and his cousin runs the quarry now.
He takes us in his truck through marble caverns,
long tunnels, and winds us up past gray-veined blocks
and calcite dust to where we can see the sea.
Later he offers us crostini with tomatoes and
herb-infused marble-cured lard from Colonnata.

To the north in Ficarolo, a tower leans into
the main piazza at the end of market day.
Vendors pack up meats and cheeses,
artichokes and oranges, and hand me a sweet apple
for the asking. I meet a man with all the names,
yet there is no way to know if we are family.
Grandpa left too long ago. Though it's springtime,
the Po River still is low, winter brought so little rain,
and in the mountains, little snow.

Downstream to the west the river flattens,
widens to a delta drained and filled
fished and farmed and built upon for centuries.
Here Etruscans traded Baltic amber with the Greeks.
Canals are lined with blue-gray heron and snowy egret feeding,
grouse shuffle in the grass by cormorant and ibis.
In dusty rose lagoons, flamingoes shimmer in the sun.

She rises slowly, spreads her wings,
unfolds her stick-like legs and dances on the water.
A silent crimson flame, she disappears into the sky.

Seaweed and Stones   *Matt Witt*

Helena Fagan

Ebb Tide

Sneaking up on autumn, cool breezes, chilly nights
cocoon our beach house, whisper of what's ahead.
The house knows, despite the gathered summer heat,
stands steady every winter, bears the wind's blast
and the heavy rains that sodden the silvered cedar siding.

This house, this dear house,
waits patiently for me
season after season, year after year.
Does the melancholy I touch
today belong to me or the house?

The pulse of our next generation moves forward
in a tide of cribs and surfboards,
a clearing of old dressers with stuck drawers,
out of date cat food, barbecue rarely used:
tide in, tide out.

The tide hurries me along,
my beach walks shorter, knees aching,
words sometimes darting from me
like the tiny silver fish in tide pools.

Thirty-four years ago, you told me the house
was mine alone. "Do what you want with it,"
you whispered from your death bed,
then let go, of everything, and floated out, beyond us.

Now, if I squint, I see my own ride
out on the tide, perhaps a long wait away,
perhaps not, but the letting go,
I recognize, begins now.

Libby Ferrara

My body's own keeper

You say that it isn't
enough that—
but I've stopped listening.
At 34, after so many
enoughs not being met,
I've stopped listening for
the part where I play
the part of being
enough defined by
someone or something
that is not a part of
me. Why should I
have listened before?
No, it is enough—
It is enough for me
and it is my life that
I am measuring, my
life I must answer to,
my face that I can
choose to turn towards
the sun and permit its
penetrating warmth
engulf me in it's sweet,
lazy embrace. It is my
eyelids that grow red
as I bask, relaxing into
this radiance.
It is enough.
It is enough to inhale
deeply, the damp-tannic
atmosphere, pregnant with
the coming spring, in these
coastal woods. To feel
the wisdom of these elders
and briefly transpire
among them.
It is more than enough.
It is a gift to rise each
day I am given and
find myself once more
sustained, once more
witness to incomprehensible
musings of birds, once
more enveloped in a
living body in a sensuous
world, it is enough!
It is enough.

Jan Jung

David Foster

Monsters versus Sapiens

When I die, my wish is to be
    devoured by flesh and blood monsters.
Let them be like Hollywood's finest:
    Utterly terrifying. Ugly!
Tearing me in the Square, ghost-white
    septum from coal-black shriek.
In that redemptive, undoubtful death,
    no eroding confusion, no stewing shame.

*Vapor escapes from the white raven's breath on a
subzero day, Nov. 23, 2023, along Tudor Road in
Anchorage*   Mike Lewis

In the Desert   Jack Broom

Jason Gabbert

The day my gods died

The day my gods died I was afraid
they would take me with them.
I turned from prophets to poets,
and my church became
a coffee shop named after a saint.
I went from right to wrong,
and all the wrongs became
questions, not sentences.
There's a ball of ants at my feet,
pulling some leftovers toward a hole
too small to permit it entrance
but they'll keep at it until dusk.
And I'll keep pushing these things
until the lights go out or a bird shows up.

Jim Hanlen

Ice Fishing

The city is starved for light.
I write a short line
Dropped through snow.

I'm eager to pull out
What holds all deep, dark
And cold, all that's beneath.

The silvery sky hangs
A frost-rimmed moon
And stars like frozen trout.

I stand and shiver
Unsure and holding to doubt
Waiting a winter poem.

Alaska's Rare White Raven Faces Off in Spenard   *Cynthia Steele*

Scott Hanson

Mahogany Chairs

I rose with bright sunshine breaking through
the sides of the drapes
dust reflected in the air already warm with summer.

I traveled through the open frame
            down the hall
past the bathroom where I took warm baths
then hot showers
and all of the things that teenage boys do
            behind locked doors.

Smoothly I moved down wooden stairs
            past dining room table
mahogany chairs

to countertops clean
and kitchen empty
but pregnant with the
smell of toast and butter,
and sound of boiling water.
Wooden table for four
            but only two of the chairs well worn
for homework at night,
a safe place to fill my hungry mind
and hungry belly.

Filtered   *Cheryl Stadig*

No layer of fear
or change in atmosphere
to front yard or back
inside or out
day or night,
lawn darts slicing all around
legs itchy from lying in the grass
catching shooting stars.

Basement piano up against the wall,
drum set in the back room
Zeppelin blasting through headphones,
couch and T.V.
just playing and lounging and dozing off
for days and days and forever days
of laziness, plus

cool rounded concrete on washroom floor
and only those things
and nothing more.

And never once did my mother appear
in this dream,
this dream I had about my mother.
I opened my eyes with a lightness of being
only remembered:
a time traveler back half a century
to a Saturday with no plans.

Thomas Hedt

The Question

Split these lines
      braid this land
           this cacophony of images

altostratus clouds

        an endless lake-dotted floodplain

    metal buildings
        dirt and gravel on snowbanks
        plowed over enveloped cars.

    Plastic bags blow
in the white cold wind, distracting
the mind from the jarring violence
        of tires slamming through potholes.

It is early spring, fractal
    hibernation slowly
    begins to break.

***

There were times
when people would move
      as land or river shifted.

      Then infrastructure hardened.

At migration's end

    we may find metastatic
      indifference
        imposed
          structure

    engineered solutions
    to compulsory
      problems.

    Houses, structures, pipelines
      designed and hardened to survive
      in a land of permafrost.

***

In Bethel, on an April afternoon,
families hang their salmon
      on lines between thin sticks,
      to dry outside their homes.

Children play around sewer pipes
      elevated above ground, laid out
      like Habitrails through town.

Inside a meeting hall,
     there is a circle of tables,
     a man speaks in Yup'ik,
     the interpreter relays his statement, and his question,
     through headphones to all those gathered:

          "the fish, when we catch the fish
          they have growths
          on them
          in their flesh
          that they never
          had before
          can anyone tell me
          what is happening
          to our fish?"

Donnie's Buoys   *Janet Klein*

Amanda Hiland

Tidal

At night
the entire planet moves by water,
and you wake up
buffered by its currents.
Being washed ashore is gentle,
wave by wave returning you from your depths
to a surface land can fathom.

The house where you were born
is smothered by the sea.
Jellyfish pulse
around the empty cradle where you slept,
glowing like dreams.

The sea has chasms that run deeper
than your mother's smile, and peaks
that cut sharper than her tongue.
It has devoured mountains
long before memory
was a flickering lamp inside our skulls.

The thoughts of the sea
swim in the shape
of algal blooms, of whalesong,
coral blazes and shoals of herring.
Its spine sways with the life
streaming through its water column.

The sea opens its mouth
to drink the river of your body.
Its rising swells swallow
your footprints,
transforming *I am here*
into *I am here, dissolving.*

Fish Caligraphy   *Jim Thiele*

Madronna Holden

Turtle House

Her shell is tough, it is true:
It is patterned on stone.

Her teeth that have chewed bitter herbs
know all too well how to draw blood.

But this is what it takes
to protect the insides
of the one said
to carry the earth
on her back.

To be such a refuge
requires the calcium
of the heart.

Hold her up to your listening:
you will be safe from her teeth

So long you do not harm
her tender tongue.

And do not disturb her children.

She knows curses for that—
curses to protect embattled seas
with their storms—

curses that make her violators
swallow sand—

curses that may yet
save our world.

Lichen and Moss, Arctic National Wildlife Refuge

Nancy Deschu

Jan Jung

Lucinda Huffine

The Old Days

We were young and lived in a house we called the shack
behind the Motel 6 off Powell Boulevard.
We were poor but optimistic – I found a twenty dollar bill
on the ground, and we both got jobs that paid the rent.
One time we scrounged cans to get money to buy beer
at the Trolley Inn. An exquisite pale pink rose
grew lustily in our front yard.
One winter day we drove to Tolovana Beach with our dog, Daisy,
a thermos of tea, and some sandwiches. The wind gusted,
rain blew sideways at us as we walked. (I remember the fedora hat
you wore, holding it down so it wouldn't blow off.)
There was no one else on the beach, except a photographer
from the Oregonian, who asked to take our picture.
It got in the paper and I still have it.
I wonder if that hat still exists. The shack was bulldozed for condos
years ago, same with the pink rose, and all of our life in that house.
I've been back there, and nothing at all remains.

Marc Janssen

Elegy For A Holiday Retirement Operations Regional Manager

At one time
     All eyes were drawn to the occupancy report
At one time
     You juggled a stack of P&Ls
At one time
     You walked into a building to replace a manager, a co-manager
     Discuss the food, meet with the housekeep staff
     Exchange a word with a resident
At one time
     You closed out the budget for the year
     You walked out of the doors that smelled like fresh baked bread
     You sat in your car and looked at the building that housed so many people, told so many stories,
waved at the activity director and drove home and never went back again.

People who live with people
     Live better
     Live longer
People who live with people
     Eat better
          While complaining about the food
     There is life there
     Someone laughs
     Shares a picture of a grandchild
     A manager pours a cup of coffee

          No one looks at 10-year-old P&Ls
          No one cares about the occupancy report for a company that no longer exists.

          The vital tasks
          One to the next
          Handwritten marketing plans executed long ago
          30-60-90s

          The proper cogs
          Inside the proper wheels
          They turn and hum
          They cachunk, even break once in a while

          And the documentation
          It goes on or it stops
          It really doesn't matter at this distance
          All these years later
          The fingerprints, the plans, the budgets, and human resources carbons,
          The operational detritus
          Has all evaporated in time.

All the buildings south of Portland
- Hidden Lakes
- Madronna Hills
- Stoneybrook Lodge
- The Regent
- Shelden Oaks
- Solvang
- Garden Valley
- Rogue Valley
- Quail Valley
- Stone Lodge

Ten manager teams
Equal number of co-managers
Kitchen staff
Housekeeping
Maintenance
Activities
Hundreds and hundreds of apartments
Hundreds and hundreds of lives

Well run
On budget
Clean
Set expectations
Managed staff
Hired people, had to fire some,
Had to stay at more than one building over night to give the resident managers a break
Great food
Happy residents

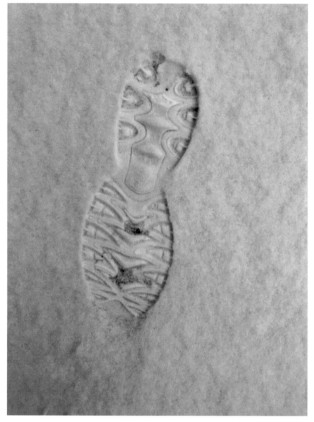

Track in Snow   *Richard Stokes*

We train each other
One to the next
On purpose
Or by mistake

We set the tone
Day to day
Moment to moment
As a regional
As a person

All that ended long ago before the company was sold into oblivion
Every metric captured
          In myriad reports
An accountant in a cube kept
A historical record of achievements
Sung across green-bar in a banker's box or in a storage unit next to a dead person's memos.
But even that accountant has been thoughtlessly fired or retired.

Really all that is left is memories
Not of residents
They are gone as well
Instead it's the memories of all the grandchildren
Who had more time with their grandmothers
Because of the work of just another regional operations manager
Who did his job.

Bark and Sky   *Lucy Tyrrell*

Eric Gordon Johnson

Afterlife

after Bruce Snider

I wake to untrimmed branches reaching out
to close the driveway. Her trimmer still

hangs on her scooter basket, sharp.
I choose books from those she chose

for the Little Free Library she asked me to
build on the snow. Later I sank a permanent post

after spring breakup thawed frost.
The willow grows green up to the red

door she painted. I take her clipper
to clear the twigs around the box.

They still come to swap books.

Susan Johnson

Let Me Remember

our walk today, hatchery road,
river-braid thaw, sky-mirror water,

wispy-tuft cattail, dusky-brown grass,
bare-branched cottonwood rooted in river.

Let me remember fallen fir tree—
a deadly spear thrust from steep bank,

and the truck who swerved to miss it.
Let me remember blue heron in dried reeds

on river's edge, the curve of her neck, her feathered
crown, her patience. How long would we have stood

there, still as she, silent as she, certain as she? How
long till she plunged her beak to feed? And yet—

you walked away, and she lifted her great wings,
rose up the channel, through the trees, out of sight.

Down the road we found fresh beaver
work across the water, a yellow gnaw

of cottonwood, surprise of light
among winter brown, a small dam,

a pond behind, a safe and hidden home,
and we, like two unsteady magnets,

faltered on our way. I had washed
the sheets this morning—and

home now, you turn to me,
the two of us thankful.

Watershield   *Lucy Tyrrell*

Keith Kennedy

Any Taste Was the Greatest

In anticipation, I had only time
To consider – briefly – that we would not
Be
Physically compatible

The sourness at the cusp of sex was
Therefore unexpected

It encouraged me to remember eager, younger times

When any taste – so long as it was flavored warm –
Was the greatest

When wetness was all delight
And newness
An extant possibility

When there was no danger of reprisal
No confusion
Because our youthful bodies sang in time
Like a tuning fork
A resonant sound dipped in hot flesh

Margaret Koger

May One

magnolia buds drip dew   finches startle
male merganser tuxedos   fade to brown
bald eagle's white   pierces grey skies

I can breathe

Make A Stand   *Sheary Clough Suiter*

John Kooistra

"Don't Be a Stranger"

for J. Davies

Night loiters outside windows
with its collar up

as the sky fills with clouds
and the dark memory of trees

crushed into strand-board
and dealt like playing cards

into subdivisions
with panoramic names.

But on Alpenglow Vista
and Blueberry Way

there's no alpenglow
or blueberries

or space between houses
where people wake

each Monday
to the taser of their alarms

and stare into mirrors
over double sinks

wondering if this
is the stranger

they told departing guests
last night not to be.

Window Trilogy   *Cheryl Stadig*

Eric le Fatte

Enchanted Valley Return

I see birches, broken and shaken,
mosses that cling to their limbs,
leaves accrued in drifts
like unsecured debts.
How far is this
from the fat days of summer?

The parsimonious sun
sifts through clouds
like a furloughed worker scanning
the want ads. I watch it reach
for the softest of landings
at the banks of the Quinault.

I take stock of the losses,
the forfeitures of fall,
as I traipse upstream.
At the turn of the river
the valley will open, and offer
white mantled mountains
that sparkle like prosperity.

Angry Sky   *Jim Thiele*

Linda Lucky

Follow

While taking a shower
I sense that I am not alone
I look down the water-streaked shower door
through the moving droplets and steam
to see a dark shape
sitting on the white rug
close to the shower door.
It is my old dog Teddy,
planted where he needs to be
close to where he knows
I can't go far.

Abigail Licad

Watteau's *Pierrot*

Even when alone
an audience is always there
although it actually never
sees you. Still you hear them
mutter *Fool, Buffoon*
as they retell the story again
and again about how she spurned you
who had blindly hoped, clinging still
to the trail of her echoing laughter.
Yet what else could you do but bear it,
keep standing there as all you wore
grew tighter with your heaving,
except for your red-ribboned shoes.
The light brightest at your belly,
you have become as the moon,
ever secondary, your glow merely
gleaned by your coarse and hollow
parts, dependent on what is
beyond. But take heart,
Pierrot, I am also you –
I, too, feel alone in the ever-present
crowd, my expression keeping still,
losses escaping to my mind
where my love follows.

Yvonne Higgins Leach

Funeral Reception

The eulogy still fresh on the tongue,
flowers abandoned at the burial site,

the black car doors slam shut.
Guests shed their coats and express

sympathy—the air between us
hard and unforgiving of mortality.

Platters of cold cuts,
homemade salads, store-bought buns

and boxed desserts—but I do not
want sustenance.

Women bring more food: a bowl of olives,
cheese and crackers, Jell-O with whipped cream topping.

Someone places her hand on my shoulder,
says: *Be sure to get yourself*

a plate, dear. I turn away,
look out the window, and cross

my arms against the world.
But it does not care.

Instead, it demands my attention
toward the blooming lilacs

and staggering bees,
to the playful voices of children

as they maneuver the swing set
under the backdrop of clouds and sunbreaks.

All this. Yet none of it will help me
find a way to live again.

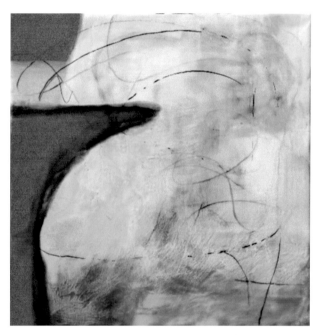

Precipice   *Sheary Clough Suiter*

Jan MacRae

Over the Dunes

We dropped acid in the winter
while living on the Oregon coast.
We walked along the beach
insisting that we didn't feel high,
finding sand dollar after sand
dollar and joked about being rich,
since finding a whole shell unbroken,
not just one, but at least five, was
abnormal. It is because we are not
normal right now, you said, and we
both realized we were high
and had walked miles, our way back uncertain,
as we had parked on the side of
the highway and clambored over the dunes.
With sudden urgency, we turned around and
right then, it started snowing. It is snowing, right?
I asked. Yes, you said, but are we having
a single hallucination between the both of us?
That made us laugh and fall for a minute into the sand.
Snowflakes on my coat: six points, not just five.

We started bushwhacking through the brush up
nearer to the road and lost sight of each other,
but leapt out of the stickery bushes and goldenrod
to find the path we had made. Our Converse
soles, you said, pointing. Then added, our verse
souls.   Profound, I said, and meant it.
Back at the A-Frame, I started a bath, climbed in,
and you sat companionably on the bathroom rug,
while I warmed myself in the tub. Yes, you drove
on acid, probably too slowly. We lit candles and
listened to the band Daddy Cool on the stereo;
we were rediscovering them.

We laid out the five sand dollars. You said, I wish there were six
Why, I asked. Three apiece, you replied, so we can each
have the same to spend. We can just spend time, I said.
We were sitting in front of the twelve-foot windows
that looked out on Woahink Lake. Snow was rimming
the deck railing and the very tall pines
had a soft coat of white. Beyond, the lake's gentle
gray ripples and the sky, low and heavy with fog and cloud.

I never spent them. I had all five for many years. Also verses we tried
to write together that night. The words were like a puzzle
of images: sky, snow, sand dollars, candles, clouds.
Our high-tops tossed off and leaned into each other. The Tartan plaid
of a blanket over our knees. Our very selves right there on paper.

Late at night, you spoke: The sand dollar is a mandala. See the spokes, the
wheel? The snowflake, our consciousness spinning from the sky.
Doesn't the ocean always represent infinity? I asked.
The beach with the waves, the snow, the larger
mandala within which we exist. And in that moment,
we felt no boundary, we were the snow, the beach,
the sand dollar and they were us and we were each other.
This is why we took acid, kids.

Spotted Medick   *Matt Witt*

David McElroy

Paris Blues

Dame Nature is whipping her trees
after a week of buttery sun on leaves.
Hot, cold, now wicked chinook—
this could be late fall or North Dakota.
You'd think the planet was bipolar.

August drags on like the Paris Peace Talks
long forgotten. No matter which way
you look, the mountains put you in your place.
Seagulls making a fuss over a bait ball in the bay
are elegant, white and gray, each one an extrovert.

In our quiet way, the outside world resolves
beyond our casements and an old film
in black and white. Paul Newman plays, but not really,
the trombone. It's Murry McEachern who really
plays it with a mood indigo to break your heart.

His lips must be tightly stressed to range
such a high, slow register of thoughtful sorrow.
Clarinet and sax console lower down
where Ellington arranged for empathy.
There's just a hint of swing to release a little joy

before the racism our lovers, our stars, Sidney
Poitier and Diahann Caroll, will face stateside
beyond the credits. Outside, willowas claw water
and lower down salmon bring their weaving.
A neighbor's chainsaw sings the only song it knows

becoming with Gunnar, wind and trombone
a part of things. He is bucking firewood.
Spruce burns fast, birch slow. He's pushing the bar
into the kerf, blowing sawdust and fragrant tang
of pitch and bark, some of the star stuff we share.

After Picasso   *Sandra Kleven*

Karla Linn Merrifield

The Swallowing

On the day of the Everglades dew,
which is every day,
I awake to realize I've been
swallowed alive.
The Universe, having chased down
half-moon shadows,
consumes me whole
like a python swallows his prey:
entire.
This is the same Universe,
the Everywhere, which my husband
reminds me – this day
of dew swallowed by crows –

is expanding. We swallow hard.
Then a minion of alligators,
a court of vultures in their black
robes, featherless gray wigs,
cloud swallow,
sun bitterns,
and gallinules of the dew,
swallow the sky.
And the Universe as it is
in the Everglades bedewed
swallows me with the morning stars.
I am the turtle taken by surprise,
plastron, carapace, soul and all.

In memoriam Roger M. Weir

Spider's Den   *Janet Klein*

Judith Mikesch-McKenzie

When We Were Truck Stop Women

The men run thick fingers down the lists on the menu, and
   laugh deep in throats made harsh from bitter coffee
   drunk late at night. The waitress shifts on her feet
   as she waits, favoring her right hip.

> *She is not you, this waitress - too old, and not tall enough. I see*
> *you in my room, tall and full, wearing my cousin's hand me*
> *downs, trying so hard to get me interested in makeup.*
>
> *I like to think you disappeared that summer with no choice, no*
> *time to tell me. I looked for you for a while - asking*
> *around town, in all of our regular places, and even*
> *at the market - only one person had anything to tell me.*
>
> *That house your parents rented was a bare wooden cave with*
> *dusty curtains. It got demolished just weeks later*
> *after a tree fell on it.*

She calls these men 'hon' and tells them she'll be right back,
   then turns to me at my table. I order quickly and she sees
   the look I turn on the men. She grins and tells me -
   they're ok, hon - they're good tippers.

> *in the freezer aisle standing near me, a woman*
> *like dust, gritty and gaping, whose voice is*
> *a storm wind split asunder,*
> *says*
> *"I know that girl, she went to work at that*
> *truck stop - she's one of those truck stop women*
> *now."*
> *and for a moment she stops, all pieces of her*
> *fighting to gather, and then the thunder*
> *strikes*
> *"Men should not tip women like that. Women*
> *like that aren't…."*
> *and she is asunder again, dust settling without*
> *purpose*

A tap on the window, a whisper, my feet landing hard as we
   run through quiet streets to the highway, where gravel
   on the shoulder rolls under us all the way to the long
   yellow building, lit up against the night, the smell
   of motor oil, coffee, and smokes drawing us like a spell.

Here the tables are in neat rows, a low wall erected between
them and the perpendicular rows of shelves offering road
food, car toys, postcards, and local artists' curios

we brush past the "seat yourself" sign and slide into a booth,
   calling out an order for coffee. One of the large men
   bent over cups at the counter mutters that the coffee
   here will put hair where we might not want it, and they
   all hunch down deeper, low rolling almost-laughter
   that fades quickly.

I curl my palms around the steaming cup she brought me
and watch the men. As the din of travelers' shopping gets
louder, they pull down the trucker caps they wear and
fold into each other around their table

Gail, our waitress, sets down our two cups with no comment.
   Sometimes she sits with us when it's slow, and we three
   spin tales into the dark, weaving into those stories the
   secrets we hope and fear the others will notice

and we are truck stop women, Gail warning us to be
   safe as we walk home while still in the dark,
   arms wrapped around each other,
         heading for sunrise.

The Power   *Sheary Clough Suiter*

John Morgan

Cremations at Varanasi

Beside the Ganges, crowds at night
as flames engulf a dozen caskets, ashes
that were people yesterday. And behind us

costumed gods and goddesses
dance, wave swords, gulp fire, a fête
for incarnations past and yet to come.

Flames that destroy the body free the soul.
Don't cry, since tears can hold the spirit near
like an unleashed dog drawn close by loyalty.

In a poor country these were not the poorest.
Stand still. I'll take your picture. Does that
make everything more real? Or less?

Last night I dreamt I was pacing a ledge
with a favorite aunt, who skipped off
and disappeared without a trace. This is the edge

we are walking, wondering are we truly
headed toward the nothing that is heaven?
Please keep one hand on your passport.

Odd Pallet   *Jim Thiele*

Linda B. Myers

Last Gift

Dead people
visit hospice rooms as lives end.
Ghostly mothers mostly
sweet sneak in
to console their grown-old young,
a moment of solace
as a brain comforts itself.
For my husband
it was dogs
tumbling, leaping, galloping
into his room that final day.
Mutts and purebreds
spaniels and doxies
paid for and rescued,
all the good girls and boys
we raised in our days together,
the mister and me.

Screaming Yellow Zonker
Northern Cider, Jack the Ripper
Lizzie Borden, Maggie J, Wheeler
Max, and poor little Charlie
yipping, yapping, growling, howling,
each according to their nature.
Their man too sick to throw sticks,
each dog too long gone to fetch
but they came as a pack
to escort him on his way.
Those wagging tongues and tails
gifted him with joy,
and he to me in his last telling
before the fade.

Eklutna Lake   *@tjinalaska Toya Brown*

Barbara Parchim

waking

there is light -
I can see it through the slits of my eyelids

quickly shutting them again
amorphous shapes writhe on the backs of my lids

pulsing and amniotic, I cling to this watery world
before consciousness fully takes hold

almost weightless - until I move,
and my body remembers gravity

they call it the crack of dawn, don't they?
silent, but relentless and insistent, nonetheless

time to rouse finally -
drinking coffee in bare feet on the front porch

I watch shadowy deer that have been up all night,
still browsing the last apple drops in the grass

we intersect here, in this moment
breathing the same air, watching the light change

dawn holds us in this tableau of stillness
before we remember we are different

Timothy Pilgrim

West of Dillon, South of Butte

Montana mist drifts off willows,
caresses day. A hung-over sun
blinks backlit clouds lighter shades

of blue-black gray. Moose thrash tall grass,
chipmunks hide, blue jays screech.
Doe, hollow ears up, stops mid-stride,

her new fawn a speckled clump
in heavy brush. Polaris sleeps.
I cease tented dreams, rise,

build fire, boil coffee, drink in
all this. Plenty of time for rod,
reel, bright flies, hungry fish.

Cloud Creek Falls   *Nard Claar*

Anne Pitkin

The Runners

skim past my house trailing the morning sun,
less bodies than a single streak carving the street.
How quickly they are gone.
How quickly the sun falls behind.
Listen. Young crows are complaining
in some tree nearby. I am complaining
under the dogwood about my life. The sun falls
on trees and runners and crows alike.
The sun falls down the sky to the other side
of the world. Falls on the lions sleeping
in the redgrass, on the termite mounds,
on the wood hoopoes chortling in the early morning.
How quickly it leaves them.
And you whom I loved and outlived
how I wish the sun had not lost interest in you
even as it chases the runners
disappearing into their own lives.

Allium   *Joe Reno*

Mandy Ramsey

Kluane

May the quaking Aspen forest wake you
from your daily slumber and sing you alive again
as you walk amongst the tribe of powdery white smooth trunks covered with eyes.

May the beauty of the wildflowers sprinkled among the forest floor bring
cheerfulness back to your cheeks and heart as
the purple lupin, yellow arnica and pale paintbrush,
wild sage and spicy rose sing your steps on.

May the blue alpine lakes and swollen glacial rivers and creeks
wash away your worries and replace your wrinkles with soft tributaries of joy.

Wild Flowering   *Shauna Potocky*

Entrance   *Janet Klein*

Richard Roberts

After Autumn

We sleep warmly in this house
we have built against storm winds
with firewood stacked and covered,
woolen clothes rediscovered,
boots at the doorway,
heavy gloves paired on a closet shelf.

Stirred by sounds of air or shifting silence,
we go to the window and watch
the first snow deepen,
our world turn from us and enter
a bear cave of exile.

Steven Schneider

Tres Orejas

Crescent moon, evening star
Hang above Tres Orejas:
Together again.

How many evenings
You have painted the gloaming sky:
Orange, blue, purple.

This Silhouette --
Many ears listening intently
Where coyotes howl.

Tres Orejas   *Reefka Schneider*

Kerstin Schulz

The Point

Bishop's Meadow, Maxville, Oregon

Sitting on the dirt dam painting yellow water lilies,
a rarity in this corner of the high desert world,
I can hear the creek circumvent my shallow dike.
If I look up I can see the deer trail slant down slope
to the stony ridge of the animal ford.

Three interns who crossed the creek downstream
over water corralled by a culvert
and who hiked a logging road through stands of juniper and pine,
bushwhack their way through prairie smoke and balsam root
to a point behind and below my seat.

They slide to the brink of the steep sided, deep drumming creek.
They don't know how to cross.
I'm tempted to tell them about the ford and the trail,
but I don't want to break the peace with a shout.

Also, they are students and I am their elder.
My job today is to stand out of their way,
let them learn the land so that they will remember.

Eventually they get there.
They even take off their shoes.

They like my painting in its bowl of bunch grass and rushes.
They don't see the missing fence, the gate
or the cattle guard, my focal point.
They see this high country grassland
as it once was and how it might be again
which is, perhaps after all, the point.

Sunset for Matilda   *Mandy Ramsey*

Sher Schwartz

First Night, Hot Night

First night, hot night cabin windows open
mortise and tenon––he joined
his piece to her piece––cabin's creation
then abandoned his work for her work
to inhabit wooden spaces––his gift––for her
to experience nature through her body––her roof
her timbers––her beams––her solid floor––her knots
her visions

first night, hot night cabin windows open

Sounds hit the metal roof
worker-voices faraway fading
harvest ended. Peewee's buzz––dog's bell
tinkles. Motorcycle roars up the county road––
crows caw embodied to their roost line––
quiver voices––Northern flicker––away
no place to go—just up and down the county road
light shines––up ahead racoons…

first night, hot night cabin windows open

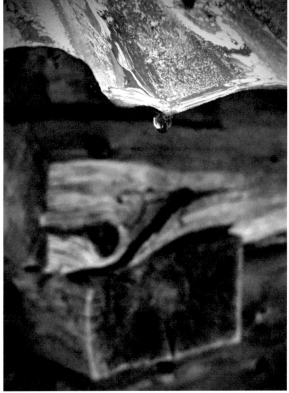

Timeless   *Shauna Potocky*

What is nature? Last whistle of the dove's wing.
Night Hawk swoop-swish folds and dives. Will she see stars
or jet lights tonight? Her cot a heat cloud––bag discarded
mosquitos seek––incense burns low––she slips––no place
to go. She sighs––smiles––Is this what she hears––
a dog's faraway yelp––shadows lengthen
screen door slams he's closing across the prairie––jumps the creek
through yellow meadow to her in his hands––old wood––his beams
his joinery.

Their coming together song…

first night, hot night cabin windows open—

Westchester Lagoon, Mountain Views   *Nancy Deschu*

Tom Sexton
Two Poems

Greed

Coffee in hand, I'm at the kitchen table
waiting for December's silvered light
to appear above the still dark mountains.
I'll roll it up like a priceless oriental scroll,
hide it in a cedar box. Claim I slept in if
someone asks if I know where it might be.

While I was poem-dreaming, it flared
the skin of a tall building downtown
built by the Hunt brothers, Texas oilmen
who almost cornered the silver market.
When I write, I keep a gold pocket watch
that I scored in a pawnshop on my desk.
I like the tick tock of its metallic heart.

Swans, July 2023

On a lagoon close to my house, a pair of trumpeter swans,
summer residents for three years now;

close by, two grey cygnets, showing a little white
feed in a patch of weeds. They must be last year's chicks.

How normal it all seems. Not a hint of what might come.
If the watchers speak, they speak of swans.

I have no idea how to end this poem.

Jake Sheff

The Hour Pulls a Muscle on a Fine Day at Cook Park

TUTTI
È bella la guerra! Evviva la guerra!
—Giuseppe Verdi, *La forza del destino*

You may like to know how open-handed medicine
Appeared on this December morning. Wind
And other weather patterns can adversely affect

A poem's taste. Have a place indoors where you
Can let this poem choo choo around the room…
It doesn't have to be a house. My twenties taught me

That my heart's garage was choosy, but it never
Did choose wisely. So I let it burn until it was
Perfectly deformed. If you decide to do this using

Matches, ignite a match and give it a moment for
The εὐεργετέω to burn off. You may like to
Understand why to the hawk on a branch hanging

Over the Tualatin River light from the rising sun
Looked like Byzantine Greek fire, while to me
It looked like a mental cha cha and to the moon,

Who was actively engaged at the time in bothsidesism,
It looked like fondue's marmoreal spirit. Wouldn't
We all take a pipe cleaner to our inner librettist

If we could? Like a policy backed by a tremendous
Amount of zeal while accomplishing zilch, a gust
Of wind railroaded the verbs in a sentence forming high,

High above the earth as I, too, was considering whether
A quest for mastery should master the person on said
Quest. Bare-breasted Liberty was laughing underneath

Ki-a-Kuts Bridge. A graffiti-artist had tagged it
With the kind of proverb that anyone with any degree
Of humanity believes should wear an eyepatch:

"The only good French monument is a well-lit one!"
A beautiful woman jogged by while her ideal
Self was museum-going. My protagonist was saying

"I'd rather die by enemy fire than live and feel
My country's ire" when the sky turned the blue of
A sugar bug vein. A bulldog with spina bifida barked,

Which, in ten seconds flat, resulted in the briefest dwy;
I don't think anyone here should like to know why.
The dwy put paid to D-minor's vision of transparent

And recession-proof perfection. The year was almost over,
But I heard it say, "I've just begun." Underneath a covered
Picnic area, worthless wisdom said to unexpectedness,

"We and ours challenge you and yours," so three-abreast,
Me, myself and I high-tailed it in the direction of the police
Department. While I was running, my protagonist shot

Eric the Cleric in the left side of his chest. A young boy
Passed me on a hoverboard as a Native American
Death song was recreated by the ghosts of butterflies

In the Tupling Butterfly Garden. You might not wish
To know what I saw next, but we do not decide
What the retina retains… Let's just pepper spray that

Memory and move on. The oleoresinous honking of geese
Was overhead when a thought occurred to me as a thought
Had occurred to me the first time I wrote a play: by

Divine inspiration – for so it must be supposed – and Eric
The Cleric lived, despite his wound, because he's living
With dextrocardia! A pocket gopher, like all gophers, booed.

Monarch   *Jim Thiele*

Eva-Maria Sher

Zwischen Zwei Stühlen Sitzen

(sitting between two chairs)

This situation
is by no means
the one Buridan's
ass experienced
when it expired between
two haystacks,
unable to decide
from which one
to munch. No, this
painful *sitting
between two chairs*
is the situation
my mother
pointed out,
were I to cast my lot
with the New World,
leaving the Old behind.

Today I find myself
sitting indeed, with
an unexpected problem
of all places, in my Zoom
poetry class:

The moon,
says the poet
Marge Piercy,
is always female,
and I agree—but only
in principle; the difficulty
is linguistic: In the country
of my birth, the moon
is *always male!*

Der gute Mond
comforts the ill
and the grieving,
cools with gentle rays
the heated word-
and-sword-play
on the playgrounds
of the world, and
sends shimmering paths
across calm waters.

Don Quixote in El Salto   *Reefka Schneider*

(On the other hand
he impartially aids
those who set out
to make mischief
when he temporarily
absents himself
from the sky.)

His silver horns
drip curative dreams
into the minds
of troubled sleepers
and when he is full
his luminous roundness
swells the vast bowl
of the night.

Consider
how faithfully
the moon's
celestial body
orbits the sun
for the benefit
of every being
on our small
planet, right down
to the tiniest ant
and the most modest
of mosses.

The good moon
pulls the tidal currents
through the oceans
and regulates
the hidden tides
ebbing and
flowing inside
women's bodies.
Scientists have mapped
the moon's face—
its waxing and waning.
Brave astronauts
have placed
their weighted feet
on its pockmarked
surface, and have returned
with rock specimens
in the pockets
of their space suits.

Did you ever wonder
whose wisdom
planted the good moon
into orbit?
Was it not done
to delight and help
us human beings
who so often
wander, lost
with nothing but
a few breadcrumbs
in our pockets?

I apologize—I lost track
of where I was going:
The point of this
torrential outpour is:
HOW on earth
did this mysterious
and benevolent friend,
how did this gentle
heavenly body
equipped with such
a plethora of feminine
virtues, how did this
praiseworthy celestial
sister end up with a masculine
article in the mother tongue
of my fatherland?

*Having researched the subject at length, the only reasonable
answer I've been able to come up with is that in Germany, "Luna"
has been, still is, and probably always will be the number-one
favorite name for female dogs.*

Below Mount Bede, Nanwalek, Alaska   *Mandy Wood*

Corinne Smith

Leaving July

Gray and green, record rain,
yet chicks still leave
the nest. Magpie, black-and-
white, flies with a wobble
across the street, following its parents
tree to tree. Green-black
and white swallows swoop
out from the nest box
on the house. A raven chick
screams from a neighbor's tree
all afternoon, like a woman knifed
in the dark. My friend lived
his best day – work plus play –
then dropped from the sky
of this life, a switch
flipped from always on
to forever off.

A month late, a robin builds
a nest on a porch beam. I see
her from the couch, where I sit
with my little dog who won't eat.
Every time I step outside
the robin flees to a tree,
calls at me to leave.

Singer   *Jim Thiele*

Craig Smith

Goodwill T-shirt

OK, used T-shirt at Goodwill
Tell me your story
How did you wind up
On this rack for $3.99?

I am buying you as a gym shirt
And you are going to get sweaty
I don't need to look stylish
Just presentable – and that's a low bar

And that's why I'm here
Instead of at Nordstrom's
I am a cheapskate
Always looking for a bargain

So, how did you get here?
Did he outgrow you?
Get tired of you?
Or did he die and you went in the "donate" pile?

Maybe his wife hated your color
"Get that stupid shirt out of here!"
And off you went to Goodwill with other rejects
Such as unread books and bad furniture

Well, your new life has started with me
You'll be part of a T-shirt gym rotation
And here's a special treat
You might get to do yardwork, too.

Not Quite Spring   *Mandy Ramsey*

Allie Spikes

You Can Take Your Bunny Rabbit Sleeping Mask & Go Back to Your Husband Now -or- K, Bye

Bewitch me, hellcat—nude, high-
　　　ponied eyes. Behind your blockade, draw a crowd and ask
me, roséd in flannel & shades, *am I a ten?*
　　　Boomerang me, blonde. Crazed, you

glittered angel: lead-painted, wings clipped.
　　　Borderline broken in that hotel room, you
cracked me, cajoling—*my nails are too wet*—you begged me, bae!
　　　to pull that black leather skirt up over your ass with my quaking

freckled fingers that change diapers, iron and fold my husband's
　　　expectations. Catch a glimpse, kitten: me trying not to
look at you like a creep. Pour me—
　　　against Mormon sensibility—champagne,

& lick my chantilly flame
　　　birthday fingers in cream. Pluck pink berries
from my fluttering tines—I'll avert my eyes.
　　　Selfie your kibitz, your kissy-face cruelty—

insta that shit. Snap it down south
　　　to your husband in Texas
while I sweat, fly-hatched
　　　& yellow, dreaming of you in jeans.

Playtime in the Garden of Good and Evil　　　　　　　　　　　*Tami Phelps*

Cynthia Steele

Kona's Landscape

A Great Dane limits one's breath
But this is the trust we place
That they won't crush us with love
They just push our boundaries
Lean on us in abandon
To meet our own pooling gaze

I live but so long they say
Won't you care for me always?
Most of us do, but there are
those for whom the life of dogs
is not such a sacred thing
But we—you and I—take care

Now til the day when they pass
their breaths draw in and wane out
their happy-tailed moments go
Wagging along as they do
Those luminous eyes look up
The spark in their eyes just there

that's irreplaceable right?
Circulation—what is that?
Mine's never been all that great
So what does it matter if this dog
circumvents a little flow
It's not changing my life much

Her left, white paw curls inward
the other sprawls my shoulder
Oh, you should've seen her run
up and down that trail along
the water splashing me hard
Her eyes boring in on me

She loves to pounce, make me shriek

It's November now, ice cracks
The trail's slick but not to her
She has no gravity no
ground constraints, sure footed girl
delighted that we are out
blue sky, sunset, pink mist light

She play fights a massive hound
Down, then springs, massive missile
The dog does not begrudge her
tête-à-tête over the lip
of the ledge Heathcliff, Catherine
they'll be, dramatically

mouthing each other, standing
Their battle a vicious sort
of presence, later laying
Snoring as they do, twitching
and yip yip yipping at some kind
of dreamed up apparition

Beluga Point Bore Tide Viewing   *Cynthia Steele*

Richard Stokes

Juneau's 2023 Jökulhlaup

Call me Ishmael if you must name me,
but know me simply as a water molecule,
very small, and when alone, of little note.

But this summer I joined
billions of billions of others like me
in a basin between two glaciers.
Some came from rain or snow,
I from the upper glacier during the spring thaw.

During the summer some of my colleagues sneaked
through cracks and crevices in the lower glacier
into the lake below and eased out the river into the sea,
but the icy dam stymied most of us.

But with rain and melt we got more crowded
and the basin too confining.
Some of us tried to climb over the blocking ice,
other tried to find ways around and under.

Eventually we found a weakness in the ice dam.
We poured out in a frenzy, quickly filled the lake
past overflowing, then rampaged down the river.
Together we sluiced away the river banks,
ripped trees out by their roots, undermined
some houses and pulled others into our midst
as the mob of us muscled our way to the sea.

I may stay in the vast and peaceful sea forever.
Or I may return in the rain to the mountains,
join others in the ice and do this all over again.

Castner Creek

@tjinalaska Toya Brown

Scott Stolnack

Plants of the Pacific Northwest Coast

I once heard someone describe
the climate here in Seattle
as Mediterranean
which is odd because I don't see
any olive trees and I doubt
that there are seven hundred species
of moss on Santorini
and I'm pretty sure
there were never salmon
the size of cocker spaniels
paddling the wine-dark sea.

It's interesting to consider
that with climate change
the sequoias
and redwoods down in California
are moving north –
a great migration of trees
the size of office buildings
headed for Seattle
calling to mind
the Oklahoma land rush
or the big
thunderous
rolling convoy
in *Mad Max*
only waaaaaay slower
of course
but still
super fast
if you think
in geologic time…
all those giant trees
racing up the Coast Highway
and Interstate 5
wanting to be the first
to score the waterfront views
on Magnolia
or Mercer Island
or Medina.

And the big trees here now
all packing their suitcases
full of lichens
and the last few spotted owls
and marbled murrelets
and lining up at the Canada border
in a nice
orderly
queue
applying for asylum
as climate refugees.

Perhaps Seattle
will become the next Athens
only with bigger trees
and we'll all be wearing fisherman's caps
and sipping retsina
and eating calamari
down along the waterfront.
We already have a Mount Olympus
so maybe the oracles have already seen it
at the Temple of Apollo
but
the message went to spam
instead of queued up in our inbox
waiting
patiently
to be read.

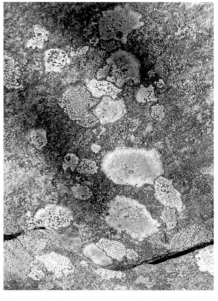

Lichen on Rock   Annekathrin Hansen

Elizabeth L Thompson

Don't *Ever* Fall in Love with a Poet. . .

She'll tack your eyelids to stars,
then tease you with slumber…
She'll exorcize blackness from midnight
and expect forgiveness…
She'll claim stability, as she
sells fiery conscience to Lucifer…
She'll fancy whoredom,
then allege nunnery….

She'll pin your heartstrings to a chord chart
and lead you to a feast of fantasy,
promising role-play, roast, and rum,
then fall with rhythmic ecstasy
into a bed of pillow-top, pillow-talk prosody,
prepositions, and pentameter,
contriving a punctuated word blizzard
amidst a sultry reckoning….

Don't ever fall in love with a poet!

Northern Lights Seen from Our Front Porch   *Annekathrin Hansen*

Georgia Tiffany

This Fish

This fish has no bones.
By night her lithe intimacies
reinvent water
shy and sigh against the glass
loosen, untie

slink and shake
disambiguate

    comin' alive

all lung and taper
recapitulate

oh
   oh
      comin' alive.

Diviner currents
all nacre and nerve
(this fish has no barnacles)
loop and lure
these dreams she's dreaming

breathe and purr
oscillate

   comin' alive.

These scales and scars
oh significant eye
reflect refract
these hooks and barbs
oh lateral line

  oh
    stayin' alive

emancipate
assimilate

no coda no fuss
no cajoling touch
oh imperative gills

to insist on bones
might ask too much

  coming
    staying
       alive.

Pay No Attention to the Groove Behind the Curtain   *Tami Phelps*

Lucy Tyrrell

Dusk Angels

Pointing the scarlet canoe upriver,
I paddle alongside floodplain silver maples.
Broken ash trees tilt and touch water;
arcs of branches dimple the surface.
Swamp smell hovers in the cooling air.

As delicate curling tongues of white
catch at brittle stems of beggar-ticks,
swirl in the backwaters,
gather on green pools of duckweed,
speckle the muddy shore,
I wonder whose feathers these are.
Then when I round a bend,
beyond the bittern and the sandpiper,
I see the answer, their white forms
unmistakable in the distance.

Disturbed by my presence,
the two swans slap their webbed feet
on the dim-light water—
their heavy shapes reluctant to rise—
before they sail down the river-tree canyon,
coming my way.
Six-foot wingspans
and trumpeting oh-OHs
burn the holy sky-path above me.

Along the Water   *Nard Claar*

When my father was hospitalized—
pneumonia in his lungs,
sepsis in his blood—
he said, *I've seen angels,*
but I'm not ready to die.

Now within a paddle's reach,
they beckon to a wild life,
clutch me to a quickening sense
of cycles and creatures and time.

Bead   *Nard Claar*

Miles Varana

Waukegan

North Chicago suburbs: scrap of light on the rehab kitchen, kielbasa, softball cults drinking by the lakeshore, echoes of 80s mall concerts, pretty femmes in hairnets coming home from work, rusty Chevy Novas kept off the cinderblocks by Polish boys in Jordan jerseys, balcony parties and arrests, tears for the Oscar Mayer Weinermobile spun-out on Edison. Run away from rehab with a fake mustache and a pair of blue Chuck Taylors and lend your heart to this place, and you could win second prize in a beauty contest, just like I did.

Alan Weltzien

Viva il Papa!

On the main street
of lower Bergamo
motorcycled police guard
cordoned off lanes
of blocked traffic
and we join
hundreds of Italians
who rush an open bed
truck bearing the body
of twice-embalmed
Pope John XXIII
en route to Bergamo's *Duomo*
in the Citta Alta
where he'll rest
a few days
then ride to his home village
18 km. away.

My eyes wave.

Dead fifty-five years
"the good Pope"
rides in style,
blesses this frantic surge
from his recumbent pose.
In a pope's afterlife
he's allowed to pay
a visit home.
Canonized years ago,
humble Giuseppi Roncalli
includes us all
in the sign of the cross
and, lifelong Protestant
who tries to sing
Tom Lehrer's
"Vatican Rag" on the piano,
I cross myself
as the crowd exhales.

Savannah   *@tjinalaska Toya Brown*

Tim Whitsel

Adoptee

The rescued Husky groans from his snooze below the table.

It is impossible to tabulate
the human wrongs in a combat zone.

You cannot fathom why
mass graves deepen or annotate who'll fill the absence.

When offenders depart the rubble,
their truncheons and bare electric leads

linger in empty rooms that will
never be empty.

To remain impressionable you must groan like a new dog
whose sleep is insecure.

The world is too beautiful to gnaw, too
smelly not to bury and rebury on the outskirts.

Strays witness everything from the fringe, hungry as owls.

Airing Out the Memories   *Cheryl Stadig*

Wanda Wilson

You Want

You so want to be in love again
that maddening crazy feeling
so strong it makes you scratch

The ache for one another when apart
that almost tears you into scattered pieces
like glass breaking inside
all the way to your toes

You want desperate hugs that squeeze
the breath to small sips
constricts the eyes

You want kisses soft as warm creme
on a summer morning
Hard as though the tongue has stabbing muscles
as you watch his jaw
break your latitudes into passion

If the world explodes you don't want to know
when he's offering himself in you
You won't care while he's lifting you to him

You want sweet roses, yellow spring violets
You want to dance & swing to
music so soft & so loud that it splits your thoughts
to nothings

You want to laugh and laugh and love
as though the kettle drums of symphonies carry you on
wings of desire & compassion

You want your life to stop flowing out between your legs
killing your kidneys, stopping your heart
You want your lovers not to be doctors

Kiss of the March Moon   *Sandra Kleven*

Kids on the Beach   *Joe Reno*

Robin Woolman

Sea You

—for Nic and Lil

Sister, that's it. You win all
the breath-holding contests
in oceans, pools and shared baths
over our lives of love and rivalry.
Competition has always been
a happy undertow of who we are:
drawing us together and better.
We dunked in turns, counting for the other
--one mississippi, two-- or measuring distance
or depth reached beneath the water.

Sister, since Wednesday, death
holds your breath for you, while I
must work to stop the persistent air,
even gulp it in the ebb between sobs.
First, blood filled your lungs, then cancer
filled your blood so fast…so fast.
You were always the fastest.

Sister, you have left me boxes
organized and labeled. You beat me there too.
My past is scattered like the plastics
in this beach sand: colorful, toxic.
I'm here on your Florida shore
looking for your footprints. I invite the sand flies
to dine on my ankles knowing their itch and pain
will keep me company in my grief.

Sister, watch me race into the sea,
as if at your heels, suck my lungs full
and plunge and count--one mississippi, two--
while the waves gently shove me,
like a good sister, back home.

Arctic Heat   Tami Phelps

FEATURES
Artists of *CIRQUE*

Cynthia Steele

Cold Wax and Poetry—Disturbing the Surface
An Interview with Tami Phelps & Kerry Dean Feldman

The painter, like the archaeologist, is a watcher, a supervisor of accident; patiently disturbing the surface of things until…A whole image, a whatness, may with luck gradually emerge almost spontaneously.

— Louis le Brocquy— Irish artist

Largely self-taught via an ongoing process of taking and teaching numerous workshops, Tami Phelps has become a serious artist. She rarely does prints. Her art takes time and has won multiple awards. Her website is a vivid, immersive experience. Yet, talking with her is easy.

I pull on my courses in Art Appreciation, Drawing, Art Exploration (printmaking, etc.), Painting, and Photography from UAA and U Dub. Tami piqued all these interests and brought back multiple memories. By the end of the interview, her positivity and work ethic made me wish I hadn't ditched a waist-high self-portrait oil painting in a dorm room closet because my nose wasn't just right.

She practices her craft in a loft art studio in the five-level townhouse she has shared with her husband and creative partner, Kerry Dean Feldman, for over two decades. Kerry, Professor Emeritus of Cultural Anthropology at the University of Alaska Anchorage as well as creative writer, and Tami Phelps, former Montessori schoolteacher and now a fulltime artist, mutually support one another's gifts.

Tami's art loft is "a hodgepodge of different sorts of possibilities," Tami said. She uses heavy rods and hangs a "living wall" of current projects. There, textile clothing made with homemade paper and denim-colored lint from the dryer rises from a page, and I reach out to touch it. She encourages me to do so. It reminds me of the clothing designs I've sketched half my life.

I spoke to Tami about a homemade paper project done in a Sheldon Jackson College Humanities course in Sitka in the 80s; much of the learning was physical. Until the unchecked pollution began harming local inhabitants' health in 1993, the Alaska Pulp Corporation (APC) pulp mill operated on the shores of Sawmill Cove. "We didn't know about the sludge and byproducts of the mills going into landfills and water."

"At 19, just the idea of easily making paper from pulp was phenomenal," I told her.

"Hold On"

Tami learned the process of making paper from Natalie Chomyk-Daniels, which included ripping up post-consumer, recycled paper, helping to eliminate the need for harvesting virgin materials, blending them, then sifting them through a screen (deckle). "Submerge the *screen*, and slowly raise it, letting the *pulp* settle on the *deckle*, thin and evenly. Then, I collected dryer lint and made the clothing. That was really fun."

"I used to be super involved with photography and served on the board of the Alaska Photographic Center from 2009 until 2017. Kerry, a fine photographer, taught me a lot."

Tami's art grew from straight b/w photography, to hand colored photography, to cold wax, where it exists now in many forms, but she still has a passion for hand-colored photography. Explaining the process, she said: "It has to be black and white. It's printed on textured paper; it has to have 'tooth,' so that when you paint, it has something to grip onto."

Tami's work runs the gamut of human emotions as well.

A memorial photographic piece Tami created has a graveyard scene and a mirror. Looking at it, she said, breaks her own heart. Her mother, Ardis, a stained-glass artist, passed away in her sixties, a life shortened by Alzheimer's.

"Mom was extremely creative and artistic in her own way and very resourceful. She had a huge influence on my work."

Tami showed me one of her art works entitled, "They Say I Look Like Her." "This is my mom's headstone. See the little mirror." Tami worked with me to catch her own reflection in the round mirror, which pleased her.

Her family didn't have a lot of money growing up. "I thought glue really was flour and water. Mom was a homemaker with five kids. A very early memory was going downstairs in this small, dank basement in South Dakota. While mom did laundry, my sister and I mixed up detergent to make a paste with our doll clothes and slap 'em up on the cement walls. There it was—an installment. It didn't come to mind when I was doing the work that became *The Woman Within*, [her and Kerry's book that utilizes cold wax, antique baby clothing, and his poetry] "but there's got to be a connection there."

Tami's own artwork began in earnest in the 90s when she and Kerry had purchased art that was then lost in transit (stolen) on a trip from Italy. "Oh, it wasn't really expensive stuff, but work I really liked. Only one piece made it back. I had that piece framed. I decided I could frame art. Then I decided I could do photographs, hand color them, and it kind of built from there."

She took a class at Blaine's Art with Janet Hickok, well-known Anchorage artist and restaurateur. Hickok and her husband, John Parker, both professional chefs, owned and operated Doriola's in Anchorage for many years, where they decorated the restaurant in encaustics—hot and cold wax in vibrant colors, which Hickok had either created or had invited others to show.

Other opportunities ensued. She took a class with peer and friend, Sheary Clough Suiter, Springfield, Oregon contemporary visual artist specializing in mixed media encaustic paintings and sculptures. The class was taught by Eve-Marie Bergen at the Girdwood Center for the Arts in 2003. Suiter, 35-year former Alaskan encaustic artis, is now living and painting in the Pacific Northwest with her artist partner, Nard Claar; both were featured in *Cirque* (13.1).

"I liked encaustic (pigments and hot wax) a lot. You have to have certain ventilation for that. I don't have that here in my studio. I thought, well, I love the wax."

So, Tami made cold wax her forte because it doesn't need ventilation.

"Cold wax paint gains this pudding-like or different types of textures, whatever you're searching for. It's about 50/50 cold wax to oils or less, depending on how thin or thick you want it. The look is glue or something between lard and frosting. Then you mix that with oils. It can be done on paper, but I typically paint on a wooden substrate. You don't want it to crinkle and fall off. Basically, you build up layers with cold wax and oil paint."

Tricks of the trade include a great deal of freezer paper and blue tape. "Without them, I couldn't do what I do. Kerry bought me six rolls of blue tape for Christmas because I asked him to, and I was like, 'Oh, I love you.'"

"Another tool is squeegees, which are used to load up paint and wax. They're soft and like a cooking tool, a bowl scraper, and then you layer. You want to get lots and lots of different layers of wax. Depending on how dry it is, you can do different things with it. Cold wax cures by evaporation. It takes quite a long time to dry, depending on the mixture and the number of layers. If I paint a first layer today, depending on how thick it is, I will need to wait until tomorrow-ish, or maybe a little bit longer to do my second layer and so on."

The process of layering is seen in the five images of Tami's newest piece, "Arctic Vestiges," which shows the surreal effects on the earth due to climate change. She uses wood-grained, arrow-shaped, blood-spotted, surreal trees on a red background with white tundra rising from below.

"Royal Whimsy Chair"

Layer 1 "Arctic Vestiges"

Layer 2 "Arctic Vestiges"

Layer 3 "Arctic Vestiges"

Top Layer "Arctic Vestiges"

The cloud figure in the sky is strongly reminiscent of her stated inspiration for this work by Salvador Dali— "Atavistic Vestiges after the Rain" (1934), a later version of Millets 'Architectonic Angelus" (1933). The "Atavistic Vestiges" is almost an inset of Dali's earlier painting.

Dali's "Vestiges" represents his fascination with a scene completed by French painter Jean-François Millet in 1859 in which a couple, field peasants, bow over a basket of potatoes to say the prayer "The Angelus" at the workday's end. Human figures metamorphose into white, amorphic sculptures on a field of blue sky and white cloud. Dali declared "The Angelus of Millet" to be "the most troubling, the most enigmatic, the most dense, and the richest in unconscious thoughts that I had ever seen."

I tell her what I saw growing up. "The Angelus of Millet"—so often in American homes—hung on my own father's wall, along with Eric Enstrom's "Grace." I recall how the paintings symbolized an expected religious reverence and humility.

Ironically, what most bothered Dali was what lay beneath Millet's painting: the unseen casket of a small child. Millet had painted over the casket to increase the salability of his painting. Dali looked beneath the painting via x-ray because he was sure he felt its presence.

Dali, the Spanish surrealist renowned for his technical skill, precise draftsmanship, and striking and bizarre images, had his own demons.

Tami, whose Dali painting, "Vestiges ataviques après la pluie" ("Atavistic Vestiges after the Rain") hangs in their home, said, "While I don't agree with Dali's politics (he was fascinated by Fascism and Naziism), there are things about his artwork that I like a great deal. Dali was brilliant in artistic ways. We can't let that go. He's a part of the lineage that can't be abandoned. He's been an inspiration for a couple new pieces that I've done."

Tami hopes her paintings signifying climate change and global warming move audiences and make them think, as Dali's artwork continues to do. Her fascination with Surrealism may be close to Dali's quote: "Surrealism is destructive, but it destroys only what it considers to be shackles limiting our vision."

Final Cold Wax and Oil Painting "Arctic Vestiges"

Creating the Layers of *Arctic Heat*

The artist is a receptacle for emotions that come from all over the place: from the sky, from the earth, from a scrap of paper, from a passing shape, from a spider's web.

— Pablo Picasso

Tami explains how to start the complex process of cold wax. "First off, prepare your board with gesso, which has chalk in it, and more or less primes your wood substrate so that the wax will stick.

"I have painted the gesso and then on top of that I use my squeegee to add whatever layers of wax I want."

The layers of wax are not necessarily a single solid color.

Pointing to her current project, I see a shoulder-high painting of "Arctic Heat"—a tall, spindly moose on a deep orange-red background. She says, "I'm super-excited about that one."

"Arctic Heat"

I tell her I like his knees—red circles showing the brown beneath.

"Arctic Heat" carries a hint of Dali's "Les Elephants," which also has a top layer of brilliant orange red. Beneath are layers of a whiteish-yellow, then brownish, then turquoise and so on.

She scratches back to the other layers.

I ask her: "So the white on here, is that part of the substrate, the gesso, or no?"

"It could be. But cold wax is under there, and you can feel it. In fact, it would be nice to feel it. You can feel the depth of how many layers of wax are on there."

I reach my fingers out and feel the levels of paint.

She stated she wants to be careful not to make her work look "too Dr. Seuss-like."

The painting reminds me of Cubists' work, which broke down the real world into flat, geometric shapes, somewhat like the trees of "Arctic Heat." They emphasized that the two-dimensional flatness of a painting should not pretend to be a window to a realistic scene. *Cirque* editor Sandra Kleven has recently done cubist work, so I've been reawakened to it, I told Tami. I studied WW I and the Interwar period (Pablo Picasso, Marc Chagall, and Salvador Dali).

I also noted that Tami needn't worry. She'd be in good company with Theodor Seuss Geisel (Dr. Seuss) who revered Dadaist and Surrealist work. For example, *The Lorax* book advocates environmental conservation, *The Sneetches* criticizes anti-Semitism, and the *Butter Battle Book* agitates against nuclear proliferation. Seuss wished to provoke his readers into rethinking the beliefs of dominant society. The goal of Tami's use of various movements and methods is to further the ideas on change regarding global warming.

Like most art, cold wax isn't entirely painless. "Let me tell you what, my fingers are killing me, partly because I let this one dry a little longer. Christmas happened, and I couldn't get to it as fast as I wanted. Every day it becomes harder, so I had to use some solvent to be able to get back to it. That's where I am with this. Last night, I scratched back to the layers for the trees."

She explains her code of meticulous side mapping written in blue tape protecting the sides of the cradle board.

"I have to think backwards. When I am finished, I know what I'll find when I scratch back. I knew that this was going to be green for these trees beneath the red because of the mapping. I also take pictures. It's kind of a road map, and sometimes, I do want it to be exact, but sometimes it's a great little treasure hunt, and I don't care what's back there."

I told Tami that when my children were growing up, we did lots of art projects, and I'd tell them, "There's no such thing as a mistake in art. It's just going to be something different than what you first imagined."

"But that's true," Tami said. At the same time, some parts require continued exploration.

Tami's moose head was playing hard to get, but eventually she found what she was looking for. I suggested that she was perhaps playing with an edge of reality.

"I do want surreal; it was too comic book. It just didn't work, so that's why I painted over it. And I'll be painting over it again. When I don't sleep, I know that I'm processing something, and I'm trying to figure out what's going on. The thinking behind this (white) is permafrost. I want to kind of make it my own, not just an abstract that copies Salvador's. I want it to mean something to me. I've painted many pieces that have to do with climate change—this being one of them—but it looks more like boulders and not like permafrost, but maybe that's okay. Or, maybe I've got to tweak it."

Italian educator Maria Montessori's influence on Tami, a former long-term teacher, is evident. Montessori wrote, "The hand is the instrument of intelligence." Tami's language always shows the reverence she has for her teaching life.

"I like to create paintings that tell stories and make people think, that have a conceptual aspect. I know what it means to me, but I like people to be able to look at it and walk away with their own thoughts about it. Or, maybe, just ponder the piece."

The Happy Thought That Became a Book

> The girl is mother of the woman,
> from seed to glorious stories
> stored in limbs, tired legs, and longings
> > — Kerry Dean Feldman
> > Accompanying Tami Phelps' Art piece: "Grounded in Winter" from *The Woman Within: Memory as Muse*

Few people get the chance to retire together and write books with their equals. Tami and Kerry are lucky enough to regularly ping ideas off one another in their spare time and take hours doing endeavors they cherish.

Kerry and Tami, both children of teachers, serve today as a valuable resource for one another's individual and joined creative outlets. This work culminated in the collaboration on the respect due to women in *The Woman Within: Memory as Muse,* an art and poetry book, done with renowned fine art photographer Richard J. Murphy. *The Woman Within* includes cold wax paintings on vintage children's dresses. Some include additional mixed media and assemblage. Each of the 14-piece art collection is paired with poems by Kerry.

Kerry, now primarily a fiction writer, has mixed the ideas of anthropology and writing, having taught an upper division Anthropology Through Literature course in the 80s. He said that Alaska Native people were his best students in this class and some others "because they understood that you can learn through a story. Western people, they just want to be entertained. The short story helps people understand concepts like kinship systems." Of note, Kerry continues to assist with research so that the Alaska Natives of Seward, Alaska may gain recognition as a tribe.

"Catch and Release"

Kerry has written a few novels of his own in addition to the collaboration with Tami: *Drunk on Love: Twelve Stories to Savor Responsibly* (Cirque Press, 2019) and *Kettle Dance: A Big Sky Murder* (Cirque Press, 2022). Told through the eyes of a mixed descent woman, *Alice's Trading Post: A Novel of the West* (Five Star/Cengage, 2022) explores the impact of Manifest Destiny beliefs on Western Indigenous peoples, and specifically the invasion of his home state, Montana, by hordes of Euro-American soldiers, miners, railroads, bordellos, towns, Christian churches, farmers, cowboys, capitalists, and, like his own beloved ancestors, homesteaders.

Kerry's writing award crossed over his discipline line in 1989 when he received an award in an anthropology short story competition, sponsored by the journal *Anthropology and Humanism Quarterly* (14.4). The fun title, a bit of a tongue twister, is "The Phaedra, or A Socratic Dialogue on Man and Woman in Make-Believe Costume Rental, Inc., Pico Street, Santa Monica." In the story, a female mannequin lacking a vagina and womb has a debate with Socrates about the notion of love in Western society and how if a person lives in a culture, they are not aware that their mind has been culturized or colonized.

Always the wordsmith, Kerry became entranced with poetry because "poetry condensed reality into something very special." Kerry and Tami, largely self-taught creatives appreciative of the written word, are often visitors to Poetry Parley and Cirque Press launch events.

Kerry's collaboration with Tami, however, is also born of his education by his feisty mother, Kathryn, a horsewoman who could stone a rattlesnake. Kathryn rebelled to get the education she was told was unnecessary. Kathryn (née Hauk) Feldman taught in a one-room schoolhouse in rural Montana and wrote her second novel after she was 60. Her novels are entitled *The Spring Tender* and *Mathilda;* Tami hand colored her own photographs for both of her mother-in-law's book covers.

Tami's work is likewise award winning. Her "Catch and Release" piece was juried into the London Art Biennale 2023 and sold on opening night. "Methane Blues" was selected for inclusion in the 5th Annual National Climate Assessment Report from Washington, DC, which was a huge honor for her (https://www.tamiphelps.com for a catalogue of awards)

Their main collaborative work occurred because one of Tami's projects got canceled, like over a million other people's did—due to COVID. In this case, Tami's solo show at Cyrano's Gallery in Anchorage, Alaska was cancelled after being invited by KN Goodrich.

Kerry explained to Tami, "Well, look, I'll write some poems and we'll do a book. The only thing is I'll write the poems, not necessarily about your art, about whatever is important to me about women."

"Methane Blues"

Kerry believes that women are "biologically superior to men in just so many ways" and wanted a forum to talk about it.

"Anthropologically, I think I can demonstrate that men are susceptible to more diseases than women. And our educational system teaches patriarchal nonsense. What's a female? XX sex chromosome. People ask, 'What's on the X?' 'Everything,' I tell them. What's a man? A man is X and Y. What's on the Y chromosome? Not much. Probably leftover stuff from when we were plants. Elementary and high schools don't teach that, they are often slim on teaching science about sexual difference."

Each piece in *The Woman Within: Memory as Muse* tells a story through cold wax. Some paintings also include additional mixed media and assemblage. Tami's *Woman Within* art collection continues to grow, but the 14-piece book collection paired with poems by Kerry is a permanent fixed piece.

The book presents a chance for Kerry to become ultimately and publicly vulnerable in a way that pulls tears from the reader as he remembers raising children. This is how we all must someday let go of our children, to let them become themselves. A portion of Kerry's poem "What Do You Say" for Tami's piece "HER METAMORPHOSIS" reads: "Helping her grow up, / feel Grampa love, / and presents—an Elsa dress, / caterpillars to nurture to winged miracles. / Her announcing, "I'm a mother, now, too." /

Her Metamorphosis

Age three. She feeds her babies / leaves, then sugar power / in oranges for flight muscles. / One day she announces, "It's time," / time to set them free / like mothers must do, / and fathers, though we cry / inside."

Kerry imagines the female world, the vulnerability, the strength, and allows it to filter through his words, his experiences, even his tears, which have interrupted a few of his readings.

He reminisces, "I watched her work on these art pieces. I'd grown up surrounded by women—cousins, grandmothers, sisters. And I was taught to take care of them. So I took care of women. I didn't realize women took care of me. Women are relational. I'm not. I am achievement oriented. I've achieved a bunch of stuff in life. I think men need to feel in control more than women do. Women's bodies bleed, and they don't ask for it. There's a lot that happens to a woman. You make love; you have a baby. I mean, your body's suddenly got something in it. You don't ask for it. It's not part of the male experience. So I wanted to write these poems."

As a woman who has not given birth, I appreciate the effort for another's perspective, one that enriches our own experiences and makes us stretch what it means for us all to be human.

The joined poems and images were met by a wall-to-wall crowd at Georgia Blue Gallery in Anchorage where the poems and art flowered and the room buzzed with conversation.

Kerry admitted, "I didn't know there would be a book. It was just sort of a happy thought. And then Sandy (Kleven) came over and saw and said, 'Hey, let's do a book.' I really didn't know they were that good."

The poems themselves are prosaic and story-like. And, as Kerry says, "Human beings are not made for reality. We were made for stories."

The Brilliance of Artistic Diversity

It took me four years to paint like Raphael, but a lifetime to paint like a child.

— Pablo Picasso, one of the first to use collage: newspaper cuttings, parts of musical instruments, music scores, tobacco boxes, fabrics, and metal.

Kerry says the diversity of Tami's artwork is what keeps it fresh.

She is not alone. Pablo Picasso would use anything and everything to create his works, and this collage practice is what held his audience's attention.

Tami's artistic style varies from one piece to another and from one series to another. "I've always been interested in Tami's work because one item is quite different from another. And that's not always true of artists."

Kerry added, "You see different things in it. I love the idea that the artwork itself has multiple layers. It shows the talent of the artist when you can create something that's so different from one another and still such a piece, such a beautiful piece, a striking piece. As everybody's starting to see, it's a true talent."

"Take Five, Dave," Tami's cold wax painting after Dave Brubeck's biggest-selling jazz song of all time, is significantly different from her other pieces. Kerry proclaimed that the piece "looks similar to the work of a famous Modern artist, maybe Paul Klee"(b. 1879, Swiss-German—Expressionism, Cubism, Surrealism), and I proclaimed it to be like work of Wassily Kandinsky, well-known Father of Abstract Art (b. 1866 Russia).

"Take Five, Dave"

Dave Brubeck captivated Tami because of her father's professional music career which included creating programs within the Anchorage School District. Sid Phelps, a 31-year music teacher in three states (Nebraska, South Dakota, and Alaska), also taught at the University of Alaska Anchorage. Always active as a trumpet player, he'd played the Bob Hope shows and the Ice Capades as well as having his own jazz band. He was inducted into the South Dakota Musician's Association Hall of Fame in 2002. Her artistic piece is a way to feel close to her father, who was an inspiration to her teaching and art. He died in 2023.

Full Circle to Italy

Your gifts lie in the place where your values, passions and strengths meet.
Discovering that place is the first step toward sculpting your masterpiece, your life.

— Michelangelo

Tami was by 2017 already amidst a two-year term as co-President of Alaska Wax (Alaska chapter of International Encaustic Artists) with Terisia Chleborad. Still, she was eager to learn more. Tami spoke of the 2017 Drezzo, Italy workshop she attended that year.

"Without a doubt, the most impactful learning that I've done was learn from the authors of the book *Cold Wax Medium*, Rebecca Crowell and Jerry McLaughlin," which Tami calls The Bible of cold wax.

Of note, Jerry and Rebecca post a great deal of learning videos online as well.

"It sounds totally goofball to say this, but it really did change my life. It really did. First of all, because I traveled by myself to Italy. It's like, oh my gosh. That's huge. I grew as a person; first of all, with my confidence and my ability. I thought, 'Hey, yes, I can do this.' That was phenomenal. It was so cool because there were people from all over."

Tami's mastery of cold wax has taken a great deal of trial and error. "A lot of things are happy accidents, which is very wonderful. I love happy accidents, but what I love most is when I can repeat them. Then, I own it. I know what to do. Then it becomes a technique."

Choosing to participate intentionally in a particular "call for art" is a difficult decision because these opportunities matter in the great scheme of things.

The greatest thing about Tami is her sense of fun, of play. Her serious side was influenced by Montessori, who states that we must respect within the child the humanity that is intellectual splendor "with a kind of religious veneration."

Tami and Kerry have long been fishing people, though not so much anymore, and a recent call for art appeals to Tami's past adventures of fishing. The call, in Italy, is titled "Art of fishing…Fishing in Art," put on by the Italian Fly-Fishing School (SIM) and the Italian International Museum of Flyfishing. The event includes a juried art exhibition and creation of a wine label.

Tami once caught a 60-pound king salmon on the Deshka River, where the couple had gone with a guide. The Deshka, a 44-mile-long Southcentral stretch, has salmon runs and holds resident grayling, burbot, northern pike, and rainbow trout. Although they don't fish much anymore, they have fished for silvers on the Kenai and trout in New Zealand.

"Part of how I decide if I'm going to apply for a call for art or not is where it is! There's a call for art in Italy for fly fishing," she laughs. "I'm gonna throw my hat in the ring."

Trout she knows well, and Italy has brought her amazing growth.

While looking at a cold wax image, she says, "It looks like an underpainting for a fly-fishing thing." It does. "I don't know what it's really going to turn out like, but that's so cool. It has to be small because shipping overseas is outrageously expensive."

She looks at all the wax pieces she painted, hanging in the room, and says, "I can paint over this one, and it'll be fine with me. Sometimes there are things like, oh, there's no way I will ever paint over that. And, they're like, your babies, you know? Sure. It's just really hard sometimes to sell them. In fact, that's why I have so much of my art in my home."

At the time of this interview, Tami's piece for the call for art in Italy was not complete; it was, in fact, scales. Now, it is the gorgeous, tall, narrow image of a trout: "Viva La Santa Nonna" (Long Live the Holy Grandma). We are happy to include her full circle achievement.

"Viva La Santa Nonna"
(Long Live the Holy Grandma)

"The Child is Father of the Man"

A part of the English Romantic poet William Wordsworth's famous 1802 poem, "My Heart Leaps Up" or "The Rainbow," reads: "My heart leaps up when I behold / A rainbow in the sky / So was it when my life began; / So is it now I am a man." In essence, for life to be worth living, the awe and joy of a child should accompany it. This is paraphrased by Cormac McCarthy in *Blood Meridian* as, "All history present in that visage, the child is father of the man."

Seated purposefully inside Tami's imagination is a vision—a child, pigments, whisps of white around a blue sky, and paint that creates a final scene in a way no one else could imagine, so complex yet so simple. We are attracted to the image, perhaps as former children, as people who raised or taught children. The stories that explain how each piece came to be are not our stories. There is a universality. The stories of her art are necessarily both meaningful and anecdotal. When the art is as compelling as hers, we still want to know its story.

One such piece is "The Child is Father of the Man," and it is not for sale, though she does prints. It's personal, but it's well admired—one of my favorites. The piece was selected for inclusion in "Vignettes in Wax and Words"—the International Encaustic Artists first international juried exhibition in digital magazine format. The image is comprised of cold wax, oil, and photo transfers.

At a glimpse, a boy stands atop the head of a daisy, planted in center, on its disk florets. The flower grows from between the pages of a book with a large circle on its cover. The boy, about seven, clad in speedos, pours a clear liquid from a dark container. Through the bottom of the book and around it, dry, wild, gold grass grows.

Tami tells the story, "The little boy is one of my nephews. At that time, he was six or seven. We were in Hawaii. He had found this coconut shell, filled it with water. There was a post by the ocean. His dad lifted him up on the post. He poured the water out. It became a game where he would jump off into his dad's—my brother's—arms. Oh my, my youngest brother's arms. It was just the sweetest."

Tami took the image and incorporated it into a photo collage, including a daisy she'd gathered from along the Anchorage coastal trail. The collage turned into a visual scrapbook of keepsakes. The story itself grows more and more intriguing.

The image's book originated from a Bible in Russell, in the Bay of Islands in New Zealand from the oldest Anglican church there—Christ Church (1835).

"Next to it was a guest register signed by Charles Darwin. I morphed the outline of the book with some photo magic. Then there's Kerry's head." Tami burnished a photo transfer of his head with the book image. The photo transfers look like ink drawings.

This final, superimposed image of different mediums, which are collaged together, are startlingly clear and simple. The image is an impression of a moment, of different moments, all belonging to her but now belonging to an audience who sees them as one. The interpretation is open. It's as compelling as the quote the art represents: "The child is father of the man."

The piece is at once recognizable as an image 20-year teachers and avid readers may form in their minds. Or, as she explains, an aunt, overwhelmed by the love of her brother and his interaction with his child, the familial line, awe and joy at its

"The Child is Father of the Man"

core. That essence is what draws the eye, but then there is that pure blue color as well and the muted warm tones.

Tami's artwork is "a photo montage on cold wax" in which she prints the photos in black and white on a toner printer. "Then, invert it and get a spoon and rub it off. I mean, I rub, rub, rub it off onto the cold wax."

These are the types of moments captured in Tami's artistic creations. For her, these moments have no price high enough to sell them. This is why, as she says, she keeps so many. It's no small wonder. ◪

"Birch Walk on a Sunny Day"

REVIEWS

Heather Lende

Thoughts on Rachel Epstein's *May the Owl Call Again: A Return to Poet John Meade Haines 1924-2011* (Cirque Press, 2023)

An intimate correspondence of words, writings, and letters
with reflections on life, death, and friendship

If the Owl Calls Again

at dusk
from the island in the river,
and it's not too cold,

I'll wait for the moon
to rise,
then take wing and glide
to meet him.

We will not speak,
but hooded against the frost
soar above
the alder flats, searching
with tawny eyes.

And then we'll sit
in the shadowy spruce
and pick the bones
of careless mice,

while the long moon drifts
toward Asia
and the river mutters
in its icy bed.

And when the morning climbs
the limbs
we'll part without a sound,

fulfilled, floating
homeward as
the cold world awakens.

　　　　—John Meade Haines

When former Alaska poet laureate John Meade Haines died in 2011, writer Dan O'Neill told the *Fairbanks Daily News-Miner* that Haines was, "the best poet, writer and author Alaska has ever produced." The paper also reported that in Haines' final hours old friend John Kooistra read to him from the poet's first and critically acclaimed book, *Winter News*. It's a lovely image. Then Kooistra sums up Haines for the obituary this way: "He was a cantankerous, insufferable, unbendable old bastard, but he was damn good writer. He is Alaska's best writer."

Rachel Epstein became Haines' close friend and champion in the final years of his life and has a very different perspective. "It was unusual how our friendship developed through the exchange of letters," she writes in the introduction of this volume in which she publishes them.

"We shared a hunger for critical historical discourse and a natural love of literature. Our stars crossed for two years and his laughter and curious intellect are gifts he left me. Others knew John Haines in different settings. Many unfamiliar to me."

She felt the world should know the John Haines that she did.

But first, the basics:

In 1947 after serving in the Navy during WW II and attending art school, Haines bought a 160-acre homestead claim in Richardson, eighty miles from Fairbanks. His paints froze so he wrote poems. His Alaska life was never linear, there was much to-ing and fro-ing between here and the Lower Forty Eight and beyond. In 1948 he returned to Washington, DC where he had attended high school (his father was a career Navy officer) and enrolled in American University, took more art classes, worked as a Navy draftsman, went to New York City and studied and made art with some of the great modern painters. (A timely essay about sleeping on the street due to his brief homelessness there is included in the book.) He returned to the homestead from 1954-1969, was appointed the Poet Laureate of Alaska in 1969 (since changed to Writer Laureate), taught graduate level and honors English classes at the University of Alaska Fairbanks and was a writer in residence at a half-dozen colleges before returning to Fairbanks where he died. Haines wrote a dozen books of poems, essays and memoir, was made a fellow of the Academy of American Poets in 1997 and earned many honors, including the 2008 Aiken Taylor Award for Modern American Poetry, the 2007 USA Rasmuson Fellow from United States Artists, two Guggenheim Fellowships and a National Endowment for the Arts Fellowship. He was the 2005 Rasmuson Foundation Distinguished Artist.

At Richardson, Haines built a 12-by-16-foot cabin from timbers salvaged off an unused bridge, according the *New York Times* obituary that also observes that his "experience hunting, trapping and surviving as a homesteader in the Alaskan wilderness fueled his outpouring of haunting poetry of endless cold nights, howling wolves and deep, primitive dreams."

Rachel Epstein was the Special Events Coordinator at the University of Alaska Campus bookstore from 1999-2020. In 2012 she received a Contributions to Literacy in Alaska Award, in 2020 the Alaska Governor's Award for Distinguished Service to the Humanities, and in 2023 the University of Alaska Meritorious Award.

In an early poem from his Richardson days that Epstein includes in her compilation, Haines wrote:

> If you ask me why
> I live here on
> This lonely hillside,
>
> I will smile and say:
>
> the autumn leaves
> drift on the moving
> water, and
> the world of men
> is far away.

May the Owl Call Again opens with a transcript of a recording of an Alaska Laureate panel Haines was on that Epstein organized. They met for the first time then. It continues with the letters he later wrote to her, all interspersed with selected poems and essays Haines wrote. The focus is on Haines. An appendix includes photographs of his Richardson homestead and additional resources.

Still, try as she might to make this a story about the poet, it really is about an unlikely, inspiring end-of-life friendship between two very different people through letters and even silly cards.

You may be uncomfortable with reading "Rachel's" mail from "John." You may think it is a violation of privacy. We can make that call individually. Rachel was the events coordinator at the UAA Campus Bookstore for over twenty years. They met through her job. She championed Alaskan writers and writing of every genre. Haines wrote her many letters-- on paper-- and mailed them to his relatively new friend with an abiding interest in his work. As far as I know, he didn't instruct her to burn them. Epstein writes that she edited out the more personal ones. I choose to trust her judgement.

Their first "letter" is an email concerning that Alaska Laureate panel. Thank you notes become regular correspondence, and a friendship bloomed. It continued until his death. Although Haines noted that he planned to return in spirit, so we will see.

One of the consequences of mixing Haines' friendly and routine correspondence with his poems is that it's clear what an artist and craftsman he was. "Winter News" did not just pop onto the page fully formed. Of course we know that, but reading a great writer's letters illustrates it.

Epstein notes that Haines' poems are not for everyone, but believes they were, "written and shared for anyone willing to open their world to a kind wildness that comforts and confronts day-to-day existence. It is written in appreciation. It is poetry beyond poetry. It is poetry in friendship."

Friendship. That's what charmed me. This extraordinary relationship.

Epstein hopes that "By compiling *May the Owl Call Again,* my hope is that more people will discover John Meade Haines and become intrigued by his life and literary accomplishments." She succeeds.

"I wanted John to be in the present, even with his recollections of younger days. To be in the present not the past. Old age, being alone, wondering what one can share when dependent for basic care, was the stark reality he faced," she writes. We all, if we are lucky, will grow old. How will we respond? It's helpful to learn how others have.

Their first exchange is so normal. An email. "John, have you gotten your ticket?" She asks. He says he has. In the beginning there were words. Just words. It made me wonder what friendships I have missed because I didn't keep replying, asking questions, checking-in, mailing pretty cards and long, thoughtful handwritten letters?

I imagine the bookstore manager meeting the famous elderly poet at the airport, the drive through Anchorage, the small and big things she does that make a visiting author feel at home. It's clear in these letters that even a writer of Haines stature, even an old man with nothing to prove, appreciates her attention. Writers lift our hearts from our chests and place them still beating on the page and then, when we read them aloud, on the podium for all to dissect. *Nothing stains like blood, nothing whitens like snow*, Haines wrote. Epstein shows us, in Haines' own words, that while five ex-wives made good obit copy, it is still a world of hurt. When Haines read his poem about his first wife leaving at Epstein's Laureate event, she tells us the room was "swept with a sad quiet."

Untitled

I see you going down
a dusty road
in the amber light;

the sun is setting
and I close
the greenhouse door.

New vines will grow again
next summer, but you

will not come back.

Later, once they became friends, Epstein apparently asked Haines about her. "I can tell you that my first wife, Peggy Davis, remains a close friend. We met as art students in New York in 1950, were married a year later, and moved out to California in 1952, a long story, but I will not tell it all here. In 1954 I packed things up, and drove us up to Alaska, to my homestead here, and which I knew I needed to reclaim and begin a new life. Well, Alaska was not for Peg," Haines replied.

I say apparently, because I assumed it from his letter. Epstein's letters, aside from that very first email, are not included. This bothered me so much (mainly in the woman not being good enough way) that I called up Epstein and asked her why she didn't share her words? Haines repeatedly praises her writing and intellect. Her limited editorial comments are crisp and clear. She's plenty worthy.

"I don't have them!" She said, laughing.

She mailed them to *him.*

She saved the letters he mailed to *her.* Who makes carbon copies in a friendship? (Is there even such a thing anymore?) She said he told her he had kept them, but after his death his place was cleaned out and they were lost.

John is a writer. Rachel is a reader. The letters make that clear. It's a perfect pairing. That we can make new friends at any age is inspiring. Loneliness is endemic in our culture, especially among the elderly. Having a friend waiting for your letter makes life better. Rachel has many questions and John has a lifetime of answers, softened I suspect, by age and infirmity.

I took care of my father in his last years, and in reading the letters recognized similar thought patterns: memories, opinions, health concerns, forgetfulness, denial, preaching, occasional bitterness and especially a vulnerability that produced unexpected tenderness. There is very little written from the perspective of ordinary old age, the kind as my father said that "Is not like the movies." The kind of aging where a man who once built a cabin and hunted game, butchered, preserved it and cooked it on a wood stove, struggled to grocery shop or get to doctor appointments.

"Thanks for writing, Rachel, and don't quit on it! The mail is something I need and rely on in these late years. My best wishes to your cats. . .
    —John"

"As for my reading of Irene Nemirovsky, the impression I had from the stories in Dimanche sent me back to the other collections of her writing, and I've been very impressed by it all. I have not gone back to Suite Francaise yet…
    — John"

"Dear Rachel,

I have your Jan 13 card, one of the best you have sent me, and to know that you continue [to] care about this old bard, stricken as he is at this time…

Love, as always. . .

John"

Rachel wrote as a kind of summation: "From cards and letters, we established a correspondence that may sound more or less than what it was. I found someone to converse with about things that, at one time, had been on my mind—questions left unresolved by overthinking or put aside due to the demands of daily life. And John found someone who respected what he thought and had a genuine concern for him."

Turns out that in the end, John Meade Haines did not want to be far away from people. He wanted a friend, and Rachel was there. ◪

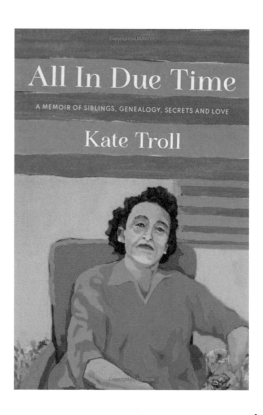

Monica Devine

A Review of Kate Troll's *All In Due Time, A Memoir of Siblings, Genealogy, Secrets and Love* (Cirque Press, 2023)

Kate Troll, from Ketchikan, Alaska begins her book *All In Due Time* with a dig through her dresser drawers looking for her passport in order to renew it for a trip to England. Upon viewing the required original birth certificate, she is shocked to learn her family is not comprised of who she thought. In fact, the certificate indicated her mother had given birth to seven children, and maybe even eight. Besides Kate and the five siblings she grew up with, two full siblings were unaccounted for. Who were these children? Were they both still alive? Had they been adopted into families years and miles away? Where were they now? Did they have families of their own? Why, for decades, had this information been kept secret? And on a more personal level, an immediate concern. Pregnant at the time, Kate yearns to know of possible genetic influences that could affect her unborn child. Met with resistance upon questioning her mother, Kate's curiosity grows as she continues her somewhat desperate, though earnest sleuthing to unravel her family's history.

Never spoken of were the details of her parents' marriage and courtship. Kate's father, an Irish Catholic, and retired military judge, was a pilot in World War II. Her mother served in the Women's Army Corp. Looking back, Kate questioned why there were no photographs of her parents' marriage, no wedding anniversaries celebrated over the years. Both of the "mystery" children were born before Kate's oldest sibling, and before her parents were legally married. Maybe the information was hidden due to shame. The merging of relations can be complicated, especially during a time in history when an out-of-wedlock mother was censured. It was a stoic and commonplace gesture in those days, to not talk about the war, or to question any detrimental effects social-cultural expectations may have had on families.

All in Due Time was a joy to read. Sprinkled with stories of Kate's formative years with her siblings, family reunions at their favorite lake, anecdotes of their work lives (Kate was a columnist for the *Anchorage Daily News* writing on energy and climate issues.), and conversations around the dinner table endear us to them. We learn Kate's mother was a kind and abiding woman of strength, and her father a genuine and present source of love to his children. They were honorable people, unwavering in their guidance and hopes for their children's futures. The tension lies in Kate's desire to find the truth.

After years of searching, the Troll siblings successfully welcome a sister and brother, complete with their own families, into their world. The enduring friendships spawned in Kate's new family constellation would have made her parents proud had they lived to see it. We will never know what a shattering loss it was for Kate's mother to give up her children; how it feels to hold a newborn in your arms, only to give it up and walk away. We will never know the reasons these secrets were not revealed. Like in so many families, hidden motivations go to the grave with their makers.

This is a lovingly rendered book, sharp in its clarity. It brilliantly illustrates how each member of the Troll family is not merely an individual, but a robust, valuable cog in a much greater familial love story. Kate's tenacity cannot be overlooked. She chose not to leave well enough alone, and many of us readers are glad she didn't. ◧

Janis Lull

A Review of John Morgan's *The Hungers of the World: New and Collected Later Poems* (Salmon Poetry, 2023)

Many of the poems in John Morgan's new book are set in Alaska, and they will resonate with northwest readers. In "The Attack," for example, a chickadee—that tough northern bird—tries to harvest the poet's hair for a nest. In a more somber state of mind, Morgan memorializes the dead in several poems called "Above the Tanana." A longer work about a river trip turns into a dialog between the writer and a fifteenth-century Indian mystic ("River of Light: A Conversation with Kabir").

Northern settings summon many different stories in this collection. A caribou herd runs up against the apparatus of corporate oil ("Counting Caribou—Prudhoe Bay, Alaska"). A poem about migrating cranes offers a portrait of a "guy who knows more about cranes / than they know about themselves ("Archives of the Air"). "The Denali Wolf" takes a surprising turn. Camping near the Toklat River, the poet hears "a noise like trash in the suburbs / being clattered away." When he opens his tent, the hooves that made the clattering have fled, but the wolf that chased them is still there, ten feet away. The writer looks at the wolf and thinks:

> Once I'd wanted to paint a canvas
> Some huge fanatical blue
> Where the hungers of the world
> Could settle and be soothed.

Face-to-face with a wolf "like a fury sculpted in ice," why does the narrator suddenly think about painting? Maybe it's because he's an artist—although usually an artist with words—and the wolf reminds him of earlier ambitions to soothe hunger with art. Unexpectedly, the poet reacts to the wolf as a hungry individual rather than a threat.

Reading this book, I assume the narrator of the poems is usually the writer himself, or some version of him. Poems aren't memoirs, but much of this work is personal in a way that connects the narrator to the actual poet. Morgan has lived in Alaska since 1976. He has floated rivers and stood above the Tanana. The narrator calls himself a poet more than once. There are enough clues here to say that the individual represented in many of the poems is meant to be a lot like the real-life writer.

Morgan doesn't always set his poems in Alaska, but even those that don't mention geography at all evoke some sense of place—a porch, a hospital room, a battlefield. "And Never Look Back," for example, happens in a garden; we don't know exactly where. A granddaughter is asking how her grandparents met, and the grandfather blurts, "It was love at first sight!" Meanwhile, in the bushes, one butterfly chases another and "fiery linkages / recur." It was love at first sight for the bugs, too, and like the grandparents, they'll probably stick together: "He'll find her again, and off they'll go."

This quietly lovely poem about gardens and humans and butterflies takes the shape of what Morgan has called a "cheater's sonnet." It's an unobtrusive bow to the history of poetry. A traditional sonnet follows lots of rules: it must have fourteen lines; it must use a prescribed pattern of meter and rhyme; it must be about love. This poem meets a few of those criteria: it does have fourteen lines, and it is about love. Some of the lines rhyme. If readers notice these echoes of the sonnet form, they can appreciate Morgan's skill in updating the tradition. If they don't notice, they can still hear the rhymes and realize that a lot can be said in just a few lines. And they can still appreciate the link

between a long human marriage and the love dance of two butterflies.

The tone of *The Hungers of the World* ranges from dejection to wonder, sometimes in the same poem. The narrator of "Celestial Firestorm," marveling at the Aurora, hears the Lights say: "Look out, mortals, things could get much worse." When the poet looks over the Tanana, he feels both grief and consolation. The river below presents him with "an island like a coffin." But the black spruce trees shooting up from the island remind him "to trust in life / not death" ("Above the Tanana: for Jim Simmerman").

Throughout his book, Morgan aims to show the interaction of mind and place. Readers who have experienced the environments portrayed here can find new ways of looking at familiar settings. Those who haven't can make some challenging new associations. All readers can feel the movement of Morgan's mind as he ties his writing to the landscapes of the world. **◖**

Sean Ulman

A Review of Nicholas Bradley's *Before Combustion* (Gaspereau Press, 2023)

I was quite delighted by the collection *Before Combustion* by Victoria, BC poet Nicholas Bradley. Drum kit music, wit, breadth, heart, moments, art, arc, etc. drove its overall effect above the banks of the scorched-earth doomsday that oozes into the second half. I'd have to say it's sad. And yet, gotta admit, I smiled within every poem.

I do indeed recommend reading it. And why not all at once, the way we watch movies. That's what I did on a flight from Seattle to Anchorage. After absorbing the impact of the ending, I took a moment to look up out of the planet of the book, one that celebrates nature's splendor while mourning its decay. Passengers on their phones. Meanwhile my hand held a precious brain/heart-made experience. Feeling its electric vitality through the textured dust jacket, I arrogantly returned to the first poem and began again.

The more times you read this book, or Bradley's previous

collection of poetry *Rain Shadow* (University of Alberta Press, 2018), the more you get. Layers, prizes, games, soul. Every go earns the reader a new angle. Expectations. Like anticipating favorite scenes in treasured films.

As I read it the third time, to prepare to write this review, I looked out for things. Oak leaves, birds, the story of a father and son, perils of climate change, snaps and pops of sharp wordplay. As I became more of a scholar on *Before Combustion* (Gaspereau Press, 2023) the shine of its design hopped in wattage.

The first poem is a camping story about how people can cause more harm than bears. It's addressed to the poet's newborn son. With poems I often wonder if the story aspects are true. I thought the first three were nonfiction. Straight from the poet's life. Neat. A tidy plank to spring from, earn style points. And Bradley stays with this guiding POV quite a bit, signing off on a letter poem in Part 3 (of 4) as "Nick."

By page 49 (of 84) the camera eye has zoomed out from family life to the run-rampant effects of climate change. A looming grim set to be reaped. A key dilemma of this day and age is juxtaposed just so.

To raise a child on dying Earth.

Such a thesis merits a book project.
I also reveled in diversions from the lead thread—a mother's inscription in a Field Guide to Birds, a fading fan's swan song to cycling, the bliss of doing laundry as expertly as tennis stars serve and volley.

> Federer
>
> of the soiled,
> Nadal of spin
>
> cycles, I sort
> and separate
>
> with aplomb

But these strays from center always rocked back to the cradle's precious contents shadowed by polluted skies.

Notable notions strike the poet while he is in transit—on a plane or ferry—and especially in the whopper that opens Part 4: "Crossing the Strait." Being on a plane as I read this line made it hit home with extra spin:

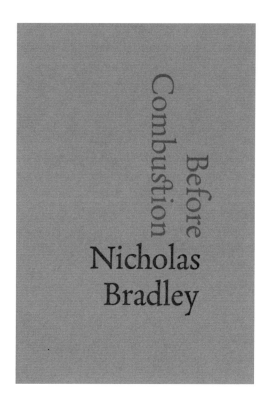

> A swell, and a dog-eared novel
> tumbled from my dozing hands

How I relish jolting awake with a book locked in my hands. And like Bradley, I recall the heft of my first trip away from my first child. While traveling I have also pined to return home while feeling:

> …fickle
> as a Zodiac
>
> with the motor cut, the wind
> picking up…

In an early poem called "Being Archaic," Bradley, an English professor at the University of Victoria (areas of expertise: Canadian Literature, American Literature, Literature of the West Coast), reflects on his days as a student and wonders if his pupils, like him before (or even now as their instructor), do not understand the old poems they are discussing.

To understand a poem... Not so simple. And is that the point of reading poetry? To crack a code? I don't think so.

I connected to more lines and sentiments in *Before Combustion* than I typically do in poetry collections. I also did not understand plenty. I didn't mind. Poems need mystery.

Like warblers, a poet must sing. Open mouth, uncap pen; spill. Refine. I got the sense that Bradley appraised every syllable with a jeweler's loupe. Whetted the diamond cutter; and edited until every note sounded spot-on. Then the gift of the published collection untaps our chance as audience.

Readers connect to works of art in ways the author may not have intended. One of my favorite poems is "Salamandra, Salamandra". The words alone:

> Fakir, thirstless, he dwells
> in a preposterous
> clime, his forecast
>
> either leaden or ablaze.
> He kips on slag and tar,
> squats on hearth…

…like rain patter, lynx pawprints on snow, staccato guitar plucks. But also where the poem took me. Childhood reveries. Turning slate slabs on endless afternoons. Catching salamanders. Legged worms with lava-striped bellies. Knowing this would be the closest I'd ever come to holding a dragon. Sequestering them in a terrarium to extend their magic. I doubt Bradley foresaw his poem returning me to childhood gold. However he did conduct it. The poem continues:

> calm despite the outlook,
> unruffled whether he burns
> or steams. All summer
>
> we lie under flimsy walls
> of silicone-treated ripstop
> peering out the mesh
>
> at the reddish haze
> of wildfire season.
> or in rented cabins.
>
> hide from parched cities,
> sleep fitfully and wait
> for morning's citrine
>
> skies…

These stanzas conjured for me the effects of Alaska's Cooper Landing wildfire of 2019. Smoggy summer in Seward, anvil-weighted air, pre-COVID scratchy throat. Hot enough to swim. A galling pall that screamed—something is off!

Better odds the poet anticipated readers rendering their personal images of wildfire effects. How it hit them and theirs. Once the poet speaks the reader can render.

In the last poem of Part 2 "Being on Fire," the emphasis oscillated from the salad days of early parenthood, oak leaves, and the simple joys of chores to the smoggy backdrop made by warming temps, storms, a worn-out water planet.

Here's are clips from four poems in Part 3 to tease out a saturnine teaser.

—"You tell me it's drier than normal on your side of the Rockies. The rain got stuck in traffic."
—"…yaks are sweating to death in summer pastures, their milk run dry."
—"…the creatures who inched out of the embers were coated in mud."
—"…the fire reddening the waves."

Surely those might ignite readers' connections; gloomy futures for withered mother Earth.

Gripping, balanced sweet and acidic, and sprinkled with delectably enigmatic stanzas, *Before Combustion* is a recipe to revisit. Devour it soon. Go for seconds.   ◪

Kerry Dean Feldman

A Review of Georgia Tiffany's *Body Be Sound* (Encircle Publications, 2023)

Georgia Tiffany's *Body Be Sound* offers words in the form of poems that enter deeply into time(s) and space(s) of a woman's lived life on the western prairie and other rural Northwest lands in the U.S.

Like my beginnings in eastern Montana.

I am not a poet though I have published some. The words in these poems occasionally challenge my ability to pierce through to their meaning, as with "Night Fishing," which begins with a kind of Zen koan for meditation: "Is a man thinking in the night, the night?"—Li-Young Lee. For me, the answer to the question is NO: thinking about night is a thought, but the reality is the absence of sunlight on one side of our spinning planet, and night occurs whether we think about it or not.

Here you see my empirical background as an anthropologist intruding on a discussion of artistic expression. Empirical thinking like that required of a physical scientist must be abandoned, put aside, to let in complex and often metaphysical conceits reflecting on family life, coyotes howling at night ("song dogs"), wondering about a mother's attraction to a milkman, or how to let Beethoven enter one's fingers to play his music properly. Also a classical piano musician, Georgia Tiffany writes, in "Chopin in the Rain": "Pianissimo, it says / What it means is: soft as frost / at the edge of feathers falling." She writes about riding to her first year in college, seeing wash hanging on a prairie line: "I shall never be ordinary, I vowed / to the woman, to the laundry, / to my mother in the rearview mirror. / I bleached and bleached it all away, / and hung from the line."

Each poem delivers aspects of resonant sounds related to words, what her famous blurbist poets describe as their "music" or "musicality." I had to do some research about the "sound" of a poem in that, unless one hears it recited, there's zero heard-sounds, there are only words seen on paper or on an electronic device. Poets, even a straightforward poet like Robert Frost ("Whose woods these are I think I know"), note that the "musicality" of words in a poem can be more important than the meaning conveyed. I suspect when poets read a poem to themselves, without even reciting it out loud, they "hear" what it would sound like. This seems similar to physicists who marvel at the "beauty" of some complex mathematical representation of forces at work in the universe, while the rest of us see only scribbled gobbledygook.

Georga Tiffany's phenomenal poems invite lovers of poetry to ascend with her to awareness of hidden connections in the flotsam and jetsam of the quiet flow and fury called our everyday life. The ooze of moments of perhaps pure understanding becomes apparent in what in some ways Kant claimed in his *Critique of Pure Reason*. The tension between mind and body, their duels and contradictions, become grasped for a moment in words that are measured and conform to the subtle rules of free verse poetry, for poems (of whatever cultural construction, including free verse) must conform to culturally recognized standards to be appreciated. How Tiffany does this can delight,

sometimes mystify, but usually takes you right "there" in her experiences in a way only a poet of rare ability can do.

These poems invite reading again, to discover perhaps nuances of meaning or ways to think about something similar in one's own life. For me, this happens in "Summoned": "All the bones of the ear are tested here / the river so quiet I can hear / spiders weaving their lives together, / fish kissing the stones." I fish a lot in Alaska, where I live. I think this book offers a significant moment in U.S. poetry today. Ponder only the title and epigraph of "Relearning the Appassionata": "He is of himself alone, and it is to this aloneness that all music owes its being." Egyptian inscription quoted in Schiller's "The Mission of Moses."

Don't miss this book if you love poetry. Get ready for a ride to places unknown that, you might discover, you actually do know.   ◪

Erin Coughlin Hollowell

Tribute to Jo Going

I lost a friend.

She chose "intelligent euthanasia" in Switzerland because she wanted to live her life on her terms, right down to the terminology of her final choice.

She was the kind of playful person who's hard to forget, her bright colored clothing, iridescent hair strands, amazing art in the most incredible neon colors. She was also a private person, holding her past and her private life and her spirituality quietly.

We are lucky because she left behind a recording for Storycorps about her choice. She chose to tell just a very few people in person before she departed. I think that she knew that we would want her to stay, and she knew that her life needed to end. In the interview, she tried to explain that she wasn't afraid of death like most people because she had aligned herself with the overall presence of energy in the world. Plus, pragmatically, she said, "We're all going to die."

She wanted everyone to be able to cuddle up to death which would help them choose better how to spend their time now. To get the "me" out of the way in order to foster a deeper relationship with the world, to quiet one's inner voice to allow a bigger voice to move through.

At the end of the interview, she talked about Agape, unconditional love that transcends the individual, suggesting that each small act of love, even as small as a smile to a cashier, is a drop. And those drops add up to a cosmic ocean of love that will heal the world.

In the morning after I found out, I wrote this scrap of poem:

Keep loving

—Jo Going's last words in her message to us all.

Each morning, the sky vivids itself pinker,
like a bet placed by some benevolent god
who doesn't even believe in themselves but
loves us all just the same. It's hard not to think
that somewhere there is a big party and the
breathing aren't invited. Jo always wanted
to make space for animals. Revered and reveled
their bones. So many people don't even think
of what once lived here. There's a snowshoe hare
sleeping under my greenhouse. Jo could
close her blue eyes and still see the tundra.
But in the end, she didn't want that method to be
the only method. I have to admire a person
who lives on their own terms. Who loves
themselves and their way in the world
more than they want others to love them.
That pink sky is a kind of love I understand.
The hare understands it as she searches
for breakfast beneath the snow made blue by
morning. I can just about hear that party.
It sounds like the creek laughing under ice.

*

Jo Going
Saying Goodbye

From Cirque 5.1

First frost, and marten tracks
there on the morning step.
The hills now are gold and shadow;
the sky gathers swans and leaves.
Gone are the endless days, dreams like sea
tumbled stones in a rush basket.
Only winter sun shall remain, a slit
through the drawn curtain,
lighting in the cracks in the floor
the spilled glass beads.

Her bio appears in the Contributors section

FEATURE

Cynthia Steele

For Poetry's Sake: Packed Cafés and Summer Soirées

Photos and Remembrances by Cynthia Steele

On a Friday evening in mid-July, Joe Craig's jazz music set the tone for *Cirque Press'* summer book releases, celebrating four Alaska writers at the Anchorage Universal Unitarian Fellowship, an apt place for promoting love, tolerance, and social justice.

Shauna Potocky shared her poetry from *Yosemite Dawning*, and Anne Ward-Masterson read from her book *Getting Home from Here* about ethnic complexities and family. Tami Phelps displayed some of her Cold Wax and mixed media art and Kerry Feldman's verse on the strength of womens' lives from *The Woman Within: Memory as Muse*. Finally, Sandra read from Clifton Bates' *Sky Changes on the Kuskokwim*.

Shauna Potocky and Anne Ward-Masterson

At the break, conversation buzzed as authors and artists joined tables to sign books and talk about projects and recent adventures. The multitalented "maker" of image, sculpture, and verse, Monica Devine, showed her fanciful sculptures and later took the podium.

The room's pews refilled with the people's poet Jim Hanlen and artist/poet wife Brenda Jaeger and many other familiar and talented voices.

By the first week of August, Sandra and I were Seattle-bound. We visited the canvas and frame-heavy home of prolific *Cirque* artist Joe Reno whose "Maui Fire," "Goddess," and "Yellow Modern" appear in Issue #26 (13.2). We photographed his art, then thrifted for frames in Ballard.

We were off to Bellingham in the second week, which held more new releases at the Mt. Baker Theater, including the posthumous poetry collection of former Alaska Laureate Joanne Townsend—*From Promise to Sadness*—and Scott Hansen's *Infinite Meditations for Inspiration and Daily Practice*. Book signings, door prizes, and refreshments meshed with the backdrop of burgundy and cream décor and glasses of wine.

David Rowan read a bit from a new book he's crafting after the success of his novel *Loggers Don't Make Love* with its rustic settings and racy scenes. In addition, retired Montana English professor, O. Alan Weltzien, a member of Wild Montana for 30 years and a volunteer Wilderness Walks leader, read from *On the Beach: Poems 2016-2021* (Cirque Press). Numerous other writers joined us to read from the pages of *Cirque* and other works.

Only four more events before we would return to Alaska, but we had begun in full swing with Sandra's usual glorious party savvy and literary wit as well as my livestreaming and record-keeping assistance.

Cynthia, Scott Hanson, and Sandra

Alan Weltzien at Mt. Baker Theater

The evening of August 11 brought a full crowd to Kenmore's Northlake Lutheran Church, where Sandra and the late Rich Kleven were married in 1967. "Guitar Gil" Menendez strummed live, along with *Cirque's* usual program fare. Warmth, ice water, music and words flowed, and books were sold in the narthex.

Chair of the Imagine arts program, Tom Frodsham, lead off the evening. The talented Tom was putting together "Jesus Christ Superstar" (and is now amidst production of "Joseph and the Amazing Technicolor Dreamcoat") with community members, many of whom showed up at the reading with a genuine interest in *Cirque.*

Readers included *Cirque Press* authors Scott Hanson—who read emotive familial poetry—and Lynda Humphrey who read from her book *Miss Bebe Comes to America - La Bebé Llega a Estados Unidos.* Lynda, a former educator, competitive dancer, and pilot, acknowledged the trio—all from Bothell High School Class of '63, Lynda herself, Sandy Kleven, publisher, Judy Nyerges, the illustrator —that brought her book to fruition. Spanish translator Patti Sosa Hands was also *muy importante. Miss Bebe* is on shelves in Walmart and Barnes and Noble as well as other bookstores, schools, and libraries, and Lynda talks of getting it across the border into Mexico, where she often visits.

More than ten esteemed readers took the stage, some serious, some spicy. Ah well, poets. What are you going to do? Invite them in.

At Tsunami Books in Eugene, Oregon, Manny Schlaeppi played piano on the next sweltering afternoon, but we had a full crowd on hand for the reading. I stood behind a back bookshelf and peered through to see everyone in full.

Janice D. Rubin took the stage with her well received release *Crossing the Burnside Bridge & Other Poems* (*Cirque Press*, June 2023), her third poetry book, about growing up in Portland, living in Eugene and the Willamette Valley, and surviving the pandemic. The evening also featured readings from *All in Due Time: A Memoir* by Kate Troll of Juneau, AK. Kate tells the story of how she and her siblings discovered, via DNA tests, older siblings who had been adopted out. This book challenges assumptions about birth, adoption, and family.

At Mt. Baker Theater: front row, Bethany Reid, Sandra Kleven, and John Morgan; back row, Scott Hanson, Connie Feutz, Tim Pilgrim, David Rowan, and Cynthia Steele

Kenmore Church Readers and Others

Janice Ruben Reading at Tsunami Books

Marc Janssen and Crowd at Tsunami Books

After the reading, which included about eight other readers, Nard and Sheary Clough Suiter took Sandy and I out to dinner at Nazzi's where we learned of their recent travels and how they came to be happy transplants to the Pacific Northwest. See *Cirque's* profile on the talented artistic duo in *Cirque* #25 (13.1).

A few days later, we encountered triple digit heat. Nevertheless, we persisted to sally forth our way across the Pacific Northwest in our white rental sedan. Ah, the heat of poetry in Portland. To be in Ross Island Grocery and Café, surrounded by cool refrigerators but caught in a collective hot flash. We greeted a crowd of wall-to-wall people with a black-drop stage and mic, just enough seating, and a whoosh of beers and kombucha to cool us.

Georgia Tiffany reads at Ross Island

Dale Champlin reading at Ross Island Grocery and Café

Considering the numbers of the Portland Poetry contingency, the crowd was no small wonder. Janice D. Rubin set the tone, reading again for us. Numerous readers entertained and delighted us throughout the night, which was as theatrical as it was literary, and the crowds heartily applauded.

The fans kept blowing, but just pushed the hot air around. We left, surviving the festivities of wonderful people and lifelong connections, and moved by the vulnerability of poets who put themselves and their good work out there.

With our AC blowing and our hearts full, we left Portland and each of our respective sons behind in Tigard, while we listened to *The Moth*. The long-term, worldwide podcast where people tell true stories, live and without notes, standing alone under a spotlight with a microphone, which somewhat mirrored our lived experiences. Note to self: Add a Bucket List item—tell a story on *The Moth*.

The lush, suburban neighborhood of View Ridge, Seattle, was our final reading of the two-week stint and occurred at the home of Chris Balk and Karl Flaccus. Chris has agreed to be *Cirque's* next poetry contest judge for "Poetry in Motion." Their shaded back porch with its glimpses of early evening rays accompanied an inside potluck of fresh salads and a multiplicity of breads and drinks with music, again, by "Guitar Gil."

After the readings, as folks gathered coats, we talked John Morgan into a couch to share with us a few of his favorite Catholic nanny poems about first crushes and young boyhood, which delighted us all and sent us off into the night with the remembrance of cherished young people.

Remember, we live stream, so our join book tours via Cirque on Facebook.

Gathering at the home of Chris Balk and Karl Flaccus: Kay Fisher Myers,
Mary Eliza Crane, Lyn Coffin, Jim Thielman, Leah Stenson, Carolyn Wright, Karl Flaccus,
and John Morgan. Lynda Humphrey reading from *Miss Bebe*.

CONTRIBUTORS

Claire-Elise Baalke received a MA in English at the University of Alaska, Fairbanks and recently began her PhD in Medieval Studies at the University of New Mexico. Her research mainly focuses on the connections between women and dragons in Medieval literature, but she also writes fiction and occasionally poetry. She has poetry publications in *The Bangalore Review* and the Flying Ketchup Press' collection titled, *Night Forest*.

John Baalke's poems have been published in *Ice Floe, Cirque, Hummingbird, Black Bough Poetry* (Wales), and other journals. He holds an MFA from Seattle Pacific University and has worked for a small tribal village government in southwest Alaska for many years.

Christianne Balk loves open water swimming and the rhythms of everyday street talk. Her video-poem "Nets" (created with performing/visual artists Karen Yarborough, Norris Carlson, and Heather McMordie) was produced by the Creature Conserve/ Endangered Species Coalition. Books include *The Holding Hours* (UW Press), *Desiring Flight*, and *Bindweed*.

Joe Barnes' poetry has appeared in six anthologies: *TimeSlice, The Weight of Addition, Untameable City, Line Up, Enchantment of the Ordinary* and *Chaos Dive Reunion*, as well as journals such as *Bat City Review, Measure*, and *Ilya's Honey*. Barnes is also a playwright. He lives in Houston, Texas. He's had 17 play readings at the Valdez Theatre Conference in Alaska, one reading in Anchorage, and one in Homer.

Sarah Birdsall's publications include *Wild Rivers, Wild Rose* (University of Alaska Press, 2020), which was the 2021 WILLA Literary Award Winner in Historical Fiction; *The Red Mitten* (McRoy & Blackburn, 2006), which won a bronze medal for best West Coast fiction in the 2007 Independent Publishers Book Awards competition; and *The Moonflower Route* (McRoy & Blackburn, 2017). An additional novel is forthcoming from Epicenter Press. Her short fiction has appeared in *The Alaska Quarterly Review* and *Alaska Women Speak*. A former award-winning journalist, she has an MFA in creative writing from the University of Alaska Anchorage and lives in her hometown of Talkeetna, Alaska.

Ari Blatt lives on the Oregon Coast and works as a Fisheries Biologist. Her fiction can be found in the literary magazine *Shark Reef*, and articles and essays in *The Corvallis Advocate*. Ari received an MFA in Creative Writing from OSU-Cascades and is continuing to bring her thesis project, a novel in stories, to its complete form..

Eric Braman (they/them) is a poet, storyteller, and theatre maker based in Springfield, Oregon. Their work has been published by *High Shelf Press, Qu Literary Magazine, Moon Tide Press, The Coachella Review*, and more. Braman released the album "By Your Side" in collaboration with musician Cullen Vance, has performed on stages across the United States, and is an arts administrator supporting community events and education. Learn more at www.ericbraman.com.

Jack Broom is a Seattle native who retired in 2016 after 39 years as a reporter and editor at *The Seattle Times*. He earned a bachelor's degree from Western Washington University in 1974. His work in photography began in the 1970s as a reporter/photographer for *The Wenatchee World*, where he worked before going to *The Seattle Times* in 1977. In recent years, his photographs have won awards at state-fair competitions in Washington and have been featured in previous issues of *Cirque*. He is a past president of the Edmonds-based Puget Sound Camera Club.

Toya Brown is an artist who shows her cultural connection in her work. She can be found advocating for recognition of Alaskan writers while hosting workshops, panel discussions, events like Live from Storyknife or judging Poetry Out Loud. She was interviewed and featured in a piece by the Smithsonian National Museum of African American History and Culture. She recently opened for *Harriet Tubman and the Underground Railroad* at the Alaska Center for the Performing Arts. She is an executive board member for 49 Writers and an active member of the non-profit Sankofa.

Randol Bruns came to Alaska after graduation from the University of Colorado to canoe down the Yukon River. He built a cabin on the Talkeetna River and has taught in Yup'ik Eskimo communities on the Lower Yukon. He built a house on the Little Susitna River where he currently lives with his wife, Claire. His poems have been published in *Ice Floe, Cirque* and *The Alaska Quarterly Review*.

Mark Burke's work has appeared or is forthcoming in the *North American Review, Beloit Poetry Journal, Sugar House Review, Nimrod International Journal* and others. His work has recently been nominated for a Pushcart prize. Please see markanthonyburkesongsandpoems.com

Randy Bynum's work appears or is forthcoming in *Cirque, Arboreal Literary Magazine, Metonym Journal, Atticus Review, New Plains Review, Cathexis Northwest Press*, and others. He explores people, places, issues of social inequity (his mother was ½ Native American/Cherokee who hid it until late in life). His publication-ready collections include *Tulips Talking Behind My Back* and a four-volume set of magical realism poems for older children/adults entitled *Dragons Who Type: Poems of Whimsy and Wishes*. He's an award-winning playwright ("The Convert", Kennedy Center/ACTF, Region IX). He lives in Portland, OR with wife Dani and rescue dog Coop of the Dump.

Elisa Carlsen is an outsider artist and poet whose words have appeared in *SixFold, VoiceCatcher, Anti-Heroin Chic, Nevada Arts Council, Oranges Journal*, and *Brushfire*. Elisa won the Lower Columbia Regional Poetry Contest, was a finalist for the Editor's Prize at *Harbor Review*, and Best of the Net nominee. Elisa is the author of *Cormorant* (Unsolicited Press, 2023).

Teri White Carns writes haiku, haibun, tanka, and tanka prose, along with law review articles and justice system research. She came to Alaska in the summer of 1971, and has never really been able to leave.

Born and raised in Montana's beautiful Flathead Valley, **J Carraher** is a San Francisco Bay Area writer whose recent work appears in such venues as *Severance Magazine, Stanza Cannon, Footnote* & others. In 2023 she was awarded the Sunspot Lit Rigel best of essay and Goldilocks Zone best of poetry. J studied folklore at UC Berkeley, holds a Masters of Science from UC San Francisco, and now works as an obstetric nurse and forensic examiner for Sonoma County. She lives with her family on a small farm in Freestone.

Dale Champlin, a Pushcart Prize nominee and OPA first prize winner in the members category, is an Oregon poet with an MFA in fine art. Dale has poems in *Cirque, The Opiate, Timberline, Triggerfish Critical Review, Willawaw, Pif*, and many other journals and anthologies. Dale has three poetry collections: *The Barbie Diaries, Callie Comes of Age*, Cirque Press, 2021, and *Isadora*. Three collections: *Leda, Medusa*, and *Andromina, A Stranger in America* are forthcoming.

Nard Claar, nardclaar.com, is an artist, poet, speaker, and social activist who promotes non-profits who value social justice, environment, arts, and community. Nard's work is exhibited in galleries in a number of states. Nard and his partner, Sheary Clough Suiter travel extensively and spend lots of time camping and connecting to nature.

Joanne Clarkson's sixth poetry collection, *Hospice House*, was released by MoonPath Press in 2023. Her poems have been published in such journals as *Poetry Northwest, Nimrod, Western Humanities Review, American Journal of Nursing* and *Beloit Poetry Journal*. She has received an Artist Trust Grant and an NEH grant to teach poetry in rural libraries. Clarkson has Masters Degrees in English and Library Science, has taught and worked for many years as a professional librarian. After caring for her mother through a long illness, she re-careered as a Registered Nurse working in Home Health and Hospice. See more at http://Joanneclarkson.com.

Mary Eliza Crane lives in the woods in the Cascade foothills in western Washington. A regular feature at Puget Sound readings, she has read poetry from Woodstock to LA, and internationally with Siberian poets in Russia. Mary has two volumes of poetry, *What I Can Hold In My Hands* and *At First Light* published by Gazoobi Tales Press. Her work has appeared in many journals and northwest anthologies, including *Raven Chronicles, WA 129 Poets of Washington (2017)* and *Bridge Above the Falls* (2019), and has been translated into Russian. Mary co-curates and co-hosts the monthly Duvall Poetry reading series.

Nancy Deschu lives in Alaska where she writes nonfiction and poetry on natural history, science, and sense of place. She takes photographs when she travels around the state, immersed in the beauty of the Alaska wilderness.

Monica Devine is a writer and figurative ceramic artist. Her most recent book *Water Mask* (a Finalist for the Willa Literary Award) is a collection of stories that reflect on motherhood, place, memory, art, and perception in the natural world. She is a Pushcart Prize nominee, a First-Place winner in the *Alaska State Poetry Contest*, and her piece *On The Edge of Ice* won First Place in Creative Nonfiction with *New Letters* journal. Her work has appeared in four anthologies, and she has authored five children's books. monicadevine.com

Patrick Dixon is a retired educator and commercial fisherman living in Olympia, Washington. Published in *Cirque Journal, Panoplyzine, Raven Chronicles, National Fisherman magazine, The Smithsonian* and the anthologies *FISH 2015, WA129,* and *I Sing the Salmon Home*. He was also included in the Washington State Book Award anthology, *Take a Stand: Art Against Hate*. Dixon was a past poetry editor of *National Fisherman* magazine's quarterly, *North Pacific Focus*. He received an Artist Trust Grant for Artists to edit *Anchored in Deep Water: The FisherPoets Anthology* published in 2014. His poetry chapbook *Arc of Visibility* won the 2015 Alabama State Poetry Morris Memorial Award. His memoir, *Waiting to Deliver*, about his 20 years fishing for salmon on Cook Inlet, Alaska, was published in 2022.

Colten Dom is a graduate of the University of Victoria Writing Program where he won the Haig-Brown Award for Conservation Writing and received a British Columbia Arts Council scholarship. His fiction has appeared in *This Side of West, filling Station,* and *The Missouri Review*.

Judith Duncan: I have poems published in *Cirque, Volume 10, No. 1; Cirque, Volume 11, No. 1; The Madrona Project, Volume III, Number 2; Metaphor Dice,* and *Hummingbird*.

Nicole Emanuel is a PhD candidate in the Department of English at the University of Minnesota, Twin Cities. Her work brings together animal studies, weird studies, queer ecology, cultural criticism, and literary theory. She was born and raised by the foothills of the Chugach Mountains in Anchorage, Alaska, and today she resides in southeast Minneapolis with her human partner, two dogs, numerous plants, and a 3-year-old sourdough culture.

Helena Fagan lives in Juneau, Alaska where she writes poetry, memoir and young adult fiction on beaches, in coffee shops and on her husband's commercial fishing boat. Her writing has been published in *Tidal Echoes, Cirque, Alaska Women Speak, Ground, North Coast Squid,* and *Exist Otherwise*. She won the Manzanita Poetry Prize and first place in the Alaska Writers Guild Poetry Competition, second place in the Fairbanks Arts Statewide Poetry Contest, and most recently was longlisted for the Palette Sappho Poetry Prize.

Kerry Dean Feldman, author of *Alice's Trading Post: A Novel of the West,* the stories of *Drunk on Love,* and co-author of T*he Woman Within: Memory as Muse,* is Professor Emeritus of Anthropology at the University of Alaska Anchorage.

Libby Ferrara (she/her) is a full-time jewelry artist and self-taught poet hand-making her home in Seward, AK.

David Foster grew up in eastern Washington. An emotional kid, he spent a lot of time in the principal's office during kindergarten. Deciding between English and Physics was a challenge for him when it was time to look at colleges. Although he went the science route, he was always writing, at the very least doing so in his head. Several years ago, he began to get into poetry again more intensely. He is writing (and reading) regularly again because he can no longer help it.

Jason Gabbert participates with words (those things that stir and explore the vast range of what it is to "be") with simple sentences.

Jo Going taught painting for the Kachemak Bay Campus, University of Alaska, Homer, in 2003, but also taught art in Montana, California, and Rhode Island, where she was from. She won numerous awards in each of these places and held esteemed grants and fellowships. She did illustrations for numerous books and promotional materials. As a poet and essayist, she published a great deal, including in *Ice Floe: Poetry of the Circumpolar North, Alaska Quarterly Review, Wild Cranes,* and *Cirque*. She also had poems and paintings published by the National Museum of Women in the Arts, Washington, DC (Library Fellows Award 1997). Her online page lists her accomplishments in full at https://www.jogoing.net/resume.htm. An interview with Jo about her decision is here https://archive.storycorps.org/interviews/in-full-color-with-jo-going/ Four years before this interview, she learned she was going blind.

David A. Goodrum, writer/photographer, lives in Corvallis, Oregon. His chapbook, *Sparse Poetica,* is due in late 2023, and a book, *Vitals and Other Signs of Life,* is due in mid-2024. His poems are forthcoming or have been published in *Cirque Journal, Tar River Poetry, The Inflectionist Review, Passengers Journal, Scapegoat Review,* and *Triggerfish Critical Review,* among others. Additional work (poetry and photography) can be viewed at www.davidgoodrum.com.

Jim Hanlen: Jim taught 19 years in Washington State. He retired to Anchorage, Alaska; has poems in these anthologies: *The Practice of Peace, Weathered Pages, Storms of an Inland Sea, Season of Dead Water, Spokane Writes,* and *GRRR An Anthology of Bears*. He's shopping a manuscript of poems about Spokane, Washington.

Annekathrin Hansen grew up near the rugged Baltic Sea beaches in North East Germany. She attended Waldemar Kraemer's drawing and painting classes at Art School in Rostock and Heiligendamm, Germany. She studied and received an engineering degree and worked in Germany and Australia. Anne interpreted aerial photos and created many types of maps in land surveying. She is skilled in sculpturing, photography, print making, painting, mosaic and mixed media. Anne graduated from various workshops. Further self-studies led to her recent artwork. In 2010 she moved to Alaska. Her artwork can be seen at Anchorage Cafe AK Kaffeeklatsch, Georgia Blue Gallery and IGCA.

Scott Hanson is a writer, philosopher, poet and wireless professional who lives in Kingston, WA. He is a lifelong resident of the Pacific Northwest and a decades-long student of meditation and the *Tao Te Ching*. Although he has been a writer of journals, poetry, family vignettes and short stories throughout his life, *Infinite Meditations: for Inspiration and Daily Practice,* recently released by Cirque Press in 2023, is his first published book.

Thomas Hedt spent 36 years working in conservation, primarily in Washington State, Alaska, California and Arizona. His poetry has appeared in: *The Sijo International Journal of Poetry and Song, Cathexis Northwest, The Tule Review, Tiferet, The Lilly Poetry Review,* and elsewhere. His first compilation, *Artifacts and Assorted Memorabilia,* was published in September of 2020 by Cold River Press. He lives in Eureka, California.

Amanda Hiland is a queer writer living in Oregon. She is very fond of the ocean, colored pens, and chai. A Special Education teacher by day, she is also a major astronomy enthusiast at night. She spends her free time folding origami, sun printing, and advocating for immigrant and unhoused communities. Her work has appeared most recently in *VoiceCatcher, Epiphany, Willawaw Journal,* and *Cathexis*.

Madronna Holden won the 2022 Kay Snow Poetry Award, as well as two previous Pacifica awards. Her recent retirement has allowed her to concentrate on her poems, over 80 of which have appeared in *Verse Daily, the Bitter Oleander, Cold Mountain Review, Equinox Poetry* and *Prose, the Christian Science Monitor, About Place,* and others. Her chapbook, *The Goddess of Glass Mountains,* was published by Finishing Line Press (2021) and an award-winning documentary featuring the production of her play in poetic text, "The Descent of Inanna," has been aired several times on Oregon Public Broadcasting.

Erin Coughlin Hollowell is a poet and writer who lives at the end of the road in Alaska. Prior to landing in Alaska, she lived on both US coasts, in big cities and small towns, pursuing many different professions from tapestry weaving to arts administration. She is the author of *Pause, Traveler* (2013) and *Every Atom* (2018), both published by Boreal Books, and *Corvus and Crater* from Salmon Poetry (2023). She has been appointed a 2022-2025 Black Earth Institute Fellow. She is the executive director of Storyknife Writers Retreat and director of the Kachemak Bay Writers' Conference.

Lucinda Huffine is a poet and reader living in McMinnville, Oregon. She is a former librarian and bookseller.

Mike Hull spent twenty-seven years as a teacher and administrator in the remote Native villages of Alaska. He and his wife have lived and worked in Southeast Alaska, the North Slope, the Interior, and Western Alaska. His focus was on creating place-based learning that incorporated subsistence traditions and practices in the core curriculum. This program attracted the attention of other educators and lead to his students being invited to attend the World Expo in Aichi, Japan to present their culture and their school program. Many visitors to the Expo met with the students and told them they did not know that people still lived this way. The highlight of this experience was a visit with the Nobel Peace Prize winner from Kenya, Wangari Maathai, who spent time talking with the students and encouraging them in preserving their culture. Mike and his wife are retired and living in Anchorage, Alaska

My name is **Russell James**, an autistic, indigenous writer from Corvallis, where I have lived since July of 2018. I'm currently enrolled in Eastern Oregon University's MFA in Creative Writing program, and I have recently been published in *The Hopper, Paper Dragon,* and *Pretty Good Pieces*. I work in both fiction and nonfiction, although my current pieces are leaning heavily towards my fiction side. I enjoy exploring relationships. There is a truth in relationships that my neurology loves to observe but doesn't quite understand. "Gooey Ducks" is this sort of piece. Technically a flash piece, it contains the portrait of an entire relationship between a brother and sister as they sit on a rocky beach on Orcas Island. Writing out these observations I've collated over the past few decades helps me feel more comfortable with things I don't quite understand. Ecology and landscape are also important to me. "Gooey Ducks" describes the landscape where these two siblings find themselves, and their interiority. My hope is it comes off as heartwarming and prescient. Russell Tecumseh James Enrolled Member, Pamunky Indian Tribe.

Marc Janssen has been writing poems since around 1980. Some people would say that was a long time but not a dinosaur. Early decrepitude has not slowed him down much; his verse can be found scattered around the world in places like *Pinyon, Slant, Cirque Journal, Off the Coast* and *Poetry Salzburg*. Janssen also coordinates the Salem Poetry Project — a weekly reading, the occasionally occurring Salem Poetry Festival, and was a nominee for Oregon Poet Laureate.

Valkyrie Liles: I am a homesteader, writer and amateur naturalist currently living in the Cascade-Siskiyou mountains of Southern Oregon. I grew up in Seward, Alaska and have always had a deep connection with the earth. My writings are deep love letters to the natural world as well as treatises on hope and holding on to love in a changing, turbulent world.

Eric Gordon Johnson was born in Fairbanks and raised in Anchorage, Alaska. He earned an MFA in Creating Writing in poetry at the University of Alaska Anchorage in December 2020. He won an honorable mention for a short story in the University of Alaska Anchorage and *Anchorage Daily News* writing contest. He has published poems and a short story in *Cirque Literary Journal*. He published a memoir in *Anchorage Remembers* published by 49Writers. He also has several broadsides published by 49Writers. He is a member of Drumlin Poets, Poetry Parley and 49Writers. He has taught poetry classes for Opportunities for Lifelong Education.

Penny Johnson, an old woman, lives out amongst the sage and bitter brush in the high desert of central Washington at the base of a mountain with a horde of animals. Early on, Johnson was a resident of Devereux Manor, graduated from The Evergreen State College and has an MFA from Goddard. She worked as a long-haul truck driver, TESL teacher in Poland and a RN. Most recently her poems have been published in *The Yakima Herald Republic, Cirque, The Shrub-Steppe Poetry Journal, Yakima Coffeehouse Poets* winning the Tom Pier Prize and *WA 129, Poets of Washington* and lastly, an honorable mention, *Cleaver Magazine,* judged by Diane Seuss.

Susan Johnson writes in the Cascade Mountain town of Roslyn, Washington where she taught in the local schools and nearby university and participated in state and national writing initiatives. Her work has appeared in *Cirque Journal, Abbey of the Arts Monk in the World, Earth's Daughters, Raven Chronicles, Shrub-Steppe Poetry Journal, and Yakima Coffeehouse Poets,* as well as other journals and online publications. Her chapbook, *The Call Home,* a finalist for the 2022 Poetry Box Chapbook Competition, was published this spring.

Jan Jung lives in Bellingham, Washington with her husband John and their delightful dog Toby. She has worked as a licensed mental health professional and as a teacher in elementary and special education settings. She enjoys walking in nature, making music, photography, and spending time with her three children and six grandchildren. Jan continues to search for images that might otherwise go unnoticed. Her photos have been featured in the book *Bridges Cloud, Cottage Magazine,* and *Cirque*.

Carol Kaynor is originally from Massachusetts but has spent virtually her entire adult life in Fairbanks. She co-wrote the book *Skijor With Your Dog,* not quite a *New York Times* bestseller, but now in its second edition. Carol entered the University of Alaska Fairbanks MFA program in the fall of 2003 and graduated a mere seven years later in 2010. Her nonfiction essays have been published in the *Alaska Quarterly Review, The Northern Review,* and *Pilgrimage*. Her *AQR* essay was reprinted in the anthology *Wild Moments*. She also had a poem about a dog published in *Ice-Floe*. She enjoys running dogs and half marathons.

Keith Kennedy is a Pushcart and Rhysling nominee sporting seventy professional credits and sixteen pieces of flair. He has recent publications at *Barzakh, Cirque* and *Red Ogre*. Keith currently resides in Vancouver with his adorable wife and is repped by Jon Michael Darga (also adorable) at Aevitas Creative.

Janet R. Klein is celebrating over 50 years in Alaska. Her writings and photographs focus primarily on the natural and cultural history of Kachemak Bay although her latest book is about *Alaska Dinosaurs and Other Cretaceous Creatures*. It was co-authored with Deborah Klein, her daughter, and contains scientifically accurate descriptions of Alaska dinosaurs. During her 40-year career working in Alaskan museums, Janet worked primarily in Homer and Anchorage. In retirement she's enjoying her grandsons, volunteering in Homer, and exploring the abundant fossil flora of lower Cook Inlet.

Poet and essayist **Sandra Kleven** has published work in *AQR, Oklahoma Review, Topic, Praxilla, Stoneboat, F-zine* and the UAP anthology, *Cold Flashes*. She was twice nominated for the Pushcart Prize. Her writing has also won notice in the UAA Creative Writing and F'Air Words contests. In 2015, Kleven was named to the Northshore School District, Wall of Honor as an outstanding graduate. Kleven has authored four books, most recently *Defiance Street: Poems and Other Writing* (VP&D Publishing House). She works as clinical director for a Native corporation. She partners with Michael Burwell, publishing *Cirque*. In 2018, Kleven and Burwell established Cirque Press.

Margaret Koger was raised on an acreage near the Snake River after electricity came to the valley and before her parents could afford to buy her a pony. She survived and later moved to Boise, where she taught English and Composition in the Boise Schools and at Boise State University. She is a Lascaux Prize finalist and her works appear in numerous publications, including *Tiny Seed Literary Journal, The Limberlost Review, the Writers in the Attic* anthologies *Animal, Game,* and *Apple,* and the collections *What These Hands Remember* (Kelsay, 2022) and *If Seasons Were Kingdoms* (Fernwood Press, 2023).

John Kooistra's first book, *Long Voyage Gathering Light,* published by Cloudbank Books, was the winner of the 2021 Vern Rutsala Book Prize. A former commercial fisherman and university teacher of philosophy, he's served as the artist-in-residence for Denali National Park and Holland America and published poetry and essays in various journals including *Alaska Quarterly Review, Artful Dodge,* and *Cloudbank.*

Yvonne Higgins Leach: My first collection of poems, *Another Autumn,* was published in 2014 by WordTech Editions. Over the years, I have been published in literary magazines and anthologies in the United States. My work has appeared in *Cimarron Review, decomP Magazine, Hawaii Pacific Review, The MacGuffin, Midwest Quarterly, Penumbra, Pink Panther Magazine, South Carolina Review, South Dakota Review, Spoon River Poetry Review, Swifts and Slows, Virginia Normal, Wisconsin Review,* and *Whitefish Review,* among others. I earned a Master of Fine Arts in Creative Writing Poetry from Eastern Washington University. My second book of poems will be published by Kelsay Books in early 2024.

DJ Lee is a writer, scholar, artist, and regents professor of English at Washington State University. She has an MFA from the Bennington Writing Seminars and a PhD from the University of Arizona. She has published over forty essays and prose poems, the memoir *Remote: Finding Home in the Bitterroots* (Oregon State, 2020), and eight scholarly books, including *The Land Speaks* (Oxford, 2017). A hand papermaker and photographer, Lee often combines image and text. Artist residencies include the Arctic Circle Artist Residency, Women's Studio Workshop, and the Wilderness Art Collective.

Eric le Fatte was educated at MIT and Northeastern University in biology and English. He has worked correcting library catalog cards in Texas, and as the Returns King at Eastern Mountain Sports in Massachusetts, but currently hikes, writes, teaches and does research on tiny things in the Portland, Oregon area. His poems have appeared in *Rune, The Mountain Gazette, The Poeming Pigeon, The Clackamas Literary Review, The Raven Chronicles, Windfall, Verseweavers, US#1 Worksheets, Perceptions, Clover, Tiny Seed Literary Journal, Clade Song, Deep Wild, Pangyrus, Canary,* and happily enough, in *Cirque.*

Heather Lende was the 2021-2024 Alaska Writer Laureate and author of four memoirs from Algonquin Books–*Find the Good; If You Lived Here, I'd Know Your Name; Take Good Care of the Garden and the Dogs;* and most recently *Of Bears and Ballots* in 2020. She lives in Haines and blogs at heatherlende.com

Judith Lethin is an Episcopal Priest who served the villages of Anvik, Shageluk, and Grayling from 1998-2005. She graduated with her MFA in the Low Residency Program at UAA in 2014. She is the author of an upcoming collection of stories about her work on the Yukon River, *A Wonderful-Terrible God,* and a women's healing retreat, *Walking In Beauty —Roots & Wings.* She has published poems and stories in *Chaplaincy Today, Cirque Journal,* and *Alaska Dispatch News.* Judith lives with her husband of 60 years, Kris, and two golden retrievers in Seldovia, Alaska. She is still active today as a Priest, Chaplain, and Retreat Leader.

Mike Lewis is a lifetime amateur photographer who retired from the *Anchorage Daily News* in 2022 after a 37-year career as a copy editor.

Abigail Licad is a first-generation immigrant from the Philippines. She received her BA from UC Berkeley and her MPhil in literature from Oxford University. She has served as editor in chief for *Hyphen magazine* and as a Rotary Ambassadorial Scholar to Senegal. Her work has appeared in *Vassar Review, The Rumpus, LA Times,* and others. She lives and works in Portland, Oregon.

Sue Fagalde Lick escaped life as a journalist in Silicon Valley to write poetry and play music on the Oregon Coast. Author of the chapbooks *Gravel Road Ahead* and *The Widow at the Piano: Poems by a Distracted Catholic,* she has published poems in many journals, most recently in *Cirque, Triggerfish,* and *Better Than Starbucks.*

Linda Lucky: Is a retired art teacher from Huntington, Long Island where she taught art for 30 years. Lucky is a mixed media artis known for her paper-mâché animals. She is a docent at the Anchorage Museum and a member of the International Gallery of Contemporary Art where she has had a solo show and been in many group shows. She is also a monologue writer and performer and has appeared at Out North in "under 30" and twice for Arctic Entries at the Alaska Performing Arts Center. She is also a long-standing member of Poetry Parley.

Janis Lull is professor emerita of English at the University of Alaska Fairbanks.

Jan MacRae has a MFA in poetry and fiction writing from the UO in Eugene, Oregon, where she currently resides. She worked for many years as the Fiction Editor for *Northwest Review.* Her work history also includes teaching college classes to high-school students and working as a sex educator for Planned Parenthood.

Shirley Martin writes harbourside in Ucluelet, inspired by her rugged west coast surroundings. She has published five children's books. Her articles can be found in the *Westerly News* and *WordWorks Magazine.* Her poetry has been published in a handful of anthologies, including *Worth More Standing* (Caitlin Press, 2022), and *Laugh Lines* (Repartee Press, 2023).

David McElroy lives in Anchorage, Alaska. He recently retired as a bush pilot in the Arctic. He has worked as a smokejumper, teacher in Guatemala, and taxi driver in Seattle. He attended the Universities of Minnesota, Montana, and Western Washington. He has been published in national journals including *Antaeus, Cirque, The Nation, Poetry Northwest, The Chicago Review,* and *The Alaska Quarterly Review.* He has four books of poems called *Making It Simple, Mark Making, Just Between Us,* and *Water the Rocks Make.* He is a recipient of grants from the National Council on the Arts, the state of Alaska Council on the Arts and Humanities. He was given *Cirque's* Andy Hope Award for poetry.

Karla Linn Merrifield has 16 books to her credit. Following her 2018 *Psyche's Scroll* (Poetry Box Select) is the full-length book *Athabaskan Fractal: Poems of the Far North* from Cirque Press. Her newest poetry collection, *My Body the Guitar* was nominated for the 2022 National Book Award. She is a frequent contributor to *The Songs of Eretz Poetry Review.* Web site: https://www.karlalinnmerrifield.org/; blog at https://karlalinnmerrifeld.wordpress.com/; Tweet @LinnMerrifiel; https://www.facebook.com/karlalinn.merrifield.

Judith Mikesch-McKenzie is a teacher, writer, actor and producer living in the Pacific Northwest. She has traveled widely but is always drawn to the Rocky Mountains as one place that feeds her soul. Writing is her home. She has recently placed/published in two short-story contests, and her poems have been published in *Pine Row Press, Halcyone Literary Review, Plainsongs Magazine, Closed Eye Open, Wild Roof Journal, Cathexis Northwest Press, Meat for Tea Valley Review,* and several others. She is a wee bit of an Irish curmudgeon, but her friends seem to like that about her.

John Morgan: In addition to *Cirque,* my poems have appeared in *The New Yorker, Poetry, APR, The Southern Review, Prairie Schooner, The Paris Review, The New Republic,* and many other journals. I've published eight books of poetry as well as four chapbooks and a collection of essays. I won the Discovery Award of the New York Poetry Center, *The Quarterly Review of Literature* Poetry Prize, and first prize in the *Carolina Quarterly* poetry contest, among other awards, and was a writing fellow at the Fine Arts Work Center in Provincetown. In 1976, I moved with my family to Fairbanks, Alaska to direct the creative writing program at the University of Alaska. I'm still there.

Eve Müller recently moved from Maryland to Eugene, Oregon with her cat and sweetheart. She has published in *Sequestrum, The Writing Disorder, Thieving Magpie,* and *Empty House*. Her first chapbook, Guide to the Ruins, is forthcoming with Plan B Press. She was recently awarded a PLAYA residency. When she is not writing lyrical memoir and autobiographical fiction, she bakes cakes, wrangles her two feral daughters, conducts research on autism and language, and skinny dips whenever/wherever she can.

Linda B. Myers: I won my first creative contest in the sixth grade. After a Chicago marketing career, I traded in snow boots for rain books and moved to the Pacific Northwest with my Maltese, Dotty. We live in Port Angeles, WA. I have completed ten novels, the most recent of which is *Starting Over Far Away*, historical fiction set in 1920s Alaska. I'm much newer at poetry which is fast becoming my first love. I currently write a monthly opinion piece for the *Sequim Gazette* and am the co-founder of Olympic Peninsula Authors, an organization that creates events for local authors to meet each other and share work with the public.

Barbara Parchim lives on a small farm in southwest Oregon. She enjoys gardening and hiking and volunteered for several years at a wildlife rehabilitation facility caring for raptors and wolves. Writing poetry helps her understand our world and opens her heart in gratitude to nature. Her poems have appeared in *Allegro, Isacoustic, Turtle Island Quarterly, Windfall, Pedestal, Jefferson Journal, Cirque* and others. Her first book, *What Remains,* was published by Flowstone Press in October 2021.

James Pearson is a writer, photographer, and teacher living in Eugene, Oregon. He received an MFA from the University of Oregon. He has a wife, four children and a bloodhound.

Tami Phelps: I am a visual artist who has called Alaska home for over five decades. My cold wax paintings have received international and national recognition, including the London Art Biennale 2023, and the U.S. 5th Annual National Climate Assessment Report from Washington, DC, 2023. My artwork is influenced by a 20-year teaching career as a public Montessori teacher and the pedagogy of Dr. Maria Montessori. Music, nature, relationships, and antique stores are additional inspirations for me. And a dash of humor never hurts. My mixed media paintings incorporate ideas, concepts, and my life as an Alaskan woman. I invite viewers to create their own interpretations. A combination of cold wax, oils, and perhaps assemblage, brings my conceptual, sometimes representational, paintings to life. Telling authentic stories through art is a cathartic process that scratches an itch I cannot reach any other way. tamiphelps.com

Timothy Pilgrim, Montana native and Pacific Northwest poet living in Bellingham, Wash., has several hundred acceptances from U.S. journals such as *Seattle Review, Red Coyote, Sierra Nevada Review, Cirque* and *Santa Ana River Review*, and international journals such as *Windsor Review* in Canada, *Toasted Cheese* in the U.S. and Canada, *Prole Press* in the United Kingdom, and *Otoliths* in Australia. Pilgrim is the author of *Seduced by metaphor* (2021) and *Mapping Water* (2016). Pilgrim's poetry can be found at TimothyPilgrim.org.

Anne Pitkin's work has appeared, over the years, in *Poetry Chicago, Poetry Northwest, Prairie Schooner, The Alaska Quarterly Review, Rattle, One,* and many others. she has published three full-length collections: *Yellow, Winter Arguments,* and most recently, *But Still, Music* (Pleasure Boat Studios, September 2023) She is an editor emerita of *Fine Madness,* a poetry magazine that has retired after twenty successful years. She lives in Seattle.

Shauna Potocky is a poet and painter who calls Seward, Alaska home. Shauna has a deep love of high peaks, jagged ridgelines and ice. She has a strong connection to the natural world—both landscapes and seascapes with their rough or subtle edges where life unfolds. Shauna is the author of *Yosemite Dawning: Poems of the Sierra Nevada* (Cirque Press 2023). Her work appears in *Writing Through The Apocalypse* (2023), *Seward Unleashed Water and Wonder* (2023), *Beyond Words International Literary Journal* and her forthcoming book of poetry *Sea Smoke, Spindrift and Other Spells* is scheduled for publication by Cirque Press.

Katherine Poyner-Del Vento: I'm a graduate of Columbia University's School of the Arts, where I studied with Richard Howard and Lucie Brock-Broido. My poetry has appeared in *Room* and *So to Speak;* my longer work is represented by Carly Watters of P.S. Literary Agency. I live on Vancouver Island.

Mandy Ramsey is an artist, mother, photographer, and yoga teacher who loves to create and write. She self-published her first book *Grow Where You're Planted* in 2019. She has been previously published in *Cirque, Alaskan Women Speak, Tidal Echoes, Poets Choice,* and *Elephant Journal*. She holds an MA in Yoga Studies and Mindfulness Education and has been living off the grid in Haines, Alaska since 2000 in the timber frame home she built with her husband. She believes that flowers and the natural world can heal, connect, inspire, and sprout friendships. Find out more at mandyramsey.com

Native New Yorker **Diane Ray** has lived in the Seattle area 31 years, longer than anywhere. Poet and essayist, her writing appears in publications including *Poetica Magazine, Sisyphus, Canary, Voices Israel, The Jewish Literary Journal, Common Dreams, Beyond Nuclear International, Civilization in Crisis,* and elsewhere. When not writing, look for her in the alternate universe of ballet class, grandmothering, or trying to save a piece of the world.

Joe Reno is a well-known Seattle painter whose work has been published in *Cirque* several times. He paints in oil and egg tempera, favoring landscapes, florals, portraits and abstract imagery. When asked what is depicted, he has replied, "What do you want it to be?" His work appears in *The Pacific Northwest Landscape: A Painted History, 2001*. He has shown his work at several galleries including The Museum of Northwest Art, in La Conner, WA.

Warren J. Rhodes is a high school English teacher and former journalist who's lived in Alaska since 1991. A past winner and judge in the UAA/ADN Creative Writing Contest, his work has appeared in the literary journals *Permafrost, Chabot Review* and *California Quarterly,* and the newspapers *Anchorage Daily News* (nonfiction) and *Anchorage Press* (poetry). His furry companions are Dixie and Hansel.

Richard Edwin Roberts (1919-2007) was always a poet. He first published in the 1940's (an anthology, *Spring Comes in Many Ways* and *Duty to Death, LD.* in Oscar Williams' *The War Poets*), followed by works in *The Christian Science Monitor, The Educational Forum,* and *High Country News*. A native and long-time resident of Montana, his love of nature and all things wild is amply expressed in his poems, many of which were written during the last three decades of his life spent in a log home that he built off the grid in Montana. Posthumous works have appeared in *Big Sky Journal* and *Cirque*.

Joel Savishinsky is a retired anthropologist and gerontologist. He is the author of *The Trail of the Hare: Life and Stress in An Arctic Community,* as well as *Breaking the Watch: The Meanings of Retirement in America,* which won the Gerontological Society of America's book-of-the-year prize. A Pushcart Prize nominee and California State Poetry Society award winner, his poetry, fiction and essays have appeared in *Atlanta Review, Beyond Words, Cirque, The Examined Life Journal, Lit Shark Magazine, The New York Times, Passager, SLANT,* and *Windfall*. In 2023, The Poetry Box published his collection *Our Aching Bones, Our Breaking Hearts: Poems on Aging*. He lives in Seattle, helping to raise five grandchildren, and considers himself a recovering academic and unrepentant activist.

Reefka Schneider, Artist, is the creator of the artwork in the highly acclaimed Ekphrastic exhibits and books *Borderlines: Drawing Border Lives / Fronteras: dibujando las vidas fronterizas* and *The Magic of Mariachi / La Magia del Mariachi*. Her watercolors "Tres Orejas" and "Don Quixote in El Salto" are part of a series of her landscape paintings that will appear in the exhibit "Last Poet in the Woods" that she is collaborating on with her husband poet Steven Schneider. Reefka's artwork has been published in *Writing Towards Hope: Human Rights in Latin America* (Yale University Press) and many prestigious journals. Her awards include the Octavia Arneson Award in the International Art Show at the Brownsville Museum of Fine Arts and a special initiative grant from the Texas Commission on the Arts. You can see Reefka's art at reefka.com and poetry-art.com.

Steven P. Schneider is the founder of the MFA Program in Creative Writing at the University of Texas Rio Grande Valley (UTRGV). He is the co-creator with his artist wife Reefka of two bilingual, ekphrastic exhibits and books: *Borderlines: Drawing Border Lives / Fronteras: dibujando las vidas fronterizas* and *The Magic of Mariachi / La Magia del Mariachi*. He is also the author of the poetry collections *Unexpected Guests* and *Prairie Air Show*. His scholarly books on contemporary American poetry include *A.R. Ammons and the Poetics of Widening, Complexities of Motion: The Long Poems of A.R. Ammons*, and *The Contemporary Narrative Poem: Critical Crosscurrrents*. Steven is an elected member of the Texas Institute of Letters. His awards include five Big Read grants from the National Endowment for the Arts, a Nebraska Arts Council Fellowship, and a Poetry Fellowship from the Helene Wurlitzer Foundation in Taos, New Mexico.

Kerstin Schulz is a German-American writer living in Portland, Oregon. Her work can be found or is forthcoming in *Read650, Open: A Journal of Arts & Letters, River Heron Review, HerStry, The Bookends Review, The Gateway Review* and *Cathexis Northwest Press*, among other publications.

Sher Schwartz is a retired University of Alaska Southeast Assistant Professor of Humanities living on a 200-acre historic farm in eastern Oregon. She is currently working on a chapbook, plays old-time fiddle music, plants gardens for pollinators, and trains bird dogs.

Tom Sexton spends his days walking his Irish Terrier, Murphy, writing poetry, and making breakfast for his wife. Many years ago, he began the Creative Writing program at the University of Alaska, Anchorage and was the English Department Chair for many years. He is proud to say Mike Burwell was his student. His poetry collection *Cummiskey Alley: New and Selected Lowell Poems* was published in 2020 by Loom Press. In 2021 Chester Creek Press published *Snowy Egret Rising*.

Jake Sheff is a pediatrician in Oregon and veteran of the US Air Force. He's married with a daughter and crazy bulldog. Poems and short stories of Jake's have been published widely. Some have even been nominated for the Best of the Net Anthology and the Pushcart Prize. A full-length collection of formal poetry, *A Kiss to Betray the Universe*, is available from White Violet Press. He also has two chapbooks: *Looting Versailles* (Alabaster Leaves Publishing) and *The Rites of Tires* (SurVision).

Eva-Maria Sher's poetry has appeared in *After Happy Hour Review, The Adirondack Review, Apricity Magazine, Big Scream, Bluestem, Brief Wilderness, Cadillac Cicatrix, California Quarterly, Cape Rock, DASH Literary Journal, Door Is A Jar Magazine, Dos Passos Review, Doubly Mad, Drunk Monkeys, East Jasmine Review, Euphony, Forge, Free State Review, Front Range Review, GW Review, Hawaii Pacific Review, The Hollins Critic, I-70 Review, Ignatian Literary Review, ken*again, The MacGuffin, October Hill Magazine, Old Red Kimono, OxMag, The Paragon Journal, Penmen Review, Pennsylvania English, Perceptions Magazine, Poetic Sun, Poydras Review, Prism Review, riverSedge, Rougarou, Ship of Fools,* and others.

Juanita Smart's work has appeared in *River Heron Review, Rise Up Review*, and *Honeyguide Literary Magazine*, among others. She writes because writing makes her pay closer attention to the more-than-human world, and because writing brings her joy. She finds her best ideas for poems and prose while exploring local Pennsylvania game lands with her three dogs Gabe, Liberty, and Wilson.

Corinne Smith turned to poetry as a self-care practice in 2020. She won the annual poetry contest of the *Anchorage Daily News* in 2023. She lives in Talkeetna, Alaska, where she spends time outside with friends (some dogs) and plays with colorful fabric when it is dark or wet.

Craig Smith is a retired Seattle newspaperman who spent the final 32 years of his career as a sportswriter at *The Seattle Times*. He is a native of Kemore, WA, and a graduate of Bothell High School and the University of Washington, where he was editor of *The Daily*.

Allie Spikes's poetry and essays have appeared or are forthcoming in *Gulf Coast, the Los Angeles Review, the Rumpus, River Teeth, Bellingham Review*, and elsewhere. Her poetry collection manuscript was a finalist for BOA's A. Poulin, Jr. Prize, and her nonfiction has been listed as Notable in Best American Essays 2022.

Cheryl Stadig lived in Alaska for 18 years, calling several places home including Anchorage, Teller, Ketchikan, and Prince of Wales Island where her two sons were raised. Running the wilds of Maine in her youth helped prepare her for life in rural Alaska. Her Alaska resume includes work at a 5-star hotel, a university, a village general store, and as a 911 dispatcher/jail guard. She would happily consider the job of hermit should a dot on the northern map be in need. Her work has appeared in previous issues of *Cirque, Inside Passages*, and other publications. She is currently living in Maine with her 100 year-old father who is still at home and cutting firewood.

Cynthia Steele is a Pacific Northwest loving, lifelong Alaskan, except for those five concert-going years in Washington State and the bouncing around of her early childhood. She writes poetry, nonfiction, and takes hundreds of photos a week, and some of these end up in *Cirque*. Her book *30 Before 13* is in its final stages. She is a dog whisperer of seven and has fostered dozens. She holds a Medical Assisting Certification, an MA in English, and a BA in Journalism and has thrice been an editor. She has two adopted, adult children and lives with husband Bill.

Leah Stenson is the author of two chapbooks: *Heavenly Body* (2011) and *The Turquoise Bee and Other Love Poems* (2014), a full-length book of poetry *Everywhere I find Myself* (2017), and a hybrid memoir *Life Revised* (Cirque Press, 2020). She served as a regional editor of *Alive at the Center: Contemporary Poems from the Pacific Northwest* (2013), co-editor of *Reverberations from Fukushima: 50 Japanese Poets Speak Out* (2014) and editor of the second edition of *Reverberations. . .* (2021). She hosts the Studio Series Poetry Reading & Open Mic in Portland and co-hosts Drop Out Parkdale, a residency/reading series in Parkdale, Oregon.

Richard Stokes is a Juneau resident of over 50 years. His prose and poetry work usually reflects his love of nature, his aging or his boyhood in the sharply defined black-white world of rural Georgia in the 1940-50's. He graduated from Emory in Atlanta in 1961.

Scott Stolnack is a poet, fiction writer, and playwright. His poems have appeared in *Cascadia Rising Review, Prometheus Dreaming, Cathexis Northwest Press*, and elsewhere. Scott holds degrees in English literature, biology, and fisheries ecology from the University of Washington. Between 2008 and 2019, he was a senior biologist coordinating recovery of endangered salmon in the Seattle area.

Joanna Streetly's work is published in *Best Canadian Essays 2017* and upcoming in Best Canadian Poetry 2024. Her work can also be found in many anthologies and literary journals. Her memoir, *Wild Fierce Life: Dangerous Moments on the Outer Coast*, was a BC Bestseller published by Caitlin Press. She's been short-listed for the FBCW Literary Writes Poetry Contest, the Canada Writes Creative Non-fiction Prize and *The Spectator's* Shiva Naipaul award. *This Dark* (poetry) is published by Postelsia Press. She has lived in the traditional territory of the Tla-o-qui-aht people since 1990 and was the 2018-2020 Tofino Poet Laureate.

Sheary Clough Suiter grew up in Eugene, Oregon, then lived in Alaska and Colorado until her recent relocation back to the Pacific Northwest. Her encaustic fine art is represented in Anchorage, Alaska by Stephan Fine Art, in Camas, Washington by the Attic Gallery, in Green Mountain Falls, Colorado by Stones, Bones, & Wood Gallery, and in Colorado Springs, Colorado by Kreuser Gallery. When she's not traveling in her camper van along the backroads of America with her artist partner Nard Claar, Suiter works from her home studio in Springfield, Oregon near the Willamette River. Online at @shearycloughsuiter and www.sheary.me

Jim Thiele worked as a photographer for a biological textbook company for several years before moving to Alaska in 1974. He has worked for The Alaska Department of Fish and Game and the University of Alaska as a biologist. He is a recently retired financial advisor. His photographs have been seen in several publications, including *Alaska Magazine, Alaska Geographic,* and *Cirque*. He lives in Anchorage with his wife Susan. Taking photos forces him to stop and really see the world.

Elizabeth L Thompson has been writing poetry for 40 years and believes "Everything is a Poem."

Spokane native **Georgia Tiffany** holds graduate degrees from Indiana University and the University of Idaho. Her work has been recognized with Pushcart nominations and has appeared in scores of literary magazines in addition to such anthologies as *New Poets of the American West* (2010). Her lifelong devotion to the arts includes participating as scholar for Idaho's Let's Talk About It library programs, and co-creating regional interactive poetry/art projects in the Northwest. *Body Be Sound*, her first full-length book of poems, was released in 2023, by Encircle Publications.

Lucy Tyrrell's writing and photography is inspired by nature and wild landscapes, outdoor pursuits (mushing, hiking, canoeing), and travel. After 16 years in Alaska, she traded a big mountain (Denali) for a big lake (Superior). Lucy lives the spirit of Alaska deeply, even in Wisconsin. She was Bayfield Poet Laureate 2020–2021. Her essay "A Special Kind of App" from the Winter 2022 issue of *Alaska Women Speak* was nominated for a Pushcart Prize. She serves on the Wisconsin Poet Laureate Commission (2023-2025).

Sean Ulman is the author of the novel *Seward Soundboard* (Cirque Press 2020). He interviews writers on a local public radio show on 91.7 KIBH FM. He is the editor of KMTA's *Trail Mix Journal* and a new project launching this spring at the Seward Community Library - Res Bay Chapbooks.

Miles Varana's work has appeared in *Typehouse, The Penn Review,* and *Passages North.* He has worked previously as a staff reader and managing editor at *Hawai'i Pacific Review.* Miles currently works for WKBT News in La Crosse, Wisconsin, where he does his best to be a good Millennial despite disliking tandem bike rides.

O. Alan Weltzien, a retired English prof in Montana, has published lots of scholarly articles, four chapbooks, and eleven books. These include a memoir, *A Father and an Island* (Lewis-Clark Press, 2008) and three full-length poetry collections, most recently *On The Beach: Poems 2016 - 2021* (Cirque Press, 2022). Weltzien and his wife travel extensively, and he still skis in winter and hikes and backpacks in summer.

Tim Whitsel: I am a journeyman writer from Ft. Wayne. But my years since high school have been spent almost entirely on the West Coast. I am the beneficiary of a cadre of five bright women poets, who have improved my poems in a critique group for twenty years. Airlie Press published my first full-length book *Wish Meal* in October 2016. *We Say Ourselves,* a chapbook, came out earlier from Traprock Books in 2012. My poem "Whoever" was a finalist in *Cirque's* Poetry of Place contest. My poem "Hanging" was in a recent issue of *December.*

Wanda Wilson: I have been writing since I was 8. *Readers Digest* published a story I wrote on Hurricane Betsy in Thibodaux, LA in 1956. Mainly tho I've been writing poetry since I was 13 and began writing to a Vietnam Vet when he was still in the war. I met Allen Ginsberg in New York City when I was working for MTV. He invited and encouraged me to attend summer classes at Naropa which I did. Guessing somewhere around 1984. I studied with Allen & Philip Whalen and Diane Di Prima and Derek Walcott & William S Burroughs. I also took classes with Alice Notley at St. Mark's Church on the Lower East Side for about a year. Attended readings in NYC which included Carolyn Forché (just back from El Salvador with her first book) and Wendell Berry and Galway Kinnell. In 1991 in Charlottesville, VA, I began Slam Poetry sessions with a poet friend. This later was connected to the University of Virginia. I've had one tiny chapbook published and used to publish other poetry, but mainly gave readings. I taught Poetry & Writing classes for 10 years in Virginia and Colorado from 1989-2009.

Matt Witt is a writer and photographer in Talent, Oregon. His work may be seen at MattWittPhotography.com. He has been Artist in Residence at Crater Lake National Park, Absaroka-Beartooth Wilderness Foundation, Cascade-Siskiyou National Monument, Mesa Refuge, and PLAYA at Summer Lake.

Robin Woolman has long been a performer and teacher of physical theater in Portland, Oregon. She loves backpacking in the high country of the Pacific Northwest or strolling the neighborhood while playing with words in her head. She dates her passion for writing back to Miss Mataroli's second grade class...More recent works appear in *Cirque, Global Poemic, Deep Wild, Poeming Pigeon, Westchester Review,* and Red Shoe Press's 2023 and 2024 Oregon Poetry Calendars

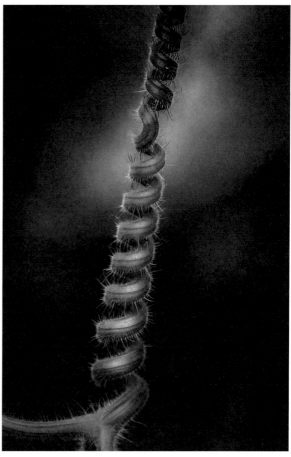

A Tall Squash Tendril   Jack Broom

Infinite Meditations ∞

FOR INSPIRATION & DAILY PRACTICE

BY SCOTT HANSON

INFINITE MEDITATIONS

For Inspiration & Daily Practice
SCOTT HANSON

THIS SURELY IS A WORK OF ART! I like that the meditations are given in a context that is useful and meaningful to the reader; in this book, the author holds a nice balance of being capable and informative, yet also humble. The first time I tried it I just "asked," and the number 33 popped into my mind, so I read Meditation 33 and chuckled at how appropriate it was. Thank you for sharing *Infinite Meditations* with me—may it have a good journey out into the world.

— Jane English, PhD, Photographer, Author of *A Rainbow of Tao*,
and co-creator with Gia-Fu Feng of an edition of *Tao Te Ching*

INFINITE MEDITATIONS **INVITES THE READER INTO** a multi-faceted, ongoing conversation with the *Tao Te Ching*, that ancient Chinese classic of mystery and sensibility. Scott Hanson's inspired reflections on the Tao and other rich founts offer compelling insights and possibilities for the reader to create a path of one's own. Here you will find ageless wisdom, new perspectives, and bountiful nourishment for an enduring meditation practice.

Drawing from an extensive range of sources as varied as multiple translations of the *Tao Te Ching*, including one by Gia-fu Feng and Jane English, to the discoveries of Isaac Newton, Albert Einstein and Stephen Hawking, Scott Hanson has created an accessible and compelling gateway to a meditation practice for a lifetime.

— Carol Ann Wilson, Author, *Still Point of the Turning World*:
The Life of Gia-fu Feng, ForewordMagazine's
2010 Book of the Year

SCOTT HANSON IS A writer, poet, philosopher and wireless professional who lives in Kingston, WA. He is a lifelong resident of the Pacific Northwest and student of meditation and the *Tao Te Ching*.

Scott has been a writer of journals, poetry, family vignettes and short stories throughout his life. *Infinite Meditations: for Inspiration and Daily Practice* is his first published book.

New From

CIRQUE PRESS

Published August 2023 on Amazon
eBook, paperback, hardback

Infinite Meditations offers techniques to:

✦ Ground yourself in times of stress and change

✦ Discover or re-kindle your spiritual journey

✦ Tap into your intuition to maximize personal joy and effectiveness

✦ Create an unlimited number of unique meditation mantras based on your beliefs and goals

49 WRITERS

CREATIVITY | COMMUNITY | CRAFT

OUR VISION

A vibrant community of diverse Alaskan writers of all levels and ages, coming together to find and share their voices.

OUR MISSION

Engaging, empowering, inspiring and expanding a statewide community of Alaskan writers.

PROGRAMS AND OFFERINGS

- FREE PUBLIC READINGS WITH ACCLAIMED AUTHORS
- CLASSES AND WORKSHOPS TO HONE YOUR SKILLS
- GENERATIVE RETREATS IN BEAUTIFUL PLACES TO FOSTER YOUR WORK

- A WEEKLY NEWSLETTER AND BLOG TO HELP YOU STAY CONNECTED
- NEED-BASED SCHOLARSHIPS FOR COURSES AND RETREATS
- A COMMUNITY OF SHARED SUPPORT

WHY BECOME A MEMBER?

Consider joining our dedicated literary community. Benefits include: discounted class tuition, early class registration, and access to members-only events.

CONTACT US

49 Writers, Inc.
P.O. Box 140014
Anchorage, AK 99514

Website: 49writers.org
Email: info@49writers.org

49 Writers

Brenda Jaeger Art Studio

PRIVATE LESSONS   ART SALES   CONSULTATIONS
INSTAGRAM.COM/BRENDAJAEGERARTSTUDIO
BRENDAJAEGERARTSTUDIO@STARTMAIL.COM

Bending Light, an exhibit of works by Brenda Jaeger, will be exhibited through the Georgia Blue Gallery at Jen's Bistro, May 13 - October 14, 2024

For a limited time, artist and educator Brenda Jaeger is offering private online or in person lessons.

Since beginning work with Brenda Jaeger, more than a year ago, I have been inspired to create art, submit work, and enter competitions. As a result, I have a painting on the current cover of Alaska Women Speak. Embrace the unexpected. Sign up for one-on-one lessons.   ~ Sandy Lantz Kleven

Book today by email brendajaegerartstudio@startmail.com | or call 907-350-4539

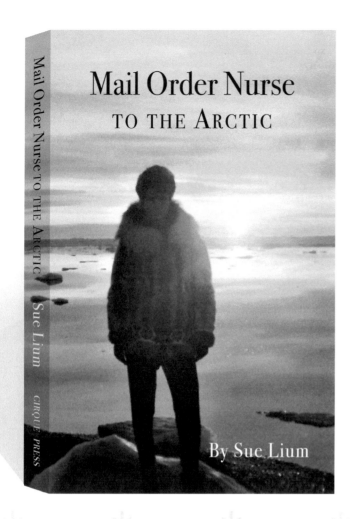

Mail Order Nurse

TO THE ARCTIC

By Sue Lium

About the Author

Sue Lium (nee Robinson) was born and raised in Calgary, Alberta, Canada. She moved to Alaska after graduating nursing school from the Misericordia Hospital in Edmonton, Alberta and worked for the U.S. Public Health Service in hospitals in Kotzebue and Barrow. After leaving the Arctic, she worked at Cottage Hospital in Santa Barbara, California before marrying and returning to Alaska. She retired after working thirty years at Bartlett Regional Hospital in Juneau, Alaska. Now widowed, she is the mother of two boys and grandmother to five grandchildren. She can be reached at suelium@hotmail.com.

CIRQUE PRESS

Sandra Kleven
Michael Burwell
Editors & Publishers

About *Mail Order Nurse*

This is the lively memoir of a young, city-bred nurse who flew to Kotzebue for her first job in 1969. It is an engaging read about ingenuity in medical care, the author's fascination with the land and her cross-cultural pleasures and mishaps. The book covers the first two years of her nursing career, including time in Barrow [Utqiavik]. It benefits from the author's photos and from her current perspective as a long-time Alaska nurse. Highly recommended for readers interested in Alaska history, medicine, and memoir.

—Sarah Crawford Isto, MD, author of *The Fur Farms of Alaska: Two Centuries of History and a Forgotten Stampede* and *Good Company: A Mining Family in Fairbanks, Alaska*

Settle in for a fascinating tour of a culture on the edge of the world, the Inupiat people of Northwest Alaska. Join Sue in fun activities from partaking in a caribou hunt, to racing across the sea ice behind a dog team, to learning cultural differences like why the Inupiat never say goodbye. Sue also shows us another side of life in this remote region, from struggles with alcohol, to culture shock to murder.

—Stan Jones, author of The Nathan Active Arctic mysteries

MISS BEBE COMES TO AMERICA
LA BEBÉ LLEGA A ESTADOS UNIDOS

Story by/ Historia escrita por Lynda Humphrey

Illustrations by/ Ilustrada por Judi Nyerges

Translated by/ Traducida por Patti Sosa Hands

"A heartwarming true story of Bebe a cat rescued in Mexico and her compelling journey to her new home in America. Charming illustrations that bring the story alive. A delightful "feel-good" read for any child."
— Corinne Ludy, M.Ed., Elementary Librarian

Lynda Whisman Humphrey is a retired Elementary Principal, former Reading Specialist, Central Office Administrator, and Administrator of a Teacher Education Program at the University of Washington.

- Considered for the Caldecott Medal for the best illustrated children's book of 2023.
- Purchased by the Oficina de Proyectos de Culturales de Puerto Vallarta, Mexico for their collection
- In the collection at El Biblioteca de Los Mangos in Puerto Vallarta, Mexico!

Circles
a Cirque Press

Available at 3rd Place Books, Amazon and other venc

JOSEPH L. KASHI
ATTORNEY AT LAW

~ Accidents and personal injury claims
~ Business sales and purchases
~ Commercial and business law
~ Real property litigation

907 – 398 – 0480
kasha@alaska.net
www.kashilaw.com
205 East Beluga
Soldotna, Alaska

CIRQUE PRESS

All In Due Time

A MEMOIR OF SIBLINGS, GENEALOGY, SECRETS AND LOVE

Kate Troll

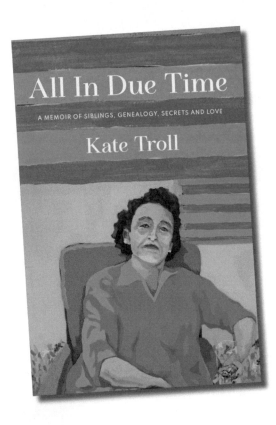

All in Due Time is about persistence, discovery, the importance of family, and the new, positive possibilities associated with DNA testing results. The writing style is both engaging and thought-provoking, as Kate weaves together relevant social topics, her family mysteries, her life, and her quest to find all of her siblings.

All in Due Time is full of surprises and puzzles, but mostly it made me wish I were a long-lost Troll.

— Heather Lende, Alaska State Writer Laureate and author of *If You Lived Here, I'd Know Your Name*

Kate Troll is an author, op-ed columnist, wilderness adventurer, and speaker on conservation and climate issues. Her opinion pieces have been published in the *Washington Post*, the *L.A. Times* and *The Nation*. For three years she was a regular columnist for Alaska's only statewide paper. In 2017, Kate published a creative nonfiction book about sustainability and climate change. Her book, *The Great Unconformity, Reflections on Hope in an Imperiled World*, led to her being invited as faculty at the Chuckanut Writer's Conference in Bellingham, WA.

Getting Home From Here offers forty-seven stunning, thought-provoking poems covering a woman's life whose personal history reflects much of the ethnic complexity, familial joys/sorrows, social strains, and natural beauty of the U.S. Anne Ward-Masterson writes of her New Hampshire girlhood, *Wading into cool water/ sinking soft sediment of the river bed oozes/sucking at our toes.* And of Alaska, her home now, *Spring cries storms against/My window all through twilight/Sunrise brings damp calm.* She also calls out the racist history of the U.S. which foisted shame and confusion upon her mixed-race childhood, but is now a source of pride. An inspiring and compelling read.

—Kerry Dean Feldman, author of *Alice's Trading Post: A Novel of the West*, and poems in *The Woman Within: Memory as Muse.*

Getting Home From Here

By Anne Ward-Masterson

CIRQUE PRESS

Sandra Kleven
Michael Burwell
Editors & Publishers

Anne Ward-Masterson grew up in New Hampshire in the tame woods, fishing, canoeing and swimming in the Lamprey River and reading books on cold rainy days. Attending Brandeis University and later marrying into the USAF gave her a broader view of people, religions and food. She currently resides in Eagle River, Alaska, where there are no tame rivers or woods.

In *Getting Home from Here*, especially her poems about race, Ward-Masterson calls out schools, the military, and people who make assumptions about her. She questions how people perceive blackness ("why won't I tone it down?"). She describes the cab of a pickup truck or a riverbed with equal clarity through sensory language. Her natural, occasional rhyme threads a consistent, melodic quality through several moments of soft, poignant sadness. A rewarding read.
—Cynthia Steele

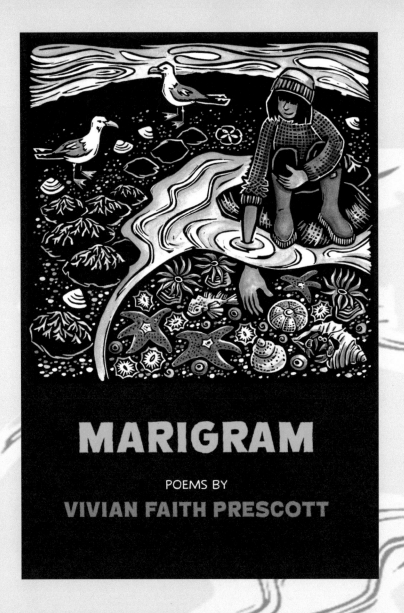

MARIGRAM

POEMS BY

VIVIAN FAITH PRESCOTT

New from Glass Lyre Press

"Eye sockets of a whale, salmonberries, rocky shoreline and seawall, crows and goldeneye, moon and tides, barnacles, dogwinkle, and limpet, krill and kelp, deer, even a mink... there is such rich imagery in Vivian Faith Prescott's Marigram that I feel physically present...
— Anne Coray, author of *Late Fall Bucolics*

Marigram: A graphic record of the tide levels at a particular coastal station.

From Glass Lyre Press, *Marigram* is a chapbook of poems about living next to the ocean in a small island community in Southeastern Alaska. Order from Glass Lyre Press, Ingram, Amazon, Barnes & Noble, and elsewhere.
Cover art by Ketchikan Alaska artist, Evon Zerbetz

Vivian Faith Prescott was born and raised on the small island of Wrangell, Kaachxana.áak'w, in Southeast Alaska on the land of the Shtax'heen Kwáan. She lives and writes in Lingít Aaní at her family's fishcamp. Along with her daughter, Vivian Mork Yéilk', Vivian co-hosts the award-winning Planet Alaska Facebook page and co-authors the Planet Alaska column appearing in the *Juneau Empire*.

Vivian is also the author of *Silty Water People* from Cirque Press, shown here.

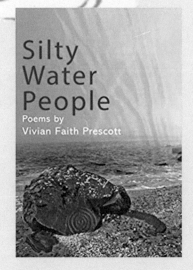

APPORTIONING THE LIGHT

BY ALASKAN POET KAREN TSCHANNEN

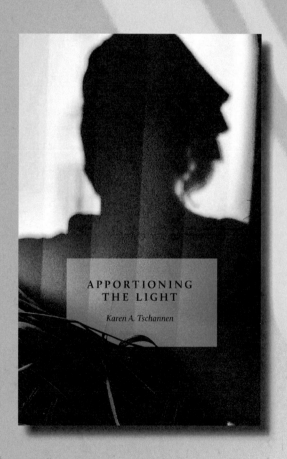

Poems so compressed the page itself trembles. So brave, in dark places, the reader clutches the poet's sure hand. *Apportioning the Light* shines. It shines.

AVAILABLE AT AMAZON OR BY EMAIL:
cirquejournal@gmail.com, $16 - CIRQUE PRESS
Sandra Kleven & Michael Burwell, CIRQUE Publishers

"A life lived to its fullest, a craft perfected so that it seems seamless, the highest compliment I can give to any writer. I read it from its beginning to its end without putting it down. Kudos to Cirque for publishing *Apportioning the Light*."

– TOM SEXTON, ALASKA POET LAUREATE

CIRQUE PRESS

Karen Tschannen has been published in *Alaska Quarterly Review, Ice-Floe, PNW Poets and Artists Calendar(s), North of Eden* (Loose Affiliation Press), *The Sky's Own Light* (Minotaur Press), *Crosscurrents North, Cirque*, and other publications. Tschannen was nominated for a Pushcart Prize in 2016. Her perceptive verse is notable for the care taken with language in both the sound of a phrase and the appearance on the page.

Water the Rocks Make
by David McElroy
Alaska Literary Series
University of Alaska Press

The poems of *Water the Rocks Make* commit into words the turbulence of emotion and thought stirred up by life's events: family trauma, psychiatric instability, the legal system, the death of a loved one, identity, cultural displacement, work, loss, creativity, and through everything, love.

David McElroy is a retired commercial pilot of small planes in the Arctic and a former smokejumper, fisherman, taxi driver, and English teacher. He is the author of four books of poetry, *Making It Simple, Mark Making, Just Between Us*, and *Water the Rocks Make*. He has been published in regional and national journals such as *Alaska Quarterly Review, Cirque, Anteaus, Poetry Northwest*, and *Chicago Review*. In 2016 he was the recipient of the Andy Hope award for poetry.

HOW TO SUBMIT TO CIRQUE

Cirque, published in Anchorage, Alaska, is a regional journal created to share the best writing in the region with the rest of the world. *Cirque* submissions are *not* restricted to a "regional" theme or setting.

Cirque invites emerging and established writers living in the North Pacific Rim—Alaska, Washington, Oregon, Idaho, Montana, Hawaii, Yukon Territory, Alberta, British Columbia and Chukotka—to submit short stories, poems, creative nonfiction, translations, plays, reviews of first books, interviews, photographs, and artwork for *Cirque's* next issue.

Issue #28—Reading Period September 30, 2024 to March 21, 2024

Issue #29—Reading Period March 22, 2024 to September 21, 2024

SUBMISSION GUIDELINES

Eligibility: you were born in, or are currently residing in, or have previously lived for a period of not less than 5 years in the aforementioned North Pacific Rim region.

-- *Poems*: 5 poems MAX
-- *Fiction, Nonfiction, Plays*: 12 pages MAX (double spaced).
-- *Artwork and Photography*: 10 images MAX accepted in JPEG or TIFF format, sent as email attachments. Please send images in the highest resolution possible; images will likely be between 2 and 10mb each. If you do not submit full-size photo files at time of submission, we will respond with an email reminder. No undersize images or thumbnails will be eligible for publication.
-- *Bio*: 100 words MAX.
-- *Contact Info*: Make sure to keep your contact email current and be sure that it is one that you check regularly. If your contact information changes, make sure to inform us at *Cirque*. To ensure that replies from *Cirque* bypass your spam filter and go to your inbox, add *Cirque* to your address book.

-- Submit to https://cirque.submittable.com
-- Replies average two to three months after deadlines, and we don't mind you checking with us about your submissions.
-- *Cirque* requires no payment or submission fees. However, *Cirque* is published by an independent press staffed by volunteers. Your donations keep Cirque Press going. You will find donation buttons on Submittable and you can also support us via PayPal to cirquejournal@gmail.com.

Thanks for your poetry, prose, images and financial support.

CIRQUE PRESS

Red Flower After O'Keefe   **Cynthia Steele**